Kilohertz

A novel by Robert Vincent

Contact: WriteVincent@gmail.com

First Available: July 2013

Prologue

Two weeks was a long time for anybody to go without sleep, but Ethan felt he was taking it exceptionally bad. The teacher at the whiteboard droned on as he prayed that it would be enough to put him out. If only until the end of the period. Instead he pressed his head into his right hand and squeezed his temples, clenching the muscles in his face and groaning.

Slowly he came back to himself. He drew in a breath slowly, feeling the air cool his tongue. Smoothing his dark hair back his hand came back greasy. Even just coming out of the shower he felt unclean. Despite his best efforts lack of sleep was translating to lack of hygiene.

"Ahhhh…." Ethan squeaked out as his senses were assaulted again. He cringed at the high-pitched keening sound that started in the audible but quickly found its way to the ultrasonic. He didn't look to the teacher as he pushed himself from his desk and stumbled toward the door, towering over the other teenagers as he passed by them at their desks.

The pain faded quickly but it left behind the same muddled feeling. The noise was everywhere. At times it was worse at times but it always had one constant, he was the only one that could hear it- the sound of some invisible rushing waterfall or construction site, it was impossible to define at times. It grew louder as he pushed the door open to the men's room; he hardly heard the door slam into the wall as he staggered to the sink.

Ethan started the water, as hot as the plumbing could muster and splashed it over his face. For a second he was back to himself more or less. He repeated the action, breathing heavily, his head pounding. The reprieve was short lived and the sound came on stronger, "Damn it!" He shouted, slamming his fists down into the sink. The old design had somehow lasted from the turn of the last century, but the cast iron meant to last several lifetimes now had two neat fist-sized holes complimenting its shape. The water quickly took the new route of least resistance and poured into the underside of the lavatory.

Ethan felt tears collect in the corner of his eyes, his throat constricting. "Damn... damn..." He knew that he was going to get blamed for it; things always turned out that way. The regret shifted easily to anger. He screamed and lashed out with his foot, striking the marble base of the sink and shattered it, going straight through to the wall.

The sound was horrible. The whole wall shook as the sink tumbled to the ground, tiles clattered from the wall one atop the other. Ethan hardly heard any of it over the bullhorn in his skull. It was building. His balance was off, he could hardly stand. He leaned heavily against one of the bathroom stalls. He had to do something. Leave school. He had to go home. Get to a doctor.

No, not a doctor, his doctor had sent him to a psychiatrist after he admitted there were occasionally voices amongst the noise and sometimes music. The psychiatrist had been even less help. They met once but she had been dismissive toward him. The only option she had given was suggesting an observation period of two weeks in the city hospital. There was no hope. He felt it, some unknown stress pressing him to act now or never. He knew he was running out of time.

It was getting had to think again, he worried that if things continued on he'd lose himself over the din. He collapsed against the stall as the feeling intensified, some unexplainable pressure in his head. Vaguely he realized there was someone in the room with him, yelling at him. He couldn't make out what they were saying. Ethan gasped out at the cold contact of the floor. As he fell forward, the world spun to darkness.

"Ethan..."
"Ethan!"
"I'm sorry, but we have to keep you sedated until we can prove you're stable." The doctor noticed that Ethan was coming to although he had yet to open his eyes.

For a moment, Ethan tried to look at the doctor before giving up; the lids felt too heavy and he wasn't in the mood to deal with the light anyway. He felt the grip on his hand tighten; he didn't have to look to know it was his mother. She'd been there every time the doctors had tried to meet with him.

"You need to talk to the doctors sweetie. They're trying to get you better again." The waver in her voice made him want to cry. Strange, it was only when he was almost completely under that he felt lucid any more. At night when the drugs started to wear off before the next injection he always felt it slip away no matter how hard he tried to hold on to that feeling.

"We've ran all the tests at our disposal Ethan but what we're still missing is your input. We're going to attempt to wean you off the benzo so that we can talk with you one on one." Ethan tried to shake his head 'no' but knew that he failed. He didn't want lucidity. If he could stay just like this forever, the nights were so quiet.

"The benzo is only a short term solution," The doctor continued to his mother, "If we need a more permanent sedative then we'll have to do some trial and error to find the best combination that allows him to function." He explained.

Ethan took a shaky breath; it had been the same thing since they'd brought him into the hospital. He was only awake a few hours a day and rarely opened his eyes, so it was impossible to determine how much time had passed. But it was still a peaceful experience. He did know however that he had been there some time. One day he noticed that his mother had been wearing boots. Before his arrival in the hospital it had just been getting into fall. Now if he had to guess it was sometime in December.

"So, I'll be able to talk to him again?" His mother asked hopeful, talking yet again as if he wasn't in the room.

"We'll see." Ethan knew from the tone the doctor used that he was thinking of the last time they had tried to wean him off the sedatives and anti-psychotics. He didn't remember any of it but knew from second hand accounts that things had unraveled similar to how things had at his school after he had passed out. More people were in the hospital, more structural damage. Despite the boasting of the orderlies that they had seen it all and their promises to take him down a peg if he should ever try something, he could tell they were afraid of him. No one, not even the doctors could explain the feats of strength he had been able to display when he was off the sedatives.

"Thank you doctor." His mother lingered for a moment and he was seized by a sudden impulse to see her again. He forced his eyes open and heard her gasp. Their eyes met and she immediately stooped down and grabbed him up in a hug, "My baby!" She cried out, holding him against her tightly, "It'll be okay sweetie, don't you worry." She rubbed her head against his and he let his eyes close, enjoying the sensation before the sedatives again did their magic, giving him the sleep he had found all too elusive before.

"Please... please... I need it!" Ethan shouted out, even though he knew no one could hear him outside those padded walls. He rocked his head forward in the dark room and brought it back with resounding force, but it was futile, the bed that he was strapped to had padding to spare.

"It's got to be time for the next injection, hello!" He called out again. Although the injections had been coming at the same time they always had, he knew from the effects that the doctor was making good on his promise and trying to wean him off the drugs. The feeling started out in the back of his head again as a low hum. Lingering like the ballast on a fluorescent bulb slowly going bad. For some time he had held out hope that maybe things had improved.

They hadn't improved. The noise had progressively gotten louder. Growing beyond what he had known before. It was only because it had grown in intensity so quickly and not had the chance to wear him down over weeks without sleep that he found himself coherent now instead of completely engulfed in the cacophony.

"Help me, please!" Ethan pulled at his restraints, the metal shackles clattering against the frame. They'd learned their lessons after the last time. He wondered if what he was going through was like coming to in the middle of brain surgery. He gritted his teeth and rocked back into the bed, "If you don't help me out..." He pulled at his restraints again, "Damn it, someone get in here!"

This time the whole bed rocked as he pulled on the shackles. "I need my injection!" The bed lifted from the ground on one side, the frame bent. Ethan didn't give it another second, pulling again the bed rocked and he cried out, screaming, it was too much.

He cried out feebly, praying to God or anyone that might help to just relieve him of his suffering. He screamed for three hours until his voice was raw and his body was limp. The last time he had been off his medications he had passed out abruptly in much the same way only to come back to himself unexpectedly.

It had taken ever available orderly on the floor and

a timely injection of phenobarbital to get him in restraints again. This time however that resistance wasn't there. This time, the only thing between him and escape was a steel chain and a brick wall. The walls don't fight back.

Chapter 1

Kazuki stretched wildly, flailing his arms as he disembarked the airplane, "*What a crappy trip!*" He cried out, dropping his bag to the floor and dragging it along on its wheels. Ahead he noticed his brother waiting which caused him to add a little extra sprint to his step.

"*That sucked.*" Kazuki called out as soon as his brother was within earshot. He ran his hand through his hair, it wasn't quite long enough to stay back so it always managed to flop back down in his face. Still, even in his face it maintained a graceful little arch, keeping it out of his eyes. It suited his rounded features.

"*At least there wasn't much of a layover.*" He nodded sagely, "*On my way back to Japan I had to sleep overnight at the airport before the connecting flight.*" Satoshi responded without a hint of sympathy.

Kazuki talked as they walked, "*You don't think something like that is going to happen on our way back do you?*" He couldn't help but worry, wondering if his brother was exaggerating.

"*Hopefully not.*" Satoshi answered keeping his pace, "Come on, we've *got to get our bags buddy.*"

The nickname still brought a smile to his face, his brother had taken to calling him that after he had gotten back from the States and it had yet to get old. It might be because he only chose to use it when they were on good terms.

Dodging the crowd, Kazuki took in his surroundings. Everything was in English. When they'd gotten off the first plane in Texas most everything was bilingual, but here... obviously this wasn't an international hub.

Down an escalator they finally made their way to the baggage carousel. It was a huge oval machine, encircled with a black plastic ring that matched five others just like it all the way down the terminal. "*So, our bags come up here?*" When they had arrived at their first airport he thought that he would have to pick up their bags and transport them themselves. He hadn't entirely believed Satoshi knew what he was talking about when he had insisted that the bags would be shuttled along to the next plane without their intervention.

"*They'll be here, give them a minute.*"

Kazuki looked around; some of the people were giving the two of them uncomfortable sidelong glances. He took a half-step toward his brother, "*Why are they looking at us*?" He asked in hushed tones.

Satoshi looked around, "*It's probably because we're talking in Japanese, they're just wondering what we're saying.*" His brother starred at him with his hazel eyes.

"*Should we be talking in English*?"

"*It wouldn't hurt. It's not like you couldn't use the practice.*"

Thinking for a moment Kazuki tried to put his question together, he'd spent so long reading English but had hardly spoken it aside from the mandatory classes at school, "How long take does this?" He asked at last, watching the sign above the baggage claim continue to flash 'Texas'. He flashed a look to his brother to see if he gave any critique of his English skills.

"It could take awhile." Satoshi answered after a moment of hesitation.

More people arrived, talking amongst themselves. Kazuki looked over at his brother; he was wearing his army shirt again. If he asked, Satoshi would insist that it wasn't for showing off his muscles. The smile on his face though would make it obvious that he was lying. He'd been proud of his physique after he'd come back from the army. It wasn't his muscles though that Kazuki was jealous of, it was his height. Kazuki had always been just about average in height but his brother still towered over him by a full head and a half. He looked American.

The sudden alarm clock buzz pulled Kazuki's attention back to the carousel. The plastic skirting lurched, the mechanism engaging with a grinding sound which gave way to clattering before spinning with slightly less fanfare. A moment later a large bag flew up from within. It carried more momentum than he expected and slammed against the plastic ribbing, sliding to the bottom and staring its journey around the oval before another smaller bag was shuttled to the top, this one landing more gracefully.

Kazuki kept an eye out. Even if his bag looked the same as others the sound it would make as it fell into place would give it away. His bag had been overweight from the start. Nonetheless it made him wonder if his abilities were always at work subconsciously. Fifty keys was a lot of luggage to be toting around without breaking a sweat.

The solid sound of the bag slamming into the carousel drew his attention. The clattering of golf clubs was absent, he knew this one was his before he even saw its nondescript features. Kazuki smoothly swiped his bag off the carousel as it went by, setting it on the ground next to his carry-on.

Moments later Satoshi snatched up his bag, immediately backing away to give an older couple access. "We're a little early." Satoshi made a point of looking at his watch as he spoke.

"Early how?"

"*Maybe a half hour.*" Satoshi responded, slipping back into his native language.

"Oh."

"We'll just wait in the loading zone." Satoshi

11

offered at last, moving smoothly back to English.

Although the airport was buzzing with activity, it was nothing in comparison to the international hubs. The layover had even involved taking a train just to make their flight on time. Still, there was plenty for Kazuki to look at as they rushed. The funny thing was that they shouldn't have even been rushing.

There was some oppressive feeling brought on by the other travelers. A contagious sensation that they forced on his sanity by running behind en-mass. Just being in the airport made him feel he was skirting the edge of tardiness despite logic dictating otherwise.

He let himself be distracted, at the edges of his mind he felt the tickle of airwaves. It felt strange after being so long without them. The cabin had been isolated during their trip across the Pacific; besides, there wasn't much need for a radio broadcast over one of the largest expanses of emptiness. And during their short layover he'd been too engaged to notice much of anything. Finally in a bit of a lull, he let the feeling encompass him, starting with the perception of a gentle touch, but finally giving way to full consonance.

The stations were different, shifted, but although it gave him an unbalanced feeling at first, he quickly settled in. In return he found himself enveloped in a plethora of new beats and songs. He felt the smile on his face but couldn't rid himself of it. He tuned from one station to another, feeling them as much as hearing them in his head. So many stations too, so much different music. Rock, rap, alternative, jazz, worlds more than he'd had in Gifu.

He'd seen it called a number of things as he browsed around the internet. 'Radio telepathy' if he had to put a name to it, but it seemed 'tuning' was a more popular choice given it's lack of notice in scientific literature.

Kazuki caught himself almost walking into a wall

as he and his brother exited the automatic doors. He tugged at his thoughts, pulling himself back to the here and now and tried to keep his focus on the music to a healthy level.

"Oh, she's already here."

Satoshi pointed and Kazuki tried to figure out exactly which of the cars he was pointing at as they weaved between one another. The pointing turned into a wild wave and suddenly it was obvious who he was trying to flag down. Kazuki had never met Miranda, heard her voice, or even saw a picture. His brother had mentioned her, albeit rarely. But those few times he'd brought her up left him wondering, there was always some note to his voice that proved had to pin down. Of all the stories he told of all the adventures he'd had while in the army, she was the only person he'd ever mentioned by name.

It was still a shock to him that they would be staying with her during their trip to America. The revelation left him with a sinking feeling that things could get awkward. He didn't stress the point. The more he heard about her, the more he realized that she was as much a part of the reason for their trip as he was.

"Satoshi!" She called out, nearly beaching the car on the curb, barely swerving at the last moment. Kazuki could see why his brother might have been taken with her; she looked the part of an American woman that television had led him to expect. Long black hair with highlights of red framed her smiling face and blue eyes. Her hair contrasted well with her skin, warmed by the slightest of tans.

"Miranda." Satoshi replied warmly, bending over to stick his head in the car window. It wasn't the largest of vehicles, more in line with what Kazuki expected from his own country. He was more surprised that he hadn't seen any of the beasts he associated with the American auto industry yet.

"Just throw your stuff in back." Her smile was accompanied by the sound of the electric locks disengaging.

Satoshi reached out and opened the door, tossing his bags into the back before reaching in and pushing them over, making room for Kazuki. He pushed himself inside and set one of his bags across his lap, wedging the other between himself and his brother's bags.

"Let me guess... Kazuki?"

Kasuki looked up from his attempts to relocate the wedged bag. Miranda had twisted in her seat belt, pushing herself between the seats and held out her hand.

Timidly Kazuki took it and gave a quick shake. "Hai."

She smiled back at him, "I hope you at least know some English." She laughed, "But I do know that was a yes." She nodded to him bubbly, "Nice to meet you."

"Nice you to meet as well." Kazuki struggled through the phrase.

Satoshi closed the door solidly, "It's nice to see you again." He trailed off awkwardly before occupying himself with his seat belt.

For a moment there was a tension there, but Kazuki did his best to ignore it. Surprisingly the conversation died away quickly despite the looks they would pass to one another. As they drove on they gradually left the city. The gentle instrumentation of music became more apparent as he allowed himself to relax. It reminded him of an old style radio his grandpa had let him play with. There was static, jumbles of voices, hints of music. He focused more to bring things into tune, rattling through the carnage in his head until he finally settled on something good.

Kazuki fumbled around with his carry-on and pulled out one of the books he'd brought with him from

Japan, "*Customs, traditions, and other American Habits - An essential guide for visiting the USA.*" He'd read it over plenty of times on the plane ride, if only to take his mind off the nervousness of his first experience, but he decided to look through it again. Finally being in the states the book felt to him like a lifeline.

The drive was a long one. Kazuki couldn't remember ever being in a car so long in one setting. He took another look out the window; there were other cars, but nothing like the traffic he was used to seeing. This type of driving almost made him want to get a license.

The stations from the big city faded away but others had replaced them, albeit in smaller numbers. Despite his tuning, he'd noticed how quiet things had been between his brother and Miranda, but the initial discomfort had thankfully abated. He wondered if they were almost to Miranda's. In synchronicity he heard the repetitive click-click of the turn signal and the smooth deceleration of the vehicle.

Kazuki felt his anticipation grow as they reached the bottom of a ramp and stopped at a traffic light. They continued from there into the city. He recognized a few places, and smiled at the fast food empires that stretched the world over. Strangely it reminded him of home. They continued onward through the city, passing more traffic laden areas and making their way into the residential districts.

Again Kazuki was taken aback. That something as simple as houses could be so strikingly different. They were built on an entirely different scale. They were huge compared to the homes where he came from. His own home was one of the largest in the area, a carry-over from old times, but some of these were even larger. How big were the rooms? Would he get his own?

The car turned suddenly before bottoming out as it climbed into one of the many driveways adjoining the street. Kazuki had only a moment to look around before Miranda announced, "And... we're here." Kazuki's head jerked forward as she engaged the parking brake.

Satoshi got out of the car wordlessly and Kazuki followed suit, before reaching back to retrieve his bags. Pulling them out he let them hang at his sides as Satoshi leaned into the vehicle for his own luggage.

The house sat atop a hill; all of the homes on this side of the street were the same in that way. But the yard was huge, and there was even more in back, with a large oak between the sidewalk and the street.

The house itself was sized to the lot. Two stories with the outside accented by a large wrap-around porch framed in lattice that went as far around back as Kazuki could see. In the front of the home Lilac bushes started along the porch and extended to cover the distance between her home and the neighbors property. Looking closer however, it was obvious that the home was in need of a little repair. The grass, though well trimmed, revealed patches of dead. The vinyl siding had obviously started several shades darker but had faded to a mottled, muted green over the years. Kazuki might have gone so far to guess that it may have even been blue at one time. The trim bordering the roof however was the most cankerous eyesore; it was decayed and weathered with some sections missing entirely.

"Come on."

Kazuki shook himself out of his reprieve, hustling to catch up with his brother who was already on the porch following Miranda. "Gomen."

Satoshi turned to his brother, "English please." It wasn't forceful, just a reminder with a playful smile. Something he wasn't used to seeing from his brother. Kazuki berated himself for the slip up. He knew English well enough to convince himself that he didn't need the practice before he left, that had been a mistake.

"Kazuki." Miranda intoned as she opened the door to her home, "Your room is to the right, through the living room and past the bathroom. The last door." Seeing his blank look she added, "Did you catch that?" She looked to Satoshi for guidance.

"Arig-- thank you." Kazuki caught himself in time and gave a bow, before he took off his shoes, setting them outside the doorway. His brother shook his head and without a word, picked them up and set them inside the doorway.

"If you do that someone might steal them." He warned Kazuki.

Kazuki nodded hesitantly before heading off into the living room. Faintly he heard Miranda and Satoshi strike up their own conversation and ascend the staircase as he left the room.

There was a dusty smell to the home that was immediately apparent. It felt like no one had been in the living room in months. There were two doors, one against the underside of the staircase and another further ahead.

Kazuki paused for a moment and contemplated the door against the staircase and after a few seconds of hesitation opened it. He'd found the bathroom. After a moment of disappointment he walked into the other door to the bedroom.

The walls were done in wood paneling that lacked continuity with what he had seen of the rest of the home. There was a window on each of the outside walls and a dresser against the living room wall. In the middle of the room was a mattress, covered with sheets and lacking pillows. The smell of neglect was strongest there.

Dropping his bags to the floor, Kazuki walked to the window, fussing with it a moment before opening it wide. The clean air immediately suffused into the room.

He gave the bed a few hard smacks, rousing a cloud of dust before sitting down. At least it was comfortable. Overhead he heard footsteps. He wasn't sure if it was his brother, Miranda, or both.

The moment of relaxation was short lived; he didn't need it after all the sitting he'd done. Standing up he switched on the lights and started going through his backpack. Unpacking his clothes into the dresser he felt a momentary worry that he might be unpacking in the wrong room. He went over the directions, sure that he was in the right room before picking up this time sure of himself.

Pushing himself up from the bed with a cough Kazuki looked to the door; he could have sworn he heard a knock, "Dare desu ka?" He coughed out, wiping the dust from his dry eyes. He didn't remember falling asleep but it was dark outside, thankfully the light was still on inside the room.

"Kazuki?"

Kazuki shook the cobwebs from his head, "Yes." He answered firmly in English, struggling to mentally switch over. "Come in please." He offered after a moment.

The door clicked open and Miranda walked inside balancing an armload of blankets and a pillow. "I thought you could use these." Then after a moment she added, "Were you sleeping?"

Grinning sheepishly, Kazuki turned to the ceiling, "Yes." He admitted, pushing himself from the bed and taking the offered bedding. He tried to move it to his bed carefully but it toppled.

"Satoshi's asleep too." She started sympathetically, "I'll bet you two have some major jet lag." This time she trailed off.

"Yes." He wasn't sure what else to say and small talk pressed his grasp of the language.

"Well, see you in the morning then." It seemed she was equally at a loss for words. "Good night."

"Good night." Kazuki replied as she exited the bedroom, closing the door behind her.

The open bedroom window had left him with a chill. But Kazuki was reluctant to close it thanks to the dusty feeling in his chest. Picking up the blankets he set them atop the dresser and beat the dust out of the bed yet again, filling the air with a micro-fine dispersion of unsavory particles.

He gave a cough and moved the pillow, grabbing a blanket he tossed it over the bed, then grabbed another and did the same. A moment later he put on his bed clothes before turning off the lights and crawling beneath the covers.

Kazuki tried to let his mind settle. He was tempted to hop on his laptop for a few minutes. Check his forums, his e-mail. He wanted to feel the different stations in the air, get a taste of the local music. But the strains of the day had taken their toll. With that thought on his mind, it wasn't long before he managed to pass out.

Rolling onto his face Kazuki tried to avoid the light streaming through the mini-blinds. In return he was gifted a lung-full of dust mites. Deciding that it was as good a time as any, he rolled out of bed and onto his feet, looking himself over in the mirror. His light brown hair was tussled and along the side of his face he had a red line where he had slept on the pillow case wrong. His brown eyes still had the look like he could pass out any second. Worst though was that he could smell himself.

As best he could, Kazuki combed his hair and changed into a fresh pair of clothes. He was anxious, excited, worried. He hoped that his brother was awake so he wouldn't have to spend time with Miranda alone.

That was always the worst about staying over anyone's home, but now he felt the awkwardness more than ever.

Kazuki rubbed his eyes one last time before turning the knob. It was quiet in the living room. But the sun was high in the sky, someone had to be up. He made his way to the foot of the staircase, looking upward. He didn't want to go up there, he wasn't sure of the layout and who was sleeping where.

Hearing water running nearby, Kazuki walked around the staircase and toward the other end of the back end of the house. The dining room and kitchen were laid out, one after another.

"Morning." His brother called out, sitting down whatever he had been drinking.

Kazuki noticed Miranda turn toward him in the kitchen before going back to washing dishes.

"How sleep did you?"

Satoshi shook his head, "No, it's 'How did you sleep?' He smiled back, "And I slept just fine. I think I even fell asleep before you."

"Good." Kazuki sat down at the table across from his brother. "I am glad."

"We saved you some leftovers." Satoshi pushed a plate in front of Kazuki covered by the lid from a pan.

Kazuki lifted the lid, sausages and eggs. It certainly seemed like American fare. "Thank you." He made sure to say it loud enough that Miranda might be able to hear in the kitchen as she put away dishes.

"So, what's the plan for today?" Satoshi asked between sips of coffee.

"Not sure." Kazuki paused to take a bit of his food and think his wording over, "Going to walk through the city."

"It's a nice city." Satoshi offered, "You want some company?"

Kazuki thought on it for a moment, having his brother around would make things more comfortable.

After all, he didn't know the area.   He wanted his brother with him. "If you want." But he decided to leave the actual decision up to his brother.

"Well, if you've got it taken care of…"   He trailed off, putting the decision back on Kazuki.

Miranda eventually finished with the dishes and left out the back door. *Do you think she'd mind if I took a shower*?" Kazuki asked as soon as Miranda walked out of earshot.

"No, why would she?"   Satoshi shook his head, "You are a guest in her house and you're going to be here awhile, she probably expects you to take several showers over the next couple weeks." Satoshi softened his expression, "And try to stick to English even when it's just the two of us, you kinda need the practice."

Kazuki felt belittled enough but his brother was right. Before they had left Japan he had been confident in his abilities, but taking tests in school and typing on the Internet were things that didn't prepare him entirely. He wished that he would have accepted his brother's offers for tutoring before they'd left.

"I will take a shower." Kazuki answered at last, just as Miranda walked back into the house and started forcing a clean bag into the garbage can.

"Okay then, you have your cell if you need me."

"Yes, will I see you later."   Kazuki answered without the slightest inflection of a question before giving a bow to Miranda and his brother and leaving the room.

The warm wind felt good blowing through Kazuki's damp hair.   Although he'd seen maps of the city, actually walking around, experiencing the sights and sounds was a different matter altogether. Yet again he was inundated by all the signs in English and he struggled to read as much as he could, especially the street signs as he was unsure of what was important.

There were plenty of places that he planned to visit, but the library was pretty high on his list. Despite being a devout technophile he could never shake the passion he had for reading old books.

Kazuki had a long walk ahead of him, but it gave him time to think and practice. Taking a deep breath, he expanded his senses, feeling the channels come to him from the air. He tuned them in one at a time, trying to find something good on the airwaves. There was something different though. Some of the stations felt weaker, like when he tuned a station and it faded from broadcast. He stopped walking a moment and focused, trying to tune into one of the odd stations.

Kazuki's eyes widened, the station winked out of existence. It felt physical, like he'd been shoved. He shook the feeling off but it left him uneasy. He tried again, more probing this time. Slowly the station reappeared and started to 'feel' normal again, but it still had that overtone that it was weaker than it should have been.

Was this what it felt like to have someone else tune the same station? He though on it for a moment, could they feel his random tuning efforts, even when they weren't in earnest? He let out a deep breath feeling slightly discouraged. Wishing that somehow he could track down whoever was using the station.

As he continued walking he evaluated each station critically. Several of them felt weird. Finally though, his trepidation gave way to excitement. Yes, this was the place he wanted to be.

Eventually he settled into one of the more alternative themed stations. He'd heard most of the songs before in Japan, but they were good. And with good music the walk went much faster.

"Hey!"

Kazuki turned to the voice, realizing that he had almost passed the library.

"You!"

This time Kazuki was better able to track the voice. There was a group of teenagers by the fountain in front of the library; one of them was waving him over.

"Me?" He called out, wondering what they were getting at.

"Yeah, you, come here for a second." The guy waving him over looked like some kind of punk rocker.

Kazuki regarded them warily as he made his way down to the next crosswalk. There were two girls, three guys, and even from his distance he could tell they all belonged to the same clique. He couldn't shake the worried feeling, part of it was him being in a new place but the other part was that these people had hailed him down so aggressively.

As he approached, the same guy that flagged him over stood up and started walking toward him. Kazuki looked around, he'd heard America was a violent place, but there was a decent crowd. The smile that the kid wore though... although a bit sarcastic it still reminded him of violence.

"I can tell you're new around here..." He started out, closing the gap between the two of them. "So let me give you one warning. Stay off our station." There was less than a meter between the two of them when Kazuki stopped in time with the library native.

"Station?" Kazuki stumbled again trying to convey his words, "Your station?" Kazuki tried again, "How station yours?"

The smile dropped from the features of the kid Kazuki was facing off with, "Oh, wow, you're really not from around here." The threatening aura he had been projecting faded as well.

"Japan. That is where from."

"You're from Japan?" The spiky haired kid parroted back incredulous.

"Yes. I am trying others like me to find." Kazuki

swallowed hard, fighting to correct himself as he mentally dinged himself for his subject object verb order. "I came here to find others like myself." He breathed out, satisfied as he saw and honest smile quirk up on the punks face.

"Like you, a Channeler?" The teen offered.

Kazuki noticed the others sitting around the fountain were starring on, curious as to what they were talking about. "Yes, forum online showed a map with… others like me."

"And you came all the way here to find someone else that could tune." The smile the teen had been wearing grew, "Well, you found five of us just now." He gestured back to his compatriots, "Hey, check this guy out. He's from Japan!" Then he leaned in closer, "What's your name man?"

"Kazuki." He felt embarrassed from the attention. He tried to accept things for what they seemed and not worry that somehow this might be some ploy to take advantage of his naivety.

"Kazuki-" The punk held out his hand, Kazuki looked down at his hand, ratty leather gloves, the fingers cut off unevenly with a chain going from the cuff of his right glove to his pants pocket. Uneasily Kazuki took his hand and shook it, looking over his muscled frame, "-my name is Noe." He released his grip, "You guys, this is Kazuki. He's a Channeler from Japan."

Noe stepped out of the way, giving the others access to him. A younger looking heavier set girl who was hanging out in the right wing of the group spoke up fist, "Hi, I'm Tommie." Then after a moment of pause she added, "That's Tommie with an I - E." Kazuki looked over her black hair done up in a pony tail and her deep blue pajama pants with pink stars. If that wasn't enough, there was also something odd about her accent.

"Nice to meet you." Kazuki gave a bow, thankful

to have learned the expression verbatim in school.

The youngest looking member of the group stepped up, pushing his hand toward Kazuki. "I'm Mike." Kazuki took his hand and shook it as well, being sure to make contact with his gray eyes. He was slightly jealous that despite Mike being the shortest of the group, he was still just as tall as Kazuki himself. Even with his short cut black hair.

"Irvin." A dark hand was thrust into Kazuki's field of vision and he took it. He didn't have to shake; Irvin pumped his hand up and down a few times. But aside from the difference in skin color, buzz cut, and brown eyes, he looked eerily similar to Noe. They could almost pass for twins.

"And I'm Allene." Kazuki felt his breath catch in his throat. She was slender, but somehow managed to have an almost offensive chest. Blond hair with a few curls sticking out around her beret, blue eyes, and a short skirt.

"N-nice you to meet." Kazuki forced a larger smile, "All of you." He added after he realized he had directed the comment solely at Allene.

Allene, Irvin, Noe, Tommie, Mike. Kazuki repeated the names a few times in his head, trying to focus on each of the members of the group as he thought their name. Remembering names had always been a weakness of his and he was determined to get things right from the start.

Tommie, the peppy slender girl was the first to speak up, "So, what brings you from Japan. You visiting family or something?"

Kazuki turned to Allene, happy to focus his attention on her again, "I want to find others like me." Then after a moment he added, "Channelers."

"And..." She smiled back to him, "Now what?"

"Now..." That was a good question; he'd expected most of his trip to consist of him just trying to locate other Channelers. He hadn't given much thought as to what to do once he found them. When he thought about it though, what he wanted to know more than anything is if anyone had figured out how they could do what they did.

It took a moment but he got his bearings together, "I do not know how powers I got. How you get your powers? How many like us others?" He rushed out, "Gomen." He shook his head, mentally trying to keep with English, "I do not mean to speak so poorly."

For the second time Irvin spoke up, "It's fine, I think I got 'cha, just keep working on it." The comment caused Kazuki to look downcast.

Noe broke in, he seemed to be the leader of the group, "You can bet we've all wondered the same thing and if you hadn't have asked us then we'd of asked you the same thing." Noe nodded his head absently, "Really though, there aren't any other Channeler's in Japan?"

Kazuki shook. "No."

"Hummm..." Noe gave a slight laugh, "It just keeps getting weirder. None of us know how or why we can do what we do." He shook his head, a few of his earrings hitting against one another. "It's just something we can do… somehow. There are more like us around here though if that's what you're looking for but they're as in the dark as we are."

Kazuki struggled to keep up with the fast pace of talking, he wished they would slow down.

"Just stay off our station." This time Irvin seemed more cordial. It wasn't really a warning, just something he was trying to pass along. Kazuki struggled though with how a person could 'own' a station like that.

"Why?" Kazuki tried to make it non-threatening, he was really curious.

Mike stepped in slightly, "If you use our station, then if we need it we won't be able to use it ourselves."

His voice broke mid-way through the statement but no one else seemed to notice.

"What he means-" Tommie cut in, "Is that if we need to tune into that station completely, and you're on it, then it could be a pain in the butt on our end. So we need that station free."

Things became clearer for Kazuki. To prove to his brother that his tuning was not a trick he'd shown off by lifting a stack of concrete pavers back home. If he hadn't been able to fully tune in like he had, he probably wouldn't have been able to lift them.

A silence settled between the group that gave way to momentary awkwardness, "Anyway... If that's it-" Noe started as he began walking back to the fountain, "-nice to meet you and everything, guess we'll see you around."

"Yeah, nice to meet you." Allene waved over her shoulder as she followed Noe, and the rest of them turned and started walking back to the fountain as well.

Kazuki started to speak up but found himself at a loss for words. He really wanted to talk some more, squeeze this resource for all it was worth. But he felt so silly trying to talk to them, it felt like every word was wrong.

"Nice to meet you all." Kazuki waved to the group as they took up spots around the fountain, some of them turning on MP3 players or checking their cell phones. In response a few waved back but they looked occupied already.

Slowly Kazuki smiled, it hadn't been perfect, but the encounter had been far from bad. Probably the best he could have hoped for. With a smile on his face he headed out of the summer heat and into the library.

It was getting dark outside when Kazuki's phone rang from his brother. He hadn't realized how much time had passed. Before he could answer it however someone hushed him loudly. Kazuki grimaced and disconnected the call. Quickly he put away the books he had been reading and made his way out of the library before calling his brother back. Dinner was ready, and beyond that his brother was worried about him. He told Satoshi that he was on his way home.

There was a little spring in his step as he made his way down the main street. Things had gone well. Aside from meeting the other Channelers, he'd found a ton of books to read. If things went well he was going to be sure to meet up again with that group of Channelers the next. Or maybe even search for some of the other Channelers they had mentioned.

More deliberately this time Kazuki plodded through the stations, tuning them in one at a time. He was careful to avoid the station from earlier but the thought made him wonder about the ownership of the other stations, being the only Channeler in his area he'd never had that worry before.

Finally he settled on a rock station, some of the more classic American fare. Kazuki was making good time on his way to dinner when he felt the station distort. Someone had just tuned it in he realized. For a moment he was tempted to tune to a different station but dismissed the idea. He was there first, and besides he wasn't fully tuning the station, it was strong enough for both of them.

For a while Kazuki and whoever else was using the station shared it evenly. Without warning however the station suddenly faded out completely, leaving an empty feeling in Kazuki's head. "Nani?"

The station was gone; there was no way he could tune into it. There was just a blank space in the airwaves where it should have been. He wondered-

A sudden explosion a few blocks off shocked Kazuki from whatever thoughts he might have had. He swallowed hard, wondering what was going on before picking up his pace.

Another concussive sound echoed across town, this one not unlike a collision between two vehicles. And this one was closer. He rushed some more, trying to ensure he stayed ahead of the carnage. He felt a different station that he hadn't even been tuned into fade out. Strange vibrations reverberated through the other stations like the sound of a bell ringing. Kazuki felt the fear rise up along his spine.

He just wanted to get home. He would ask about it tomorrow at the library. He was overcome with fear. A fear he knew as irrational, the carnage was over a mile away but it felt like he was there watching it happen. Kazuki could feel the power, two different sources. Two people Kazuki realized. Fighting? He wondered.

Another sound echoed simultaneously across the city and airwaves and suddenly one of the stations was back. Then just as quickly the other, but someone was still there. He pulled himself away from the airwaves, consciously pulling inward. He looked up, in his rush he had started to run and without even realizing it he was back at Miranda's.

Chapter 2

That night Kazuki found it near impossible to shut his brain. When at last sleep did come it was fitful but still he found himself waking up later than he expected. He made his way to the library in long strides, his shoes striking soundly against the concrete sidewalk as he turned the corner.

Normally he had free rein over the radio waves, taking them in and thoughtlessly leafing through them. Now there was at least one station he was trying to avoid. Even with the other stations he tried not to pull too much, he didn't want to direct attention to himself. He wanted to meet people, but he didn't want a repeat of how he had met Noe.

Besides, Kazuki had been catching hints of others on the stations all morning. He shook off the feeling, instead focusing on what was around him. The beautiful blue sky and warmth to the morning air that had yet to be overcome by the heat of the day.

Goose bumps began to rise up on Kazuki's arms. There was someone else on his station. Quickly he changed over, from rock to rap. A moment later there was a presence on that station too. Just as quickly he tuned again, this time to a country station and step for step, a presence met him again. That same presence.

Kazuki shook his head, letting out a deep breath before mentally pulling himself from the vastness. Afterward, his walk was a little less bright. As much as he tried, he couldn't shake his uneasy feeling.

The library was a letdown. The group from before was nowhere to be found. He felt like an idiot for believing they would be in the same spot. Kazuki let out a sigh as he walked over to the fountain and set down. It was just a small fountain, a few meters across with series of square terraces increasing in size from top to bottom over which the water flowed. It was pretty to look at but that was the intention after all. He thought for a moment of distracting himself with the library, but he had plenty of books. He needed to get out; not cloister himself up in that hole.

He forced himself to keep moving. He remembered from the maps that there was a park nearby along the lake. It was as good a goal as any. There would be plenty of time for a second chance meeting.

"Hey jackass!"

Kazuki turned, afraid as he felt a strong hand firmly grabbing his shoulder.

"You wanna fight or something?" The boy said with a sing-song quality. It was a teenager, about the same height as himself, short cropped black hair, and wearing a t-shirt that would have better served as a cloth for staining furniture.

"What?" It was all Kazuki could think to say. Quickly he pulled away from the grip on his shoulder and thankfully was able to put some distance between himself and the other guy. Someone else walked up, with a smirk on his face to match and the two of them stood side by side.

"Are you the one I've been chasing all over the airwaves?" He laughed.

Kazuki blanched, realizing that he had allowed himself to settle on a channel without registering it. This person had tracked him down just like the other Channelers the day before. "I am sorry." Kazuki tried, hoping for the best.

"Sorry, for what?" He laughed off the apology, "I just wanna kick some ass."

"Sorry. I am Japan from." Kazuki bowed his head and backed away, "No offense. No offense." Whoever this guy was he felt as hostile as he sounded, and Kazuki's fighting career had been on the ropes since he was beat up by a girl as a pre-teen.

"You are Japan from?" The two of them laughed and Kazuki felt himself blush as he realized his mistake. The laughter died down and Kazuki caught the thoughtful look, "Baka kuso atama." He spouted off unexpectedly with an accent that could have grated diamonds. He moved over to his friend and muttered, "Stupid shit head." And laughed.

Kazuki's eyes lit up, "Nihongo wo hansemasu ka?"

Again that laughter, that same sardonic smile, "You think I understood a word of that?"

"But… Japanese." Kazuki mumbled perplexed.

"Shit, I learned that from watching Anime." Then after a moment he added, "Baka."

Kazuki took a moment to choose his words carefully, "What do you want? I need home go." Kazuki eyed the person behind him; it looked as if he hadn't had a good night's sleep in some time from the dark bags under each of his eyes.

"Since I learned how to do this shit with the radio, I've stomped everyone else in the ground." The two of them laughed, "You being a Channeler you're pretty much bending over and telling me, kick my ass please." It was the matter of fact delivery that worried Kazuki the most.

"I must go." Kazuki tried to move to his right but the teen who had been standing in the back stepped up and around, blocking his way.

"You don't walk away from Alden." Kazuki felt the wind leave him as he was shoved. He stumbled back and nearly fell. It took him a moment to regain his footing. Kazuki looked at his attacker, his scruffy hair continued down past his sideburns, finishing with a tuft of hair at the bottom of his chin. The look was completed by the torn denim vest he sported.

Reason had fled the scene, "Please. No. I can

not fight." Kazuki covered his face with his arms to protect himself. Against his better judgment he pulled himself out of the stations.

"Pthhh, whatever." Alden was silent for a moment and Kazuki held his position before he heard a huff, "If you're not even going to try... you're not worth the effort." Kazuki reeled back as he felt the punch connect solidly with his arm. "Come on Jayson."

Slowly Kazuki uncovered his face as he watched the two hooligans walk down the street in the opposite direction, laughing and occasionally turning back to point at him.

He hadn't let himself cry. He felt so helpless not being able to explain himself. And what he could explain was woefully inadequate. It's not that he couldn't defend himself at all, but against another Channeler, he had no illusions about winning. Kazuki wondered if that was the feeling he had the night before when the stations died. Was it that same Alden guy? Two Channelers fighting?

The only nice person he'd met in America so far was Miranda he lamented. Everyone on the street walking past him, beside him, no one gave him a glance. It was all so unfriendly.

The park reminded him of Japan, that the city could come to such an abrupt end. Across the street there were multi story buildings, but his side of the street, there was grass, trees, and further in a lake.

He smiled, though the park could do for some flowers or something with color, it was nice enough. From there it was only a short walk to the beach. There were some people in the water but not as many as he expected. Kazuki made his way along the shoreline to the edge of the swimming area, marked by an outcropping of rocks. He found a nice spot there to take a break, wedged between two boulders.

As he laid there with his eyes closed, feeling the heat from the sun penetrate his jeans and shirt, time passed quickly. More people made their way to the shore, and finally Kazuki felt comfortable enough to once again expand his powers to enjoy a little music. Slowly the sound entered into his senses, and he adjusted his tuning appropriately, careful not to take too much of the station.

The vibrating in his pocket preceded the ringing of his cellular phone, one of those old fashioned rings that mimicked a LAN line. Groggily he opened his eyes, he hadn't fallen asleep but it had been close. Scrambling he reached into his pocket and retrieved his cellular phone. It was his brother's number.

"*Hello.*" Kazuki allowed himself to answer in Japanese as a comfort for earlier.

"*Hey, how are things going?*" His brother asked, sounding pretty cheerful himself.

"*Okay, I'm just sitting down by the lake.*"

"*Having some fun?*" His brother asked jokingly before he heard him take a deep breath, "*I was just calling because Miranda was going to take us out for dinner later. Do you think you could come back a little earlier than we'd planned?*"

Kazuki smiled, "*Yeah that sounds good, what time?*"

"*About six.*"

"*See ya then.*"

"*See ya.*" Kazuki flipped his phone closed and put it back in his pocket. He settled back in, there was still plenty of time to kill before dinner. He mentally focused on the station and brought it into stronger relief.

Finally, he knew he needed to leave; he was starting to get a sun burnt. Besides, he wanted to search the internet for some of the people that he met the day before. He knew some of their first names and their city. With that he was hopeful he could find something on the message boards. If he could only talk to them over the internet, he lamented, introducing himself would be so much easier.

Kazuki pushed himself from between the two rocks, feeling his back give warnings the whole way as the pressure from the boulder he had been sitting on was removed. Squinting as he finally opened his eyes he noticed that the beach goers had been filling the beach, spreading out until there were people camped almost within arms reach.

He dusted off his butt and headed toward the city, a little spring in his step. As he walked through the forested part of the park, he noticed a presence on the stations. There was the feeling that someone was there, but it was different, someone else. Somehow it felt close by though he couldn't explain the difference. He kept walking but the feeling nagged at him. It felt like he was closing in but there was only a couple sharing a picnic lunch.

"Forgiveness please." Kazuki started as he approached the table, getting the attention of both of the occupants, "Are either of you a Channeler?"

The man and woman exchanged amused glances, "Are you?" The man spoke up first, pushing back his sandy blonde hair and eyeing Kazuki critically.

"Yes." He admitted, a hopeful smile creeping onto his face.

"Then you already knew the answer before you asked." The woman smiled back at him, her mouth a prism of perfect teeth.

"But, which of you?"

"Both of us." The man put his arm around the woman, entangling his hand in her blonde hair.

"Oh." Kazuki paused for a moment, the both of them seemed fairly approachable, he offered his hand, "I am Kazuki. From Japan."

"Casey, nice to meet you and this is my

35

girlfriend…" The man took his hand and shook it, then passed it off to the woman next to him.

"Julie." She smiled to him, nodding her head in a miniature bow.

"Very nice you both to meet." Kazuki smiled at the two of them.

"So, Japan, that's a long way away. What brings you to America?" Casey asked, holding his girlfriend close against him and offering him to sit with a gesture from his other hand.

"I want to find more like me. Channelers. To find out more about Channelers." Kazuki smiled, hoping to get his point across.

"You came all the way from Japan for that?" Julie asked, looking shocked.

"No one in Japan can do these things. It is important to me very."

"Well, there's a bunch of us around here, I mean, there's me and Julie here. Then there's Noe and his group, and Carmela-" He paused a moment glancing at Julie, "She's a Channeler right?" Julie gave him a smack on the arm and a smile, "-and... well, Alden." Casey noticed Kazuki's look, "I take it you already know about him."

"Yes." Kazuki tried to hide his melancholy, "We meet today."

"He's an asshole." Julie chimed in, keeping it light despite the insult, "He likes to think that all the stations are his, and gets all up in your face if you're tuning on the same station he is." She huffed.

"He wanted with me to fight." Kazuki lamented.

"He'll do that." Casey picked up, "And he's a good fighter too. I don't think either one of us could take him alone."

The implication clicked quickly, "You two?" Kazuki looked between them; they didn't look like fighters. Although Casey's medium build might have been that of a combatant, Julie's lithe body didn't look like it could take punch-one.

"Well, it was mostly for fun, we took some classes in martial arts and some cardio kickboxing and stuff." Julie was blushing, "But I'm glad we did, just so we can teach that guy a lesson when we need to."

Kazuki examined Julie more carefully, noticing for the first time the faint scar, starting on her neck above her collar bone, and the bit of a scar coming out from beneath her long sleeved shirt and wrapping around her hand. It did seem odd that she was wearing a long sleeved shirt in the temperatures that they were having. He wondered if the scar continued the whole length.

"There was another guy with him... Jayson?" Kazuki asked, trying to get more information.

"He's just a thug Alden hangs out with, him and Bailey. Neither one of them are Channelers, just bullies that pick on people." Julie said with disgust.

Casey took his hand from around Julie's neck and folded his hands on the table, "Just ignore them if you can."

The revelation was a relief to Kazuki and he let out the breath he had been holding. "Is there a channel that I should not use. To upset him not?"

Casey shook his head, "No, that guy is all over the place. The only people around here that lay claim to a channel are Noe's group, W.B.Z.X. We got an agreement to stay off that but other than that we tune whatever we want."

"I am glad. I was worried." Kazuki felt his jaw unclench.

"About powers though-" Julie brought her hands up to her head and ran them through her hair, "-It's not like we have anything written down, but we've learned some things over the years." Julie exchanged a look with Casey, and he took the cue to pick up the conversation.

"You know, like the more you are tuned in to a song the more power you get out of it." Casey started.

Kazuki thought back to his own experiences, "I know about that. Like you will kill radio stations."

Casey nodded, "Yeah, they completely fade out. And if you sing along with the song in your head you get even more out of it. Like you fall into sync, like a rhythm with the beat."

Julie smiled, "One time Casey broke a tree in half that was like this big around." She spread out her hands about half a meter. It was impressive and caused Casey to blush.

Julie continued with a laugh, "Alden heard about it, I think that's one of the reasons that he doesn't mess with us any more."

Casey joined in after a laugh of his own, "Yeah. And hey, you can go from one song to another when they end to keep tuning, but you'll pay for it later. You might be sore for a while."

Julie gave Casey a nudge and a smile and they exchanged looks again for a moment. "But anyway man, if you don't mind we'd like to get back to lunch before we have to go back to work." After a moment he added, "Don't worry, we'll see you around."

Julie offered her hand, and Kazuki took it, "It was nice meeting you Kazuki."

Kazuki took Casey's hand as well, "Nice meeting the two of you as well." Kazuki stood from the table and bowed in each of their directions, which Julie seemed to really enjoy before he walked off.

Casey shouted after him, "Good luck man!"

"Thank you!" Kazuki shouted back waving, before going on his way back into the city.

Pizza wasn't Kazuki's normal idea of quality restaurant food, but he had to admit it was much better than he'd expected. Around the establishment, large overhead lights lit at each table with bright red colors adorning the walls; it had the atmosphere of a bar. When he'd mentioned that his brother told him that bars sometimes had the best food in America. Indeed, the pizza was on a completely different level than the style in Japan. That was a joke by comparison. This was thick, heavy food, and very filling.

Kazuki grabbed a third slice from the tray in front of him and put it on his plate just as Miranda was grabbing her second. He looked to his brother, eating his own pizza. He wanted to tell him about his day, finding even more Channelers; he was still so excited from it all. Casey and Julie had turned everything around.

He held his tongue. Channeling itself was strange and really had to be seen to be believed. And since Miranda hadn't seen anything Kazuki held back from saying anything. Still, there was something he could talk about, "Satoshi?" Kazuki swallowed his last bite of pizza and set the rest of the slice down.

"Yeah?" Satoshi stopped eating for a moment.

"I was hope-- wondering if you would show me to fight."

"You want me to teach you how to fight?"

Miranda stopped eating momentarily to watch the exchange between the brothers but said nothing.

"Yes, please." Kazuki looked down at his food.

"I can if you want, but why?" Satoshi asked, taking another bite of his pizza.

"I will feel safer." Kazuki figured that the exact details could wait for later.

"I'll buy that." Satoshi nodded, taking another bite, "When do you want to start?" He eyed Kazuki curiously.

"Can tomorrow we start?"

"Can we start tomorrow?" His brother parroted back to him, "Yes, we can start tomorrow." Satoshi smiled back at him and Miranda decided to start eating again.

With that the conversation died again. Kazuki finished off his slice of pizza but did not go for another slice even with Satoshi and Miranda still eating.

"How did you meet Satoshi?" Kazuki asked Miranda.

She swallowed the bit of pizza in her mouth and wiped her lips with a napkin, "Well..." She seemed caught off guard by the suddenness of the question. "I met him while he was on leave from the military base." She took a drink of her soda, "My mother had just passed away -- and I was out-- at the bar."

Kazuki felt her mood shift and immediately regretted bringing it up. However Miranda just took another sip of her soda and continued.

"And well, he was at the same bar, looking out of place."

Satoshi took a moment to explain, "The guys basically dragged me there, my English was garbage, worse than yours, I knew I wouldn't fit in." He laughed to lighten the mood.

Miranda nodded, "No, his English wasn't that good. But I could figure out what he was trying to say. So, we talked for awhile, and shared a few drinks. And, I found out what a nice guy he was. So, we started hanging out after that."

Satoshi gave a hard smile, "She was one of the only locals that would take the time to talk to someone like me, there aren't many Japanese troops after all." He finished off the slice of pizza that he had been eating and drained his soda.

At the same time Miranda finished off her food, "Your brother's a cool guy to hang around with, and he had all kinds of stories."

"Good." Kazuki didn't know what else to say. He was curious now, he wanted to ask how she took his leaving but didn't want to pry more than he had. "Thank you for the food." He added with a bow of his head, noticing that the waitress had put down the bill.

Miranda smiled and slipped her credit card out of her purse, "You're welcome."

Sunlight streamed through the window, rousing Kazuki from his sleep. Even with the blinds closed the potency was hardly diminished and he had no defense against it aside from bundling his head in the blanket. Which would have worked, save the fact that the mornings did seem to be even warmer and doing so caused him to sweat profusely.

Begrudgingly he pushed himself up from his bed and into a sitting position. Looking at his laptop he couldn't help but think of the night before. He'd stayed up way too late trying to find contact information for the other Channelers he'd come across. It was frustrating but true, the internet was about useless. All of the e-mails were outdated. He would have been much better off with a few surnames and a phone book as embarrassing as it would have been.

He sighed as he pushed himself to his feet. Satoshi was going to teach him to fight today; he smiled finding himself a little excited. Kazuki put on some loose fitting clothes, his tore up jeans and a yellow shirt with a tomato stain that he had packed in case he needed to do something dirty.

The living room was vacant. If he'd been told that it hadn't been vacuumed in a year he would have believed it. His brother was at the breakfast table. He didn't see Miranda anywhere though. "Good morning." He called out as he made his way around the staircase and started heading toward the table.

"Yo." His brother waved a hand and put down his news paper. The house was dead silent.

"Where is Miranda?" Kazuki asked, her absence

feeling wrong.

"She's sleeping I think. I didn't bother to wake her." Satoshi explained, taking a sip of water.

"Okay." Kazuki sat down at the table, there wasn't any food or anything to occupy his attention so he cut straight to the chase, "*When do you want to start training me?*"

"*Anytime you're ready I guess.*" Satoshi put down the paper, "*But why do you want to lean to fight anyway? It's not as dangerous here as television and movies make it sound, not in Wisconsin at least.*"

Kazuki swallowed hard, he didn't want to make it look like he was really in danger or else his brother might feel the need to be involved, "*It's just, some of the people around here have powers like me and they use their powers to help them fight. I just want to be able to defend myself if I need to.*"

Satoshi sighed, "*It takes a long time to learn to fight properly.*" He let the pause speak for itself, "*Lucky for you I learned to fight in the military. Let's just say I had an accelerated course.*" He finished with a smug smile that proved infectious.

"*That's awesome.*" The smile faded slightly, "*But what about Miranda, does she even know why I wanted to come here?*"

"*No.*" Satoshi shook his head, "*And let's keep it that way for now, she just knows that you wanted to see an American city. That's enough.*"

"*Okay then.*" Kazuki stood from the table, "*Let me get something to drink then we can get started.*"

Lying on the bed, Kazuki rocked his feet in tune with the beat. He moved his laptop off the bed and onto the nightstand, wishing not for the first time that he had brought a CD player as a stand alone unit instead of utilizing a whole laptop just to play CD's.

Past the headphones he barely heard the knock

at the door. "Come in." He called out, pulling off the headphones and rolling onto his side.

Miranda pushed the door open, "Here, I brought you some lemonade." She offered him a glass, taking a step forward.

"Thank you." He took the glass from her gingerly, sitting it down next to his laptop. He was feeling a little thirsty. "And thank you for letting me borrow your CD's."

"No problem." She laughed, "I never listen to them anyway, not since I got my MP3 player." She stepped back into the door frame, "Anyway, I'm gonna call it a night, see you in the morning."

Kazuki gave a wave as he took a sip from the glass. "Good night."

The door closed with just the sound of the latch engaging. Kazuki gave a yawn and set down the glass. His whole body felt stiff, especially where his brother had tossed him on the ground. They hadn't gotten around to hand to hand fighting, but he was getting schooled in take downs and submission holds. He never realized though how much thinking there was to fighting. He always assumed it was mostly instinct, but from what his brother showed him, if a skilled fighter was facing off against someone who fought solely on instinct, skill would triumph. It was more a combination of takedowns and boxing than martial arts his brother explained, but it was effective.

Only Miranda's entrance made him realize how late it was so Kazuki pushed himself up and set his laptop in his lap, dragging the cursor over to shut it down for the night. The second knock at the door was more unexpected than the first.

"Yes?"

This time it was his brother who pushed open the door, "Thought I would check up on you." He gave a smile and leaned against the inside of the door frame,

43

"You know, see how your bruises are healing."

"I am fine." Kazuki set the laptop aside. He was hurting all over not that he would admit it.

"So, are we on again tomorrow?" His brother asked with that same cockiness.

"Yes, more tomorrow." Kazuki smiled realizing that his brother had enjoyed their session. He would probably be hurting even more by then. Then to heap even more injuries on top of that, Kazuki knew he was setting himself up for disaster.

"Cool, so what's up with the CD's?" His brother asked, gesturing to the stacks sitting on the dresser.

Kazuki looked over to them, he wondered if Miranda had told him that he wanted to borrow them. "I have to like the music here more." He explained, unplugging the headphones from the computer and wrapping them up.

"Why?"

"If I really like the music, I can be stronger." He shut the lid of his laptop, "I can get more power."

"Oh." His brother answered almost dismissively, "With that thing you do."

"Yes, the more music is good the better I can be." He knew his brother didn't understand. It was something unique to him, another sense he didn't have so to speak.

"Well, whatever, see you in the morning." His brother nodded heading out of the room.

"*Good night.*"

"Good night to you too." Satoshi closed the door softly, leaving Kazuki to sit and think.

After changing into his bed clothes he made sure his laptop was plugged in and charging. Turning out the lights he plunged into bed and covered up. As he relaxed Kazuki started thinking about the music. If he wanted to really be able to draw the most from it. He had to know it, verbatim. Be able to sing along with it, love it. He needed the practice as much as he needed the practice fighting if he wanted to fit in with the other Channelers and defend himself if he had to.

Still, that wasn't the half of it. After he had finished training he'd gone back to the library, and again was met with disappointment. There was no one there from Noe's group.

Kazuki had tried to feel them out through the radio waves. There were people there, other Channelers. Some of them felt familiar, and someone was on Noe's channel but nothing that he could track. Apparently no one was as close as the couple from the park had been. He hoped fervently that he would find them again. With his conversation with Casey and Julie, and beginning his training, he felt he was making progress. He wasn't sure toward what, but just by being by other Channelers he felt like he understood himself better, like he was making progress.

But he didn't have forever. And somehow all at once it felt like there was too much time left, and too little. Training with his brother, training his powers, and finding any other Channelers while all the while avoiding Alden and his crew. America was something else all together from what he expected.

Kazuki rolled over in his bed, trying to get comfortable. At least things seemed to be going well between his brother and Miranda, not at all like their first day together. Kazuki noticed the difference in the way she treated him as well.

Chapter 3

The pain was so potent that Kazuki had no choice but lay motionless, eyes turned to the sky. Unfortunately, his brother was still ready to go. Achingly Kazuki pushed himself to his side. The grass was soft, pleasant; it was the packed earth beneath that was giving him trouble. His brother had moved from showing off simple take downs to more advanced techniques coupled with the occasional jab or sucker punch.

At first Kazuki thought he'd been holding his own but that illusion had been shattered. His brother had been pulling his punches. And the worst of it was that even with his telegraphed movements and restrained attacks, Kazuki had eventually been forced backwards and toppled.

Satoshi had that smug look on his face. He'd been showing that side of himself a lot more lately, though he would never admit it. At least when they talked afterwards there was always a sense of humility. Satoshi earnestly appreciated the effort and general accolades. But while they were training, in the thick of it, his brother never lost his smile.

It was of little condolence to Kazuki that he'd yet to channel while practicing. He and Satoshi had talked before they had even started; Kazuki had promised that until he had mastered the basics, there would be none of his 'tricks'. If he could be formidable without channeling then things would fall into place once and eventually he knew he would have to combine the two arts.

Kazuki pushed himself to his feet with a groan. His hips hurt from the constant falls. His chest hurt from a few unlucky punches. And his palms hurt from catching himself mid-fall again and again and again.

For the umpteenth time that morning, Kazuki was

faced with a lob of half-paced punches. He managed to dodge several, but they only missed by the grace of God. There was no respite, the punches kept coming and eventually a few managed to thud annoyingly against his head and chest. Kazuki knew from experience that they would leave painful lumps the next day.

Actually anywhere thin skin covered hard bone he was prone to such contusions. Kazuki staggered, he hadn't even noticed the kick, he'd been too busy focusing on his brother's hands. Stumbling off to the side he collapsed with a grunt. "*G-Give me a second.*" Kazuki braced against the ground with his hands, the wind absent from his lungs. He was overheating and the humidity wasn't helping, he wanted to throw up.

He cursed inwardly to himself; every time he started to feel like he was doing well, Satoshi took it on himself to take him down a peg. Kazuki had just been getting used to the punches. The takedowns too had been simple enough to learn. Now suddenly he'd been relegated to beginner yet again, he took a shuttering breath and buried his face in his hands.

"What do ya say we call it a day?" Satoshi called out, holding his foot up off the ground and letting it swing effortlessly as he held his stance.

Kazuki looked up at his brother's smiling face. His brother could keep this up all day. But, if he kept going he was just going to get slower and sloppier. "Yes, it is enough." Kazuki took his brother's hand and utilized it for his up-righting.

"Good, I've got things to do." Satoshi gave a nod, changing the mood in an instant. "Just take it easy today, okay?" He added as an afterthought heading into the house, leaving Kazuki to himself in the yard.

Alone, Kazuki sat back down on the ground, wincing as he used his arm to slow his decent. Slowly he lay out on the long grass, watching the clouds float overhead. The coolness of the earth gave pause to his forming bruises.

He took a few deep, relaxing, breaths before allowing his senses to expand slowly. He tried to be more purposeful about it, feeling the airwaves around him. At first it had been difficult to exercise that level of control. That's why he had put forth the effort to learn it.

Systematically he tuned through the stations. He spent a few moments on each, trying to catch a glimpse of another Channeler. The most frustrating part was that although he couldn't find them physically, he could feel them on the stations. He wondered if they knew that it was him sharing the channel. Maybe they were looking for him too.

Finally he found a good song. He took a moment to feel out the channel, gently rolling the station in his mind as if forming a ball of dough. It was free. Focusing he tuned in more fully, feeling the music flow through him and enter his blood. Keeping his focus he pushed himself to his feet feeling energized anew.

Cautiously he threw a few punches, careful not to overextend his elbow. Just as deliberately he kicked at phantoms in the air. Quick enough the song was fading and the DJ destroyed his concentration. With a deep breath he simultaneously let the station free. The effect was instantaneous, his body sluggish at the loss.

Kazuki thought about it for a moment, gauging how motivated he felt. It was still early enough in the day to get some searching done. He hurt, but nothing that topical analgesic wouldn't help with.

Climbing the steps he headed inside. It was quiet. Apparently his brother was already gone. Absently he wondered what his brother had planned for the day. Grabbing a cup from the cabinet he filled it with water and quickly gulped it down. He changed his clothes, picking one of his t-shirts with huge kanji on the front and back. He wondered if anyone would ask what it said.

The weather was changing fast. Over the last few days the heat had been almost unbearable but now it was breaking in the wake of a cold front. The news said it was still a day out but the sky had been overcast all morning. It didn't matter; the dreariness was a decent trade-off for the break in temperature.

Kazuki walked as best he could to ignore the pain in his hip. The walk went quickly and as he approached the library he gently tuned to the station that Noe and his group called their own. He could feel them, several people. It was a fleeting feeling, like trying to find an unknown sound from rooms away. There were people there, more than one, but that was the limit to what he could tell.

Rounding the corner brought him within sight of the library. There area around the fountain was vacant. So many of his daily trips to the library had left him with nothing to show. Not for the first time he wondered about drawing the group to him. He knew their channel, if he tuned into the station and held it, fully absorbed it, would they come and find him? Then again they hadn't seemed happy last time when he had been squatting on their station. Would they understand him pulling a stunt like that to get their attention?

He dismissed the notion. Kazuki was anxious, not desperate. Walking up to the fountain he sat on the ledge of the stone retaining wall, holding his head in his hands. Slowly the throbbing started to pick up in his hip, inactivity feeding the injury. He debated the merits of moving.

Back at Miranda's house there wasn't much he could do. As of late he had been taxing his taste in American music, listening to the same CDs repeatedly. Instead of fostering the appreciation that he was shooting for, the opposite goal was being accomplished.

At least his brother had commented on his improved English.

Half-heartedly he stretched out his abilities again. He probed the WBZX frequency purposefully. The feel of the station. It felt cylindrical, soft with some sort of sweet smell. Wherever that feeling came from, it was unique for each station. It was a long shot, but maybe they were close by, like the day at the beach.

As Kazuki tuned he first noticed the muted, somehow muffled feeling on the station. That feeling he had when more than one person was utilizing the resource. It was a good sign. Kazuki grimaced as he got back on his feet. Experimentally he paced around the fountain, listening beyond the sound of the water splashing into the pool beneath. He felt something. It was different when he… he walked further from the fountain, crossing the street in front of the library as the traffic cleared.

He followed the street in one direction, then the other. It was hard to keep his eyes open and maintain the concentration needed but he had to in order to avoid walking into someone or causing an accident.

Toward the end of the street there was a staircase leading down from street level. Above the stairs was a shoddy neon sign. "Arcade?" Kazuki looked it over, he knew what an arcade was, but with the number of letters burned out, his guess could have been wrong.

He bit his lip; he had a strong feeling there were Channelers inside. Guardedly he descended the staircase. The place looked open; there were people inside and it did sound like an arcade. Lights flashed from behind the paper covering the window. He looked at the hours just to be sure.

Kazuki steadied himself before he stepped inside. The place was considerably more populated than he expected from the location. There were people jammed around every machine, three and four deep in some areas. The crowd relaxed him. Here he could blend in.

Simultaneously, the crowd did make his task ahead more difficult. Kazuki made his way over to the change machine and fed in a few dollars not entirely for appearances. A handful of bronze tokens tumbled out of the machine that somehow felt more genuine than the paper currency he had exchanged.

Most of the games were older. Classic would have been the most accurate description. Kazuki thought back to the last time he had been in an arcade, it'd been years. Giving another look around to get familiar with his surroundings, he started to get his bearings. He walked to the center of the room. Despite the dim lighting, he was able to see wall to wall from that vantage point. The arcade was smaller than it seemed.

There were Channelers here but the feeling wasn't precise. He gave another look around, scanning the crowd for a recognizable face. With a smile he tuned in WBZX and tuned more into it, then out, and then back again, pulsing the station. He noticed a few heads turn in his direction and in return he couldn't help but smile. Quickly he side stepped the traffic coming toward him and made his way to the far corner of the arcade.

"Hello." Kazuki greeted as he approached. Apparently the group had taken up residence in the corner, claiming the few games there as their own. There was a dance type game directly in the corner, and an arcade machine on one side of it with a fighting game across the isle-way. "I am Kazuki." He called out, stepping up to the heavier set girl of the group, the only one not playing a game, and hoping she remembered him.

In return she gave him a smile, "So, you're the one that's been messing with our station again." There was playfulness there but Kazuki wasn't sure if he could understand any subtleties over the din.

"Yes, I am sorry." He smiled in return, putting his hand to the back of his head and giving a slight bow. "I looked for you everywhere." Kazuki returned fully upright, "But I not- did not-" Kazuki corrected himself, "find you, or…" Kazuki paused, trying to remember names, "… or Noe, or…" He trailed off again, he suddenly remembered her name, Tommie, but couldn't remember anyone else from the group's name.

"We've been hanging out at the beach lately, and the arcade. The air conditioning beats all in the summer." She laughed exaggerated to be heard over the rattling of joysticks and push-buttons.

"Oh." Kazuki moved in a little closer. He struggled to find small talk but couldn't come up with any, "I want to talk with you about being Channeler."

"That reminds me!" Tommie cut him off and turned to her friends for a second before turning back to Kazuki, "Just wait here, I'll be right back." She flashed him a smile as she wandered off into the crowd.

Kazuki shrugged and moved closer to the dancing game to make his presence known. In return Noe turned slightly, "Hey man, I thought you went back to Japan or something. We haven't seen you around lately." He turned back to the screen and matched it beat for beat, pounding his feet against the ground at just the moment asked of him but nothing more.

"No." Kazuki looked around to see if Tommie had come back, "I did not know where you were at." He swallowed, "I check the library every day."

"We're there sometimes." Noe replied, beating his feet against the mat mercilessly, "Usually though we're here… or the park… or the beach... the mall." Each pause matched with a stomp on the gaming board. He spun in place with a flourish before spinning back toward the screen just as the song ended. "So, did you manage to find any others?" He asked, letting out a few deep breaths.

"Yes." Kazuki thought back, "Alden." Regrettably, that was the first person that came to his mind.

"That jerk." Noe laughed as the next round counted down and he began moving to the music. "If anything, you better avoid talking with that guy. If you do, he'll drag you into a fight and don't expect any of us to step in."

Kazuki smirked; it seemed no one had a high opinion of Alden, "And Casey and Julie."

"They're good people." The level was noticeably more difficult, Noe swore under his breath as he missed several cues in a row. "Julie could definitely teach you something, she's got a trick everyone's trying to learn."

"Learn what?" Kazuki moved in closer.

"Did you notice the scar?"

"Yes." Kazuki remembered the scar that started on her face and disappeared beneath her shirt only to reappear coiled around her hand.

The strain of the game was apparent through Noe's voice, "I don't know many... of... the... details. But she got it... through... channeling." Again, his words timed to his feet beating against the gaming floor.

Kazuki took a moment to digest the information. How? That was the largest question, but Noe had just said he didn't know the details. He figured it probably wouldn't do him much good either just going to her and asking since it seemed like she hadn't wanted to divulge the information to anyone she already knew. What reason would she have to tell a stranger?

Noe picked up the conversation again, "She was in the hospital for... like... two... months!" His feet slammed against the plastic flooring causing the machine to shutter. "Whooo!" He yelled out, "I guess Casey got all freaked out." Noe was sounding more winded and it was obvious why, he was all over the place even though he only had to move his feet a little at a time to succeed. "They used to train all the time. Fight. Practice. For fun. Until that happened." His feet thundered against the machine and his jewelry clattered together as his turn ended, "Yeah! Beat that!"

Stepping down, Noe called out, "Irvie, you're up!" Noe huffed and pushed back his hair as he took over at the fighting game mid turn. Irvin for his efforts bounded onto the machine before the next round began, rocking it momentarily to the side from the shifting weight.

Kazuki was temporarily distracted as Irvin seamlessly took over the game, playing it with considerably more grace than Noe. Though amusingly scoring considerably worse. Kazuki turned back to Noe, the frantic motions of his feet had translated to the quick constant movement of his joystick.

"Anyway, what's up with you?" Noe mumbled out, engrossed with the game even more than the previous.

"I just want to know more."

"Yeah… yeah… but we don't know anything." Noe mumbled, this time synchronized with the jamming of buttons.

Kazuki stood there a few moments as Noe played through a round before he turned to someone tapping on his shoulder. Tommie was standing next to a taller, thinner girl in a pleated black and white skirt.

"Here." Tommie started, gesturing to Kazuki, "This is the guy from Japan, the Channeler."

"Really, this guy?" She questioned, sounding disbelieving.

"And you…" Tommie started.

"Kazuki." He filled in with no prompting.

"Yeah, Kazuki, this is Ellie. She's a Channeler too."

Ellie reached her hand out with a timid smile, "Actually it's Carmela but everyone calls me Ellie."

Kazuki took her hand and shook it, looking her up and down. She might have been taller than Tommie but still seemed a little short compared to everyone else he'd met. That coupled with her long slender legs made her look fragile. What really caught his eye though was her piercing green eyes framed by her chestnut hair. The combination caught his breath in his throat.

"Your eyes," Kazuki felt compelled to say something, "They are very strong." He couldn't find the exact word but it would do.

Ellie pushed her hair back, "Thanks, I get that a lot." She answered back sheepishly.

"I like your clothes." Kazuki smiled back, seeing how well she took the last compliment.

"This is just my uniform." She stuck out her tongue slightly, "I guess it looks okay though." She pressed down her skirt. "So, Tommie tells me you came to America to find other Channelers?"

Kazuki nodded, "Yes, I found internet site with map of Wisconsin. There were Channelers here."

"Don't know if I ever saw that before." Ellie shook her head, "But there are Channelers here, you got that much right." She smiled, looking a little more comfortable with the situation, "So, why are you trying to find other Channelers?"

Kazuki hoped he wasn't blushing, Ellie seemed almost as uncomfortable as he was, "I want to know more. How, why, I am curious."

Ellie adjusted her posture, "I was curious too, but it's not like someone showed up and explained it to us either." She stopped for a moment to rest with her hand against one of the arcade machines, "I'm pretty good at it, but with some of the weird stuff that goes on lately I've been avoiding it."

"With Alden?" Kazuki asked, hoping to put himself back on even ground.

"Alden, Julie burning herself. I mean, how do we even know it's safe? Everyone I've ever told about it looks at me like I'm crazy or something." She took a moment to smooth out her skirt again, this time it didn't need it. "And with some of the teachers in my school the way they are, they'd probably think I was channeling dead spirits, not the billboard top ten."

"Do you have school now?" Kazuki asked, wondering why she was wearing her uniform in the middle of summer.

"Just in the morning." After Kazuki gave a strange look she clarified, "It's mostly bible stuff."

Kazuki nodded, he hadn't known that they had school during the summer but he had heard of those types of schools. He tried to get back to the subject, "So..." Kazuki paused a moment, "You avoid because of Alden?" The part about Julie burning herself was self explanatory.

"Oh, I can kick Alden's ass, it's just a matter of dealing with him and the punks he hangs out with at the same time. I mean, if I hit one of them I can really screw them up if I am tuning so that means they end up hanging in the wings until my back is turned and then come in with a brick or something." She mock grabbed the back of her head going through the motions of getting clobbered and leaving Kazuki incredulous, she looked like a brick would demolish her.

"You can fight?" Kazuki asked at last.

"Well, yeah." Her hands moved again to her skirt, gripping it and wringing it lightly, "I can fight, I had to teach myself. But, you know, when you're a Channeler you don't need much technique when you've got strength to spare." She gave a goofy smile and pulled up her sleeve a little bit, giving an over exaggerated flex of her arm. There wasn't even a bump.

"Could you show me to fight. As a Channeler?" Kazuki asked, feeling a little excited at the prospect of training with such an attractive woman.

Ellie blushed, turning away slightly, "No, no, I really can't fight. I-- I could show you some moves though, or at least offer you some advice." Slowly she turned back to him and Kazuki nodded, enticing her to continue, "Now?" She gave him a confused look but with his excited nodding she shrugged her shoulders and went on, "Well, first…" She trailed off and moved in closer, speaking in a more hushed tone, "You know when you're really tuned in and the station goes black?"

"Goes black?"

"When it fades off the radio and stuff, you know when you're fully tuned in?"

"Yes, I know about it."

"You can go even further, if you sing to the music, even hum the song along with it, you can get even more in sync with the music. I can get like twice as much strength if I know the song by heart."

"Oh." He did remember Julie or Casey mentioning something like that.

"Yeah, even if you don't know the words you can hum along, it really helps."

"Okay, thank you." Kazuki replied honestly.

"And if you're trying to take a hit, don't go limp. You have to tense up. I know, it goes against everything you've ever heard about getting in an accident, but when you're tuning your muscles are like iron. If you don't tense up you could break a bone or dislocate something." She moved away slightly, her voice picking up to compensate. "So if someone gets in a cheap shot while you're not expecting it you could easily end up down and out."

"Thank you Ellie." He repeated, not sure what else he could say.

"It's no problem." Her hands came away from her skirt again. The conversation between the two of them died as quickly as it started. Ellie took a step forward again, "Anyway, it was nice meeting you Kazuki, but there's this game I've been dying to play." She gave a little wave, "Guess I'll see you around."

Kazuki gave a timid wave in return, "Yes, see you."

Ellie laughed nervously turning on her heel and heading back off into the crowd. Kazuki let out the breath that he had been holding. Reaching into his pockets he fished out a handful of the tokens and walked over to Noe. "Here, take these." Kazuki offered the handful of coins.

"Thanks man, you're not going to play any more?" Noe was already fully focused back on his game.

"No, I have to think at home."

"That's cool." The tokens went into Noe's pocket, "Nice seeing you again though."

"Nice everyone too." Kazuki looked around, he hadn't even said hello to the rest of the group. But everyone seemed so engrossed in their games. Only Tommie caught a glimpse of him leaving and responded in kind.

As Kazuki was leaving however he noticed one of the people standing by the door giving him an odd look. He looked to be the kind of person who subsisted on mooching off others. Ready to cause some trouble.

"I know who you are." Kazuki stopped at the comment directed toward him. He tried to remember if he ever saw this guy before. His baggy shirt seemed to be hiding the bulk of his body, but there was nothing familiar about him. For a moment they were face to face, Kazuki caught his gaze, Kazuki's eyes meeting with his dark brown eyes.

"What?" Kazuki turned, the look he was getting was somewhat more sinister than one would expect in day to day life.

"You're that guy from Japan, that Channeler." The last word carried a bit more venom than Kazuki was accustomed to.

"Yes, from Japan." Kazuki replied back, casting a long glance over his shoulder to see if anyone from

Noe's group had noticed his situation. He was on his own but was hopeful he could get their attention if necessary.

"Yeah, Alden told me about you, he said you're a little pussy." Again Kazuki was subjected to that same analyzing stare. He could feel the gaze, up and down his body.

Timidly Kazuki probed the airwaves. At such a close distance he could see if this person was using any of the stations. He felt nothing. He hoped it wouldn't come to a fight but didn't expect it in such a crowded place, "I am sorry, I do not mean to anger." Kazuki tried to get past him to leave.

"You just try to run away without introducing yourself?" The hoodlum huffed, "No manners what-so-ever."

"I am Kazuki." He mumbled, hoping that someone would notice his plight.

"Kazuki... what a gay name." He laughed, "I'm Bailey, Alden's friend, and when he kicks your ass I'll be there to watch."

The image of Elli being hit in the head by a brick sprung to mind and it was accompanied by a trickle of anger. "Please, to home I want to go."

"To home you want to go?" Bailey laughed, "What are you, retarded?" Another laugh, "Oh, no, wait, I forgot, you're Japanese!" This time he gave a burst of laugher and pointed right in Kazuki's face, breaching his personal space. "You better fly back to Japan buddy because next time Alden finds you he's going to stomp you into the ground."

"What did I do?" Kazuki asked after a moment, taking the extra time to double check his question before unleashing it. Elli, Noe, Casey, they had all warned him not to fight with Alden, and he didn't want to any more than they did.

"You." Another laugh that made Kazuki grit his

teeth, another vision, this time of Elli on the ground being kicked in the side. "He's going to kick your ass just because you're someone new for him to fight, call it practice." Bailey took a step forward, "If I were you I would double down on my life insurance." And with that he turned and walked away laughing.

Quickly Kazuki scanned the crowd for any sign of Alden. He wondered and hoped that the Bailey guy wasn't traveling with him at the moment. He had so much left to learn. Thankfully, there was no sign of Alden amongst the faces in the crowd. With his heart beating deeply in his chest, giving each breath its own deep feeling, he turned out of the darkness of the arcade and stepped back outside.

The weather forecasters had been wrong, the rain was early.

Cold, wet, it was a dampness that permeated every inch of ones being. Kazuki walked through the park beneath the trees, listening to the continuous tapping of water falling atop the overhead leaves. The park was empty; it wasn't surprising considering the turn the weather had taken. It matched his mood though. It was amazing how easily one thing could ruin his good day.

The arcade had been a godsend. He'd wished to find Noe and his crew again and succeeded just when he was starting to get distressed over it. Not only that, but another Channeler as well, Elli. It had lifted him up so much that his encounter with Bailey had been an even more unexpected punch to the gut.

Kazuki bemoaned the thought of fighting Alden. He was spiteful, and from what he could tell from talking to everyone else, matched that attitude in his honor. Kazuki got the feeling that if things did go in Alden's favor he would do something dirty to regain the upper hand.

Trying to shake the thought from his head Kazuki emerged onto the beach. He looked around, out at the water and the play of the raindrops across its surface. The beach itself was barren, just a massive expanse of wet sand dotted with the occasional dugout where some child had attempted to construct a moat around a sand castle or bury a parent.

Slowly Kazuki took a deep and shuddering breath. Carefully he stooped down, touching his toes, stretching his back and his legs, ignoring the lingering pain from earlier. He pivoted his head on his shoulders, clapped his hands behind his back, and finished with a few jumping jacks. Something to get the blood flowing.

He thought back to what Elli had mentioned. Try to tense up to prevent injury. The power was channeled into the muscles. Sing along to help draw power form the music. Kazuki closed his eyes and began tuning. Purposefully he combed through the stations. Feeling each in turn before moving on. He was looking for something good, something special.

The static between the stations roared like cars through a tunnel. He took another calming breath realizing he was forcing it. He slowed, tried to give himself the time he needed, and finally he came to something. It wasn't good but it didn't have to be, whenever he used his powers it always made the hairs on the back of his neck stand up, covering his body in goose bumps. That was the way it had started the very first time. That feeling, the connection with the music that went beyond just hearing it.

He kept his eyes closed. It was easier to focus that way. In sync with the beat he bobbed his head up and down slightly. Letting the music fill him fully. The sound of the drums, a guitar, he was learning to really enjoy American rock. He tightened his hold on the station, tuning it fully.

The joining of himself and music was less

superficial now, he felt even his heart beating in time to the song. He hummed along as best he could. In return he felt overtaken with the drumming.

He opened his eyes and darted toward the center of the beach. It was funny, he thought to himself, with all the energy and power he felt at the moment he had no clue as to what to do with it. He smiled, turning as sharply as his body would allow and kicked up a wave of wet sand in response, his momentum causing his legs to slide almost completely out from beneath him.

Kazuki continued the turn, parlaying it into an ascending kick. After the first he gave another while still in the air, he had the time to spare and as soon as he touched down onto the sand he gave a strong jump and threw out a few more elaborate kicks. He huffed as he landed, but hardly felt the impact.

Dipping down low he brought his foot out from under himself and spun it around as if to sweep some invisible enemy off their feet. Immediately he jumped up and tumbled into the dirt, going end over end before springing to his feet, his mouth full of grit. He continued into a new tumble, throwing himself into the ground before again managing to toss himself onto the soles of his shoes.

A few more kicks, some punches. He pretended he was fighting other people, he pretended he was in a martial arts movie. He blocked, ducked, dodged, weaved. It all felt so natural with the music in his veins.

Giving a strong jump backward he cleared some space for himself with an elaborate series of kicks. Simple straight kicks had been extrapolated into round houses. As the beat of the song reached new proportions he struck out again at invisible opponents, spinning back fists, concerted uppercuts, and blocks all mixed in.

Kazuki tumbled again but this time caught himself, instead doing a front flip using his hand as a pivot. He'd never done anything like it before. He tried again but misjudged his center of balance and slammed face first into the ground, rattling his brain and sending horrid vibrations into his clenched teeth. But he just rolled again to his feet, his vigor hardly doused.

Finally the song was winding down; he made his way to the water. Stepping into the water to his ankle he unleashed a kick, sending a crescent-shaped splash out and away. He stepped in yet deeper, then again, this time with another kick with the water up to mid-shin. Another gout of water sent toward the middle of the lake.

He kept it up, a few more steps in, up to his knees. This time the kick was harder but far from impossible, it was almost as fast as it was unencumbered. Deeper into the water, mid-thigh he tried again, the song was nearly over but his kick was still fast enough to leave a vacuum in its wake, slicing through the water.

Finally he was in to his waist, the fabric of his jeans felt tight against his skin. He kicked, sending out a ferocious diffusion of water. Then again he kicked, this time with his other foot, and again the water sprayed high into the air. Around him the water roared, frothing and boiling as it rushed and foamed from the beating it was taking. He picked up the pace, one kick, then another, then another, he could hardly keep his eyes open but he no longer felt the resistance of water slowing his kicks, somehow the lake was at bay despite him being waist deep.

He grunted as fatigue attacked, giving one last futile kick that hardly made it to knee height before being restrained in the sudden quagmire of water that rushed in to engulf him as his song ended.

Slowly, ever so slowly, Kazuki made his way to the beach, trudging through the lake in soaked denim jeans. His quads not so much feeling weak as simply unable to carry his weight. He was soaked to the core, his hair dripping into his eyes, his shoes sprayed water with every step. He gave a little cough, sending spittle everywhere before falling onto his butt and laying down in the wet sand.

Time passed quickly, his perception altered by the frantic beating of his heart in his ears. His body aching, Kazuki tried to wipe the water from the eyes and only succeeded in wiping sandy grit into them. He gave up and just let the rain fall over him.

His phone was vibrating; he opened his eyes on reflex and cried out from the sudden invasion of water. Kazuki shook his head to clear the water away and let out a sigh, forcing his hand into his soaked jeans. The feeling of wet denim tight against him as he fished out his cellular phone.

"*Four missed calls*?" He mumbled to himself, scrolling through the numbers, he must have fallen asleep. They were all from his brother. Maybe the water was screwing up the circuits. He hoped it wasn't as he punched a button and dialed his brother's phone.

Chapter 4

Usually the walk was about an hour, but the next day it took the better part of two hours for Kazuki to hobble from Miranda's to the beach. Letting out a wheezing breath he lowered himself onto a bench, starring out at the expanse of sand. The sun was out, and although it was still early the beach was starting to fill up. There were people walking and talking, kids playing in the waves, building sand castles. Others were wading in the water splashing one another or trying wrestling moves.

Kazuki looked across the lake. From his vantage point he could see the other side easily. A puddle compared to the ocean. The only reason any of the lake was hidden from view was that the lake circled back on itself like a kidney bean.

Despite its size, it still did a good job of keeping people cool. Back home the closest Kazuki had been a rocky shoreline that was unforgiving on the feet. Still, the cool water made any foot pain completely worth it on a hot summer day.

He looked over to where some children were running around a rut in the sand. It was a relic of his 'training' the day before, a place where he had tried an axe kick and succeeded in blowing a hole in the sand. The beach of today was nothing like the empty, wet, dreary atmosphere it had harbored.

When he thought back on it though it hadn't been training at all. Granted, it was practice at using his powers but there hadn't been any technique to it. No methodology. When he let himself be overcome by the music the one thing he hadn't had was control. Had he even tried to control the power?

Experimentally he stretched his legs, already they were cramping from the walk. He needed to get moving or risk having a pointless day. With the exception of the few e-mails that he'd sent after breakfast he hadn't done anything to make this day in America count.

His friends back in Japan were curious about America and wanted to know every little detail. On top of that they kept adding to the list of things they wanted him to bring back. All said it was enough to tie Kazuki up on an all day scavenger hunt.

That would be a waste. Already he felt crummy for missing practice with his brother. He wanted to get the most out of it, he knew that if he tried training with Satoshi at home his mother would be too worried. That being the case they would have to train secretly. Kazuki doubted Satoshi would be willing to do something like that, if only because of his inherent laziness. Even his time in the service had done little to improve that aspect of his personality.

No, this was his only chance to train with his brother. This was his only chance to meet other Channelers. This was his chance to figure out what his powers meant. Even if no one else had any clue either he thought glumly.

Kazuki brushed some hair out of his face, he'd really run the gambit of people. Alden used his powers for fighting. Elli tended to ignore her powers. Noe and his group segregated themselves out from everyone because of them and used them as a glue to hold their band together, and Casey and Julie used them as common ground upon which to build a relationship.

Still, no one had any idea of how they got their abilities, or why they had them. Unless they were lying, they were all just as in the dark as he was. Was there really anything to find out? He'd met more people like himself and learned a few things about his powers. Could he parlay that into justification to himself for the money and time spent?

Kazuki leaned back fully against the bench and

looked to the sky. The sun wasn't overhead quite yet. At least the breeze off the lake felt nice. Graciously he let his shoulders slouch as he took another deep breath. He could forgive himself for taking it easy for the day. Kazuki brought his arms up, resting them on the back of the bench as he allowed himself to sink down. Just a few more minutes and he would attempt to accomplish… something.

Satoshi stepped out of the back door with his usual cocky smirk. Behind him the door swung shut with a muted thud, the sound of which was lost as he trounced down the stairs. Deliberately Kazuki ran his bare feet through the grass trying to find any stray pebbles before he found them on his back.

"Think you're ready for this?" Satoshi asked sarcastically, bobbling in a half-circle around Kazuki as he stretched his arms above his head and cracked his neck. A moment later he stripped off his shirt leaving him in just his jeans. Showing off the tiger tattoo on his shoulder from his last time in America.

Kazuki grinned back at him. "I am ready." The day before he'd found Noe and his group at one of the buffets and spent lunch with them, mostly listening. After that he'd wrapped up the rest of the day at Miranda's listening to CD's. Today he felt a hundred percent better.

"Let's see if you remember everything we've gone over." Satoshi crouched slightly, lowering his shoulders and going into his boxing stance, bringing his hands in front of his face, bobbing between his feet, exaggerating the effort for Kazuki's benefit.

Recognizing the stance Kazuki copied it himself; taking a deep breath he let it expand in his lungs, focusing himself. The punch came suddenly, but traveled with a purposeful telegraph. He dodged to the side and took a step back forcing Satoshi to close the

67

gap.

Absently Kazuki remembered reading about the amount of time that it took the brain to recognize that a punch was coming. By the time the brain recognizes the punch, it has already landed. The only way to block a punch is to understand the signs that the person is preparing and anticipate where it will land.

That's not how Kazuki felt though as he dodged to the side of another punch, this one aimed at his face. Kazuki brought around his own fist, pegging his brother lightly on the side. He still didn't have the nerve or aggressiveness to hit his brother in the face even a tap.

Satoshi didn't even pretend to notice the strike and brought forward his hands to put his brother in a clench. Kazuki twisted out of it and brought up his knee, catching Satoshi in his knee.

"Ow!" Kazuki hobbled backward and Satoshi reached down and rubbed his own knee a moment before the two shared a goofy smile.

Satoshi recovered quickly and brought himself upright again. He swung out his leg in a wide arc. Kazuki knew the move was showier than anything else since his foot could easily be caught. That's why it really irked him that his brother went to great pains to use it every time they sparred.

The kick was too fast to dodge so Kazuki blocked it with his forearm. He brought his other hand around and tagged his brother in his arm at least hard enough to make him back off. Satoshi slammed down his attacking foot and pivoted on it heavily, spinning into his brother with a kick gifted with centrifugal force.

With Kazuki's hand still in motion from the punch the kick landed fully against Kazuki and threw him to the side. He pushed to catch himself and managed to keep upright but the next punch almost made it to Kazuki's face. His defenses were eroding rapidly. Dodge to one side, then the other. A repetition that he was used to, but he hardly had time to process what was going on.

Satoshi's attention was focused at eye level; Kazuki changed his strategy, bringing his knee up intending to take out his brother's solar plexus. The knee was poorly aimed with almost no range and with the combination of dodging that he was doing only hit Satoshi in the hip. It was a meaty hard impact but it failed to slow the action.

Kazuki tried hard to retain all of the teaching his brother had beat into him. Bits and pieces would come back to him suddenly. Usually a moment after the information would have been useful. Just as one of the punches came forward Kazuki reached out and snaked his arm around his brother's wrist and brought him forward, locking his arm.

Trying to pull himself away, Satoshi almost tripped and Kazuki pressed his momentary advantage by applying his full weight to the trapped arm. *"Got you!"*

In desperation Satoshi swung his free arm out and up, into Kazuki's solar plexus. It missed its target, sending its energy fully in his sternum, there was a deep thudding, and sputtering spittle from his mouth but it wasn't enough to cause the necessary loss of breath requisite to win his freedom.

Satoshi tried to repeat the feat but this time Kazuki reached out and grabbed his forearm just before it landed. They twisted, Satoshi trying to regain the advantage kicked out at his brother's legs.

The both of them tumbled to the ground. Kazuki, lost his hold on his brother and tried to roll away but Satoshi wouldn't let up, pushing himself roughly toward Kazuki and digging his knees into the grass he tried for a wrestling pin, grabbing his brother by the leg and twisting.

Kazuki rolled, Satoshi applied pressure again and Kazuki rolled in the other direction. Kazuki kicked out, his foot catching Satoshi in the face, dragging down his nose, skinning it. Satoshi tried to stand while holding Kazuki's foot, barely catching his footing at all. Kazuki crooked his free foot in between his brother's legs and pulled, caused him to tumble back to the ground.

Pushing himself to his feet, Kazuki tried to put some distance between himself and his brother, nearly tumbling while backpedaling. Satoshi was back on this feet too quickly, hardly giving Kazuki time to move his fall zone to some place other than the concrete driveway.

Rushing forward, Satoshi slammed his larger body into Kazuki, lifting him with his shoulder. Kazuki staggered back but was struck again by Satoshi's outstretched hands, almost causing him crash completely to the ground.

Satoshi shot out his hand and Kazuki tried to pull away but failed. His wrist tightly held by his brother. He was trying to make it a grappling game. Kazuki knew that if he was taken down he wouldn't be able to keep up and it would be game over. Doubling up his hold with his other hand, Satoshi twisted, trying to wrestle his brother's arm around his back. Kazuki struggled against it and managed to shake off one of Satoshi's hands. The effort was wasted as Satoshi simply used the free hand to grab Kazuki's other hand.

Desperate, Kazuki doubled over, causing his brother to do the same and lowered his center of gravity. Kazuki gasped as the knee was driven into his chest, then again. Kazuki was frantic; things had never escalated so far.

Suddenly there was a song there, it wasn't intentional but the notes came to the forefront of Kazuki's thoughts like the sound of a knocking engine. Instinctively he tuned more fully, focusing on the music. It didn't matter what it was. Another hit nearly made Kazuki lose the station. He felt Satoshi's grip slipping, his forearms and wrists were slick with sweat and dirt.

Kazuki yanked at his right hand, but unlike before it came free easily. Instantly he twisted his other hand around and brought his brother's hand with it, grabbing him by the wrist. Quickly sidestepping, Satoshi almost fell over from the change in balance but Kazuki moved with the momentum, pivoting his body he lifted his brother up and off his feet, spinning him in mid air and throwing him onto his back.

Satoshi bounced painfully, his body shaking the ground before laying flat on his back. The two of them didn't move, just held their ground breathing heavily. Kazuki let loose his hold on the song, letting himself fall to the ground a moment later, landing on his butt.

"You're getting better." Satoshi said at last, his breathing still heavy, "But you cheated at the end there."

Kazuki gave a light laugh, "How would you know?" As far as he knew there was nothing obvious about when he was channeling and when he wasn't.

"Are you kidding, it was like I got hit by a bus. One second I was on my feet the next I was on my back." Satoshi pushed himself onto his butt, "I thought we agreed you weren't going to do stunts like that."

"I try to not do that. But I need to practice sometime."

Satoshi cracked his neck from side to side, "Well... I guess we did get a little carried away. But... at least warn me next time." He pushed himself to his feet, "Geezee..." He held his back as he rose up, grunting. He sucked air roughly though his nose, "It's like you knocked all of my snot into my throat..." A moment later he offered his brother a hand and pulled him up as well.

"Thank you." Kazuki grunted as he was pulled up. His skin still feeling extra hot, he was coming down from a wonderful exhilaration that one only gets from a truly satisfying workout.

"Hey, you wanna head out with me and Miranda

for lunch or something?"

Kazuki shook his head, "That sounds good."

"Well, let's go hit the showers." Satoshi bobbed a little as he cleared the four steps in one leap and headed inside, holding the door open for Kazuki.

Lunch wasn't anything special, just one of those hole in the wall restaurants whose name wasn't spoken outside a select radius. But once the food was in front of Kazuki it spoke for itself. He was starting to get hooked on American fare. He'd ordered one of the large hamburgers, onions, pickles, bacon, cheese, he wasn't sure what else. But it was stacked, and next to it was a large heap of fries to go with a giant soda.

Kazuki moved in closer to his brother, "*Is this where you guys go every day for lunch*?"

Satoshi answered back in a hushed tone, "*No, this is my first time here.*"

"What was that?" Miranda asked from across the table, momentarily stopping her eating.

"He just asked if you eat here everyday."

Miranda laughed, "If I ate here every day I wouldn't make it through my bedroom door at night."

Kazuki smiled, that had been exactly what he had been thinking. Now that he thought about it though, he wasn't sure what his brother and Miranda did all day. He knew that Miranda had a job doing data entry that had her work odd hours. Whatever it was, it was erratic at best, six hours one day, maybe three the next, then nothing, it was all random. Some kind of fly-by-night operation.

"So, did you check out the beach yet?" Miranda asked.

Kazuki gave a little nod, "Yes, more than one time."

Satoshi spoke up, "Maybe we should all head down there one of these days."

Miranda nodded, "Yeah, before you guys leave, at least once." She managed out before hefting her hamburger and burying her face in it, a strange sight for such a small girl.

Looking around, Kazuki tried to recognize anyone but failed. He wondered what everyone was up to. Noe and his crew seemed to take each day as it came with no real plan so he had no clue what they were doing at the moment.

Satoshi set down his hamburger and took a drink of his soda, "Maybe I should take you to the base for a tour." He said looking at his brother.

"Can you still do that?" Miranda wondered aloud.

"Probably, I bet there's still someone there that I know that could let us in." Satoshi flashed a smile.

"Sounds like fun." Kazuki mussed. It didn't sound all that exciting but it could be interesting.

Looking out the window, it was amazing how fast the days went. Soon enough it would be time for bed, for his near daily call to Japan to wish his mom and dad good afternoon while they wished him good night.

He was finally used to the difference in time zones but it was going to be hard going back again. It might be even harder than the change in the first place.

"Do you have any plans for today?" Miranda popped a fry in her mouth directing her question to Kazuki.

"I will go to the library, arcade. Maybe someplace else." The usual palaces he reasoned to himself. Honestly he wanted to talk to Julie after what Noe had told him in the arcade about her abilities. But he also didn't think he would get very far.

"Humm… okay." Miranda went back to her meal as the conversation stalled. Kazuki left it at that and took another big bite out of his hamburger watching cars drive by outside the window.

Kazuki dragged his feet as he walked down the deserted street. He'd been trying to find at least one other Channeler since lunch and eventually found Casey and Julie in the middle of grocery shopping. All he managed was a 'hello' before they continued on their way. They felt like they were on the other side of some imaginary divide between being a Channeler and just being a normal person. He let them be.

They had been on their stations, he'd felt people over the airwaves throughout the day but he'd overestimated his ability to track the others through their tuning. He'd think that he was getting close but would lose it just as he felt he was making progress. He wasn't sure if it was a concentration issue or just the people tuning again when a song ended but he met with failure again and again.

He cut across a parking lot to shave a few minutes off his return trip. The lights overhead came on about half-way across. Kazuki frowned, he knew he could find his way home but still wasn't sure he liked the city at night. He distracted himself by tuning the stations nearby.

It reminded him of his first night wandering around. There was a strange feeling, the sound of something going beyond human hearing, a sinking feeling in his head.

"I see you haven't swum back to Japan yet."

Kazuki turned on his heel, a little slow with the comeback but certain of its message, "No, not yet."

Alden was just walking out from between a parked car and SUV. "So, are you going to cover your head and beg for mercy again?" Alden laughed and Kazuki looked around cautiously, he didn't see any one else. If it came to a fight it would make things a little less scary.

"No. Just will not fight you." Kazuki shook his head and crossed his arms standing more upright.

"Won't fight me? So that means you'll just stand there and take the beating." Again that shameless laugh. "Because I will kick your ass with a smile on my face."

"Please, no." Kazuki stood his ground but could feel his heartbeat picking up. Gently he tried to probe the stations to find something useful. He had to be careful, he was sure that if Alden figured it out he would pounce on him. "I want to go."

"You can go." Alden started, purposefully raising his fists up and cracking his knuckles one by one, "If you promise to go right back to Japan and never show your face here again. Can you understand that or is your English too screwed up."

"Not yet. Four weeks." Kazuki tried to release his clenched fists; he hadn't found anything useful on the stations yet. At the level of Channeling he was using, everything was so weak that he could hardly tell what was playing; they were just ghosts of beats and fragments of sounds. To make matters worse the station that he had been listening to most of the day was nowhere to be found.

Kazuki saw a flash of emotion across Alden's face and his smile curled up amused. He knew for sure that Alden had just found him out. "Oh?" Alden mocked, "Find anything good?" Kazuki grimaced as Alden continued, "I'll give you to the count of five to run or fight."

Kazuki felt his feet glued in position.

"Five." Kazuki struggled openly through the stations, trying to find "Four" something, anything familiar that he could use for fuel "Three" in the upcoming fight. He was running out of "Two" time too quickly though, he'd have to settle for the "One" next station that he ran across.

Kazuki tuned in fully to the station, immediately thankful that it wasn't a commercial, a DJ or something worthless. The punch came faster than anything that his brother had ever thrown. Country, it was country music. He hated country music. He tried to dodge again, this one aimed at his head, the edge of Alden's fist connected with his temple; he felt the hair and skin there scrape away from his scalp.

Another punch came at Kazuki's face, and because of the angle he couldn't judge the distance correctly. It nailed him right on the forehead, causing him to rock back with the blow. It was crippling, his neck was going to snap, and he heard things crack all down his spine as the shockwave cascaded. His world spun, his vision blurred, but he still managed to side step out of instinct and put some distance between himself and Alden.

In desperation he tried humming along to the song, anything for that added boost. He felt the kick to the shin but it was the kick to his side that threw him like a rag doll against the dumpster. His body hammered into it, the incredibly loud gong of metal momentarily distracting him enough to suffer another hit of the same caliper. Literally lifting him off the ground and throwing him several feet.

The feeling was strange, he was trying to keep all of his muscles tensed as he was told, it was easier than going limp, but it was doing a number on his body. A number of the smaller muscles of his back felt like they were torn, pulled, something. Hurriedly he pushed himself up from the crumbled blacktop, damning any injuries for the time. Before he even made it to his feet he caught another kick, this time to the chest, tossing him backwards.

"Punk." Alden laughed at him. "Bet you thought you were something, eh?" He continued between sharp breaths.

Kazuki pushed himself up to reach out for Alden's leg to take him down but instead Alden shot his foot up in an attempt to catch Kazuki under the chin. At the last moment Kazuki turned his head missing the kick which Alden dropped down like a sledgehammer to his back, sending Kazuki to the ground. Winded, and pained.

His hold on the station became fleeting, he was having a hard time holding it or any coherent thought. And just as quickly, it was gone all together sputtering out of his grasp.

"Feh." Alden laughed, spitting on Kazuki's back. "You idiot. Never let me see you again or next time I might fight for real."

Kazuki laid there face down against the blacktop. The abrasive stone pressed into his skin, each breath drawing pebbles off the ground and into his nose. His fingers were cut up from scattered leftovers from broken bottles. His chest hurt to breath, his ribs, and sternum. He hurt all over, even the places he hadn't been hit. "Heeee." Kazuki rolled himself over onto his side. A moment later the dumpster caught his eye. The side was dented badly; the leading edge looked like it was hit by a truck, not his back.

A few more shuddering breaths didn't help to make Kazuki any more confident in his ability to get home. The muscle spasms in his back were getting worse and his stomach muscles felt like they were trying to break free form his body and run away. The thought made him laugh or wince, he couldn't really tell the difference between the two.

Timidly he reached down, trying to find his cellular phone. A few people had filtered out of the building nearby but they didn't seemed to notice him on the ground. He decided to keep comments about rude Americans to himself and keep holding out hope.

Eventually he retrieved the electronics out of his pocket, in pieces. He would have laughed to himself but it was too painful.

"Kazuki?"

The act of twisting his neck around proved to be too painful so he abandoned it mid-way. Deciding to just guess who it was based on the voice. "Elli?"

"Yeah." She paused, surveying the damage, "I guess I'm too late." She walked around in front of Kazuki so he could get a look at her. She was wearing a large over-sized night shirt and pajama pants with no socks or shoes.

"Why you here?" Kazuki wheezed, trying again to push himself up and succeeding part way, at least enough to prop himself up on his arm.

"I was just getting ready to take a shower when I felt the stations get all funny… I just had this feeling that it was you and Alden about to face off." She paused a little winded, "Looks like I was right. Did you at least manage to get in a few good hits?"

Kazuki stopped to think about it, but the fight itself had been over in an instant. He'd moved so much faster than Satoshi, "I do not think so."

"That sucks." She frowned before reaching out a hand, "Here, let me help."

Taking the offer, Kazuki was pulled to his feet, it hurt as much as taking another kick from Alden and he hardly managed not to topple once he got up. Carefully she pulled away her hand and somehow he managed to stay upright.

"Let me guess." She started again, "Nothing good on the radio when you needed it?"

"Yes." Kazuki couldn't help but smile that had been it exactly.

"Want me to help you home?"

Despite his condition, his pride conspired against him, "No, I am okay."

"Whatever." Elli countered dismissively, stepping in she bent down and scooped his legs out from beneath him, lifting him into the air as if he were an infant.

"I am too heavy!" Kazuki called out, more out of shock at being picked up so easily.

"Duh! I'm a Channeler too, and you don't look that heavy anyway." She smirked at him.

"It is a long distance to the house." Kazuki tried again, feeling helpless.

"We're not going to your house. I live like two blocks from here. I'll carry you there then I can drive you home."

Kazuki felt stupid, everyone had a driver's license in the country. "Oh." He decided to keep his mouth shut for the moment as Elli carried him out of the parking lot.

Throughout the walk Kazuki worried about Elli's bare feet but kept his comments to himself. Actually allowing himself to sink fully into her arms as she effortlessly carried him to her home. He felt Elli shift strangely and realized that she had lifted her leg, turning slightly he watched her use her toes to open the car door. "Here." She offered, moving to sit him down.

Moving again brought whole new worlds of pain but Kazuki muted any outcry to a simple wince. "Thank you." Kazuki made it into the vehicle with only two limps and conformed himself to the passenger seat as Elli closed the door behind him. Absently he buckled himself in, regretting the movement and the pain it brought.

Elli held up a finger indicating that she would need a moment and ran into the house. The living room was lit but the second story was dark. Kazuki took a deep breath, the expansion of his lungs putting undue pressure against his spine which caused him to cough. He held up his hand to his face, wondering if his phlegm was bloody but couldn't tell in the weak light. It certainly felt like it should have been.

"*Damn*." He muttered to himself. For a moment

he thought back to the fight. No, it was a beating. He shook his head, that slight effort enough to make him cringe. He'd wanted the fight no matter what he had said. Training with his brother, experimenting with tuning. The power had made him cocky and for that he just got his ass handed to him. He remembered the dumpster. He was lucky to be alive. And if it wasn't for his abilities he knew he wouldn't have made it.

The driver's side door opened suddenly. Kazuki hadn't even seen anyone come up to the vehicle. Instantly Elli was in the driver's seat and the door was slowly closed. "Okay, here we go." The car rolled out of the driveway in neutral. It hadn't been started. Kazuki gave Elli a questioning look, "I don't want to have to explain to my dad where I'm going dressed for bed." She smiled as she turned over the starter and clicked on the headlights.

Kazuki looked her over, she was still wearing the same night shirt but at least she had shoes and pants now. "Thank you." He repeated again nodding to her, he felt slightly faint.

"No problem." The car sped ahead, "So, where do you live?"

Kazuki rattled off the address that he had memorized, glad that she knew where the street was.

The radio was off. The car was silent. Kazuki looked over the vehicle. It was an older car. The kind that Kazuki had always associated with America, the proverbial 'boat'. He wondered if it had been gifted to Elli or if it was her father's car but didn't want to disturb the silence.

Elli shifted in her seat slightly as she drove, "So..." She started off awkwardly, "what do you think of America?" She gave a brief laugh, realizing that the question was a bit loaded "Is it just like you expected from all the movies?"

It took him a moment to find the joke but it still

made him smile, "No, not likes movies. Good though, much like Japan but... less people." Kazuki paused to look her over

"So, if I want to imagine Japan I just have to picture downtown with more people?" She joked obviously trying to make him feel better.

"More people, taller buildings, more cars, smaller streets." He rattled off, trying to picture all the differences.

Elli took a deep breath audible to Kazuki, "When are you going back?"

"Back to Japan?" He parroted, feeling stupid but not sure what he wanted to answer. He wished he could just give up.

"Yeah, or are you just going to stick around here?"

In his head Kazuki tried to plot out the days, but their return flight wasn't set in stone, "Four weeks." It was a decent approximation.

"So you'll be around a little longer then."

Kazuki stretched his arms and let out a pained breath, "A while, yes."

"Really though, how is it back in Japan. And what's it like to just go to another country like this? I mean, aside from Mr. Psychopath?" Elli made a sharp turn that caused Kazuki to lean into the door and grimace.

"Neat..." Kazuki tried to laugh but failed, looking for the right words, "Scary, lonely. Only my brother came from Japan. Maybe better when I know more people."

"Hopefully it won't be so lonely if you find some people to hang out with." Kazuki wished the car wasn't so dark but the sun was long gone.

"Yes." He smiled back at her, he wanted to hang out with Elli more, and Noe, and everyone. Especially after what just happened he didn't want to be alone. He wasn't sure if it was fear. He didn't want to be afraid.

He just didn't want to be alone for awhile.

Kazuki's whole body twitched and he almost doubled over from a sudden spasm of pain in his back. He was thankful that Elli was so focused on the road. "This is all very nice from you." She gave him a sidelong glance, "Thank you again." The car gave another lurching turn.

"Not a problem and you don't have to keep thanking me." She paused a moment obviously embarrassed, "Besides, I wasn't going to just leave you laying there." She laughed, "Besides, you looked so sad holding your broken cell phone."

Flinching mentally Kazuki remembered the phone; it was in too many pieces to count. It had been very expensive too. He sighed, what did it matter anymore?

"So, which house is it?"

Kazuki looked intently along the side of the street. He'd never had to find the house in the dark. More than ever the architecture blended together. He strained his eyes and leaned forward in his seat, his spine protesting like mad.

"That one." Kazuki said pointing, recognizing the wrap-around porch that was characteristic of the house.

Elli nodded and brought the car up into the driveway, the bottom scraping heavily as she made the turn. A moment later they were stopped and Elli was the first to get out of the car, quickly walking around and opening the door for Kazuki.

Patiently she stood in front of the door as Kazuki carefully pivoted himself and dropped his legs onto the concrete. Graciously he took her hand as she pulled him to his feet giving him a new horrid pain down his back and into his knee that he hadn't felt up to then. He forcibly let out a breath before hobbling onto the other leg.

"Are you okay?" She asked worried.

"I will be okay." The question was obviously the

only thing she could think to ask.

Elli scooped an arm under Kazuki's arm and around his back and led him to the doorway keeping him upright. Kazuki knocked on the door firmly, causing him to notice tiny glass shards from the parking lot still embedded in his knuckles.

Kazuki heard footsteps inside, then the sound of locks opening. He looked up just as the door opened.

Miranda looked shocked, "What happened?" Her voice was just above a whisper. She turned back into the house, "Satoshi, get out here!"

Kazuki could tell that Elli was nervous; she was pulling away slightly so Kazuki pulled himself away, managing to successfully sway on his own two feet without falling. Miranda didn't look impressed, "Who hurt you? What happened?" The questions came in rapid succession.

Looking down at himself, Kazuki didn't think he looked that bad. Sure, he felt like crap, but there was nothing overtly obvious about his injuries. Well, unless his face was all cut up or something. He figured it must have been because Elli had been helping him to the doorway.

"I am okay." He smiled back at her as best he could just as Satoshi appeared in the doorway.

"*What's going on*?" Satoshi wasn't even going through the motions of English.

"*I got beat up.*" Kazuki answered readily. He hurt everywhere and every second it seemed new pains were making themselves apparent. "*I think... I think I need to lie down.*" Kazuki felt himself sway as he tried to take a step into the doorway.

"Someone beat him up." Satoshi translated to Miranda.

"Do we need to go to the hospital? No, we should call the police first." Miranda offered, looking between Kazuki and Elli. "Could you help him inside?"

"No police." Kazuki mumbled. "No police."

Chapter 5

The conversation at the table died the moment Kazuki sat down. He looked between Satoshi and Miranda, hoping to bring things back to life. Satoshi gave him a knowing look but kept quiet.

Kazuki sighed and reached out, grabbing an empty plate and loaded it up with some of the food cooling on the table. Miranda enjoyed, or at least had a habit of, making breakfast every day. It was a luxury he wasn't used to and one he was going to miss back home.

"So-" Miranda started out, sitting down her coffee, "If you're feeling better I can take you to file a police report."

Kazuki shook his head, "No, I do not want to." He rotated his shoulder to help relieve the stiffness. He'd been lying in bed the entire day before and it'd left him stiff and unmotivated. He was trying to push through it. He took another bite of sausage, it was helping things. Seeing his need, Miranda got up from the table and came back with a glass of orange juice.

"Thanks." Kazuki accepted the glass, glancing over at his brother who was keeping his nose buried in the paper. Kazuki glanced at the headline:

"LOCAL STATION PETITION TO FCC FOR VARIANCE APPROVED - PREPARATION BEGUN FOR INCREASE IN SIGNAL STRENGTH."

Kazuki was half-heartedly trying to read the story while eating when Miranda spoke up again. "You can't just do nothing." Her voice was even, nowhere near as pressuring as it had been when he had come home bloodied and bruised.

Satoshi set down the paper, taking up the fight for his brother, in part because of his more eloquent grasp of the language, "Look, it's up to him. If he doesn't want to press charges then he doesn't have to. This is just a scuffle between two boys."

"Scuffle?" Miranda questioned harshly. She had been there when Satoshi had helped Kazuki take off his shirt that night, after he had asked Elli to go home. She had seen the bruises; black, blue, purple. There was a particularly distinct bruise, a line that bisected his back diagonally about as wide as his wrist. He figured that was from his first hit into the dumpster. The cluster of bruises beneath it looked like someone had tried to paint a wall with crumpled news paper, sharp and jagged with random edges; bloodied and torn.

Those were of course just the most painful injuries. The angry bruises on his chest looked even worse but only hurt when he took a deep breath. Then there was a multitude of cuts on his hands and knees. He had to admit that he saw where her concern was coming from but his brother couldn't have put it better, it was his choice.

"I just..." She seemed flustered, "I don't know how you do things in Japan but here we try to get law enforcement involved as early as possible when something like this happens. You don't sit back and take it; you have to do something about it." She huffed, settling back into her seat she paused a moment before adding definitively, "That's it, I'm done."

Kazuki tried to relax again. He knew Satoshi was worried about him too; his brother just understood that he didn't want to get the law involved. He was thankful Satoshi understood that of all things. It was a matter of pride.

"Hey-" Kazuki heard the salutation through his door at the same time he heard the door knob turning. "Some people are here to see you."

Looking up from his laptop Kazuki pulled off his headphones. Behind his brother he could see Noe, and where there was Noe... Kazuki pushed himself off the bed and onto his feet. The pain was nowhere near what it was the day before.

"Hello." Kazuki called out, trying to look past his brother. Satoshi moved out of his way, Noe's whole crew had showed up. "What is everyone doing here?"

"We came to check up on you." Tommie intoned, walking through the doorway, followed immediately by Noe. "Elli told us what happened, but we could have guessed from the mess over the air waves."

"Sounds like you got beat pretty bad." Noe said with not a shred of tact, taking a seat at the foot of Kazuki's bed. "I mean when two Channelers fight, wham, bam!" Noe slammed his fist into his palm for emphasis, "Wish I could have been there."

Irvin, Allene, and Mike all made their appearances less dramatically, Mike taking up a position inconspicuous behind Noe, and the others standing off toward the doorway. Kazuki didn't know any of them the best, but he wondered if the last three in the room were uncomfortable for the same reasons. He'd only spoken a few words to them at lunch the other day.

"Anyway," Tommie started again, "We were wondering if we could get you out of the house, hang out or something."

"Thank you." Kazuki appreciated the offer, but it felt too much like charity.

"Come on man, we just want to hang out." Irvin offered, waving Kazuki over.

For a moment Kazuki looked the crew over, but the offer appeared genuine. It brought a smile to his face, "Yes, I can... will come."

"Cool!" Noe pushed himself up from the bed, "You want us to hang outside?" Seeing the nod he motioned his hand forward, "Come on you guys." With that Noe and his troop exited the room, closing the door behind them.

Kazuki sat there for a moment, thinking it over.

He was feeling self destructive but he still had sense enough to get away from the feeling.

As Kazuki got ready, some of the angles he found himself in brought tears to his eyes. He tried to ignore the protests from his body. Briefly he looked at himself in the mirror. All over his back the bruises where beginning to lose definition. They bled abstractly into one another contrary to the bruises on his chest which looked even worse. He sighed; there was no way he stood a chance.

He rubbed a dab of greasy mentholated ointment over his back as best as he could reach. The more he looked at himself the more he realized how tore up he still was. He'd certainly have to take it easy a few more days.

As soon as Kazuki stepped out the door, Noe was there with that same big smile on his face. "You ready man?"

Kazuki nodded, "Yes."

"Cool, let's roll." As one, Noe's crew built momentum in the same direction as their leader and Kazuki followed suit.

Tommie fell into step beside Kazuki, "So, does it hurt bad?" Without hesitation she reached out and poked the swollen spot just above the cut on his face.

Letting out a pained breath Kazuki looked her over for a hint of compassion, "Hurts a lot, not as bad as before though." He rubbed the swollen area lightly; it made a strange sensation that registered simultaneously as pain and relief.

"Sorry." She stuck her tongue out at him. "I was just curious how you were healing?"

"He'll be back up and running in no time." Noe called out from the front, "You know how fast us Channelers heal." He boasted with a cocky tone, not losing his step.

"In a heart beat." Irvin agreed with an upbeat tone, "Another day and you'll be good to go."

"I hope." Kazuki sighed, wondering if Channelers really did heal faster of if it was just idle boasting.

Mike spoke up from behind Kazuki suddenly, "I bet you took him down a peg though, right?"

Turning slightly as he walked Kazuki made eye contact for an instant before continuing ahead, "I am having a hard time remembering." He shook his head, "Maybe?" Honestly the night had turned into a blur, he wasn't sure if it was his brain over-processing things or if there was some trauma but when he tried to remember what happened he might as well have been trying to piece together a story from the excrement of a paper shredder.

"Did you black out or something?" Allene spoke up for the first time, picking up her pace a step or two and poking her head into Kazuki's field of vision.

"I do not think so." He didn't know for sure but the beating seemed pretty continuous in his mind.

"You've never really fought using your powers before have you?" Allene continued.

"No, no I not have." Kazuki confessed feeling embarrassed.

Noe broke back in, "Then it's pretty obvious why you look like you've been chewed up and spit out." Irvin scoffed to emphasize the point as well, before Noe continued, "You need to fight totally different when you're tuning. You have to fight like... well... like a Channeler." He paused sounding unsure of himself for just a moment before coming back as confident as ever, "You have to fight like a Channeler." He repeated again.

"How?" Kazuki asked curious.

From behind Kazuki saw Noe shake his head, "Later on we'll show you."

"Okay." Kazuki felt like scratching his head, Noe

had seemed so passionate but suddenly he stopped. Was there really something so different?

"Yeah." Tommie agreed excitedly, "We'll show you how to fight, that way when Alden shows his face again you can shove your foot up his ass far enough to kick out his teeth with your toes!"

From behind Kazuki heard Allene laugh lightly, bringing a smile to his face. That and Tommie's bolstering presence were helping to set his mood straight again.

"When I was fighting Alden though..." Kazuki started out, remembering the something from the fight, "I could not find my station. I was just missing."

"Was it rock?" Noe asked from the front.

"Yes." Kazuki remembered.

"WRFK?" Noe asked, saying each of the call letters slowly.

"I think." Kazuki agreed unsure of himself.

"Alden had it." Noe said succinctly.

"He had it?" Kazuki asked.

"He took the station, he was using it." Noe turned around enough to see Kazuki as he walked before adding, "It's what he was tuning."

"But why?" Kazuki felt at a loss for words for the first time in a while.

Tommie spoke up again, "If someone is fully tuned into a station, then you can't take it away from them. You can't share when you're tuned in like that. The stations just disappear." She snapped her fingers for effect.

Kazuki thought about it for a moment, "Then why can I get your station?"

It was Irvin that answered his question, "Because we're not really 'using' the station, we're just listening to it. If we were really tuning it then you'd never be able to find it."

Noe continued, "If we're really doing something

with it, we trade off who has the station, one of us will take it while the rest of us take a break then we pass it along."

"Or we can use other stations." Allene added on the tail end of Noe's comment.

"But, yeah…" Noe picked back up where he left off, "Two people can't use the same station at the same time like that, and if they try… one of them usually wins the station pretty quickly and then there's no chance to wrestle it away from them."

"Unless you knock them out." Tommie added with a grin.

The six of them reached the end of the block and the area opened up to a busy intersection. Across the street was the mall. The parking lot packed with cars and the cars on the roadway swarmed in all directions. Apparently they'd chosen one of the busier times of day to make their pilgrimage.

Without hesitation, Noe lead the way across the street and through the parking lot, dodging the occasional car. Kazuki looked all around as they approached the mall. Of all the comparisons Kazuki had made between American and Japan, the mall turned out to have the greatest differences between its overseas double. It must have been because it was such a small city that the size was less than impressive.

Even having made their way out of the summer heat and into the air conditioning, it wasn't the slightest bit larger from the inside. The number of stores was so low, the foot traffic so diminished, and the number of vacant stores so high, that he had to wonder if this mall was going to be around much longer.

He was used to malls that stretched forever. Malls with huge areas where you could get lost for hours, that was what a mall was supposed to be. But just walking into the door he was already seeing half of what it had to offer. How long would it take the six of them to make their way through everything?

"You hungry?" Noe asked, already leading the group toward the hot dog stand in the middle of the isle way.

"A little." Kazuki nodded, food did sound good.

"You ain't tried nothing till you've tried an American chili dog." Noe boasted, stepping up to the cash register.

Kazuki could tell he didn't have much say in the matter so he smiled and nodded.

"I got it on lock-down; you just find us some seats." Noe turned back to the counter leaving Kazuki wondering what it was he had on lock-down. Absently Kazuki reached into his pocket and thumbed a few bills. He had enough money for whatever he wanted on the menu if they asked for cash. Kazuki looked over the tables setup on the faux cobblestone and picked a table big enough for all of them.

Kazuki sat down heavily; his back was aching from the activity. It didn't let him forget how severely he was injured and how much longer the road to recovery could be. Settling in he looked down, the tabletop was a criss cross of steel wire, he poked at the wire, it looked cheap but managed to feel sturdy. Up at the counter the others were passing their orders along to Noe. Allene finished her order first.

"Yeah, you know..." She pulled out the chair, the steel legs screeching as they scraped over the stone, "If I'd been around I would have been there for you. I'm sure Noe's already told you the same thing... but, you know it's true."

"No." Kazuki shook his head, "You are the first."

Allene smiled, dimples in the corners of her face, the earnest expression contrasting the usual mature front she put up, "Anyway, if it hadn't been so late in the day I'm sure someone would have been around to help you. But..." She let out a sigh as Mike and Tommie sat down next to one another, "At least Ellie was able to get you taken care of."

Mike took the opportunity to join the conversation, his voice starting off timid, "That's one of the reasons we all hang out together, Alden is a bully. Before he would mess with us just because he liked to fight other Channelers." Mike let out a sigh, "At least he picked on people he could beat up, I don't think he ever really messed with Noe."

"Don't worry…" Allene broke back into the conversation, "We've all got some tricks that we can show you."

Kazuki smiled and nodded. He didn't feel like a rematch. More than anything he wanted to avoid Alden; for the rest of his trip if possible.

Allene picked up on his mood, "Being a Channeler…" She paused a moment before trying again, "It's like having a lot of power… no, like having a lot of money. If you don't know exactly what you want to do with it, it's easy to waste it all and have nothing to show for it." She paused a moment watching to see if her words were sinking in, "If you're going to be able to use your powers, you have to train to use those powers. You have to practice." She smiled wide, "You know what I'm saying?"

Actually Kazuki wasn't sure what she was getting at, he nodded anyway just as the food was arriving.

"Here we go!" Noe dropped the tray on the table and picked off a huge hot dog and set it in front of Kazuki. Kazuki looked it over with a touch of trepidation, on the side of the half-box in all capital letters it said "Foot long" and looked like it was covered with chili and mustard and onions. The chili layer was so thick he couldn't see a trace of what was beneath. For all he knew there could have been yet another layer. He looked up pleadingly as Noe dished out the rest of the food to the others before sitting down.

Carefully Kazuki pushed his hands under the hot dog and lifted it out of its box; both sides immediately drooped under the weight of the toppings and spilled themselves all over the table. The sound of laughter brought his head up and he could feel the embarrassment on his cheeks. Irvin, who was sitting next to him, patted him on his back causing Kazuki to breathe in sharply, "That's only for advanced eaters. Until then just keep it in the box and eat it out of there." Irvin lifted his own hot dog box up and slid the hot dog out of the opposite end and took a bite with as much of a smile as he could muster considering the quantity of food.

Kazuki smiled sheepishly and tried to move the hot dog back into the box, scooping some of the toppings up with his hand and planting them back in place before lifting it and taking a bite. He set the hot dog down and gave a big smile. It did taste better than the ones that he got back in Japan. It took a moment for him to determine why everyone was smiling before he quickly wiped the chili from his face.

The mall had been a welcome distraction. Despite its size there had been a number of stores that Kazuki had never seen before. Then there had been Noe and his group too. They acted completely different away from the library and arcade, just interacting with each other, always laughing and joking. They'd spent most of the day there until Mike and Tommie had to leave.

There was an uneasy feeling though and it was getting stronger. They were getting closer to the parking lot where he had fought Alden the other day. In a few hours the sun would be just as it had been then. He tried to brush off the feeling. Kazuki told himself to think of something else.

"That's where Alden beat you up, right?" Allene

asked, leaning in closer.

"Yes." The chill that crept up Kazuki's spine was the most distracting yet, but even imagined, the cold almost felt good against the bruises. He hadn't thought that they were intentionally going there, but now that they were walking across the parking lot there was no denying it.

"Here." Noe was looking down at the ground, scraping at the asphalt with his shoe. "Come here a second." Kazuki timidly crossed the distance. "What's this look like to you?" Noe asked, pointing to the asphalt with the tip of his shoe.

Kazuki looked closely; it looked like the marks left after heavy equipment was parked on blacktop. "Like something heavy was here." He answered at last.

Noe gave a chuckle, "That's what it looks like when a Nike presses into the pavement with enough force to rip the sole in half." He gave another laugh, "At least you ruined his shoes."

Kazuki let out the breath he had been holding, lowering himself to the ground he looked at the depression; it was almost big enough to fit his hand into. When he looked at it closely he could see the rubber that had been abraded against the blacktop as it had sunk in and at the very bottom the rounding where a foot had struck.

"Recognize this spot?" Noe continued, "I bet a dumpster or something was here before."

Kazuki looked up, sure enough it was the same spot where had had been beaten the other night. "No matter how much stronger tuning makes you, it doesn't matter. You always weigh the same, you hit someone strong enough and you're just going to throw yourself back." Noe again pointed with the tip of his shoe, this time at a different mark, "I like to call that the kickstand effect. You know, like on a bike?"

Again Kazuki examined the spot, comprehension

right on the edge of his senses. Noe continued, "Yeah, when you use your kickstand your bike sits at an angle and digs in, keeping it in place." Noe put his shoe into the depression, bending at an angle and extending his arm as if mid-punch, "When you punch you need to angle your body so that if you connect you dig in, that way everything you have goes into the punch and it can't throw you back. If you can ever brace yourself against something then you can really go all out."

It clicked; suddenly it made sense of the way Alden was fighting. A dark hand was in his field of vision and he took it, Irvin helping to hoist him to his feet. "If someone is coming at you with everything though, and you get out of the way they'll end up really off balance from the follow-through." Irvin smiled at him, "It's always better to move than block."

Noe shook his head, "He got you backed against a dumpster and scored all of these hits on you, and you're still up and walking around..." Noe gestured with his foot at all the depressions in the ground, "You're either really lucky or a lot tougher than you look."

Kazuki took the comment pride, even though his back was still screaming from hunching over on the ground. "I was just lucky very I think." If he had already taken the worst case scenario, it at least made him feel like less of a wimp.

"Kazuki..." Noe nodded purposefully, "When we're done with you, you'll be able to kick Alden's ass. No question about it." Noe eyed the cut above Kazuki's eye, "Until then we should probably keep hanging out so that thug doesn't get the jump on you again."

Kazuki looked between Noe, Irvin, and Allene, the looks on their faces did wonders for his confidence. No way did he want to face Alden again in the future, but he still felt better about the past.

"So, are you going to have another meeting of

your fight club today?" Miranda asked as she got up to answer the door.

Satoshi was quick to speak up, "The first rule of Fight Club is you do not talk about Fight Club."

Miranda playfully smacked Satoshi on the shoulder earning a smile from him in response. "You know what I mean." She said heading toward the door.

"Probably." Kazuki answered truthfully. Noe had been showing up at least every other day with whomever to give him training lessons since that day at the mall over a week before. If someone came then they would train, if no one did he would take it easy, though his injuries were just memories by now, allowing him to spar as well as watch.

Getting used to fighting as a Channeler was strange at first. The take downs that he'd learned from his brother still had their place, but they were just part of the equation. There was in increased risk of sudden brutal force overpowering them in their application that prevented them most of the time. Instead things devolved more often than not into simple fist fighting. Well, simple in principle, in practice the movements felt unnatural, overextended, and off-balance.

When tuning though everything felt perfect. It just took the practice to keep the movements feeling natural as unnatural as they seemed. Miranda walked out of the kitchen, the dish washer starting up, "Well, good luck anyway." She waved as she walked past and out of the room. A moment later she called out, "Kazuki, its Elli!" As the two of them headed back to the dining room together.

Kazuki walked over to greet her, "Nice you to see again."

"You too, how are you feeling?" Elli asked. It was only the second time Kazuki had seen her since she had given him a ride home.

"Better, completely recovered." He gave her a

laugh to ease her nerves, she looked stressed.

"Well, I've got to get going." Satoshi excused himself from the room as well. Kazuki still wasn't sure where he was going, maybe heading over to the base and visiting some of his old friends.

"Good luck." Kazuki wished in general as his brother nodded in his direction and headed out of the room with Miranda following not far behind. He turned his attention back to his guest, "How are you doing?" He asked after a moment of hesitation, staring a moment longer into her malachite eyes.

"Good... good..." She was looking at her tennis shoes and seemed anxious. "I hope that your trip hasn't been completely ruined by that ass."

It shocked him to hear profanities out of Elli, but he didn't let it show, "No, there were other good things."

"Really...." She let out a sigh, "How's everything else?"

Kazuki made a face, trying to condense the events of the last several days, "Things are okay, I am training with Noe and others. I think I am moving forward."

Elli nodded her head but went silent, starring off into space, or maybe forward directly at Kazuki. He wasn't sure which. Eventually she spoke up again, "So, you're on summer break right now, right?"

"Yes... yes." Kazuki's mind shifted gears, "I do not go back till August the end of." As soon as the sentence left his mouth he winced, he could tell he'd said something off.

"I thought you guys just always went to school, that's what Japan's famous for, isn't it?" She asked with a bit of a laugh, if she caught his slip she didn't show it.

Kazuki smiled back, "We go longer but we still get break." Then he tried to turn things around, "What about you? You have school now too."

"Yeah." She nodded, "But that's just me, all the

normal schools are out."

Elli cleared her throat, looking slightly nervous after looking up from her shoes she started again, "I really only have a few minutes. I've got someone in the car waiting for me. I was wondering if maybe you wanted to go to a concert tonight."

"Concert?" The invitation was unexpected.

"Yeah, Noe and a few of the others will be there, it's just over in Madison. He mentioned you'd probably like to come with us." Elli had regained some of her nerve.

"Who is playing?" Kazuki asked, wondering more about the price of the tickets than anything.

"Just a couple of local bands." Elli reached to her side and pulled out a ticket, "I have an extra ticket..."

"That sounds good." Kazuki nodded, trying to accept graciously.

"Cool." Elli said after a pause. "I guess we'll come by and pick you up..." She gave a few shallow nods and turned away partially before turning back, "Okay?"

"What time is it?" Kazuki asked.

"Oh, seven. Will that work?"

"Yes, it is good."

"Okay, well, we'll see you later then."

"Yes, good bye." Kazuki gave a little wave to match hers as she walked out of the room and heard the front door close. Kazuki walked back over to the table and dropped into the chair with a sigh, wondering if anyone else was going to be making an appearance before the concert.

It took a little bit of doing, but between Noe, Allene, Elli, Irvin, and himself, the five of them had made their way to the front of the crowd. Kazuki took in his surroundings, the band had yet to make their way on stage but the audience was already a maelstrom of activity. People pushing, yelling, there was so much energy and excitement, and Kazuki found himself right in the middle of it.

"You doing okay!" Noe yelled down at him despite being close enough to press into his arm.

"Yeah!" Kazuki yelled back, "Just excited!"

"Just wait till they start playing!" Noe yelled back, pushing back on the crowd and Kazuki a little more to open up some room and Allene and Elli did likewise. It cleared some space but not much.

Elli moved in closer to Kazuki to yell over the crowd, "See those guys over there!"

Kazuki nodded his head, not wanting to strain his voice.

"Tune around some, you'll find the station they're broadcasting on." She replied back smug.

After few moments the words from the people in the booth almost matched up with their lips. He'd found the station. There was a bit of lag, but it was hardly distracting. "They are about ready to start!" Kazuki yelled out causing Elli to smile and nod.

It was such a great feeling to be in on such an exclusive clique. For a moment his thoughts went back to his departure from the house. He had told Satoshi that he was going to a concert and when he had been leaving, Satoshi had been setting up candles around the house. It was obvious that Satoshi had been planning something between himself and Miranda. Was that how things had been before he had gone back to Japan in the first place?

A few moments later the band walked out on the stage. The singer wearing knee-high leather boots, his long hair slicked back and hanging down almost to his butt. "Are you all ready to rock!" His voice boomed over the PA as his band mates made their way to their instruments, trying to check the tune of things before settling in for their set.

The beat of drums, strumming of the guitar, suddenly the band burst into its song. Kazuki's eyes opened wide, the feeling of the music, the beat in the air, something he could feel into his bones coupled with the duality of the music he was tuning. It was incredible.

Noe must have noticed the effect the music was having, "I know, it's freaking awesome isn't it!"

Shaking his head vigorously, Kazuki agreed, "Yes, this is great!" The pounding beats were unreal, in a league reserved for Channelers alone. The heady feeling expanded, it was all connected. Somehow there was a connection between the frequencies of the radio, the music in the auditorium, the fervor of the crowd. And it was all resonating, coalescing, filling Kazuki with a feeling more powerful and accomplished than any ever before.

Chapter 6

The sound of fingers striking the keyboard echoed around the wood paneled room. Licking his lips, Kazuki flexed his fingers and paused a moment, starring at his laptop screen. He had drifted further away from daily phone calls to his parents and more toward e-mail. After picking up a cheap digital camera he'd also started attaching plenty of pictures.

They had responded in kind. Their own replies containing pictures of home. It was silly, nothing had changed that quickly. However, after his initial dismissal, he had come to expect the images. His previous computer background, a scantly dressed cartoon character, had been replaced with a photo of his dad trying to repair a window with the sun setting in the background.

Looking out of the window, the moon was hanging almost at the top of the frame. Swinging the cursor lower on the screen he brought up the calendar. There was just a little over two weeks before he would be back in Japan. Time had passed so fast, yet simultaneously it felt like forever before he would make his return trip. Though he wasn't looking forward to spending sixteen hours trapped on a stuffy airplane he missed his mom, his dad, his friends, his own city.

Shifting the laptop he clicked the 'Send' button, shooting another pulse of electrons half-way around the world in the blink of an eye. Rubbing his forehead he scrolled back around on the computer screen and started another new e-mail. It was hard keeping everyone up to date on what was going on. The thought of a blog or similar entity though was dismissed outright.

He was leading too many different strings of life at the moment. His parents only knew bits and pieces of his ability. Other friends knew the whole story, but still others knew nothing of his powers.

Unfortunately that necessitated keeping them all on their individual news feeds no matter how much of a pain in the butt it had evolved into. He took a minute to look through his last sent message to see what had changed since then. Not much, training, fighting, and getting in shape for fighting. More than ever he was sure that a rematch with Alden was inevitable.

While he was training, sweating, feeling endorphins rush through his blood he was sure that he would win no matter the odds. But at times, like now, sitting in a cold bed and worlds away from most of the people he loved he was reminded that there were no guarantees in life. He'd been beaten so thoroughly. One of the hits that had crumpled him against the dumpster had been so powerful that he was sure he was going to die. He didn't want to feel that panic ever again.

It left Kazuki with a nauseous claustrophobic feeling. He gave up on his e-mail, closing his laptop and sitting it out of the way. It wasn't long before he had changed into his night clothes and was clicking the light switch off. He settled under the covers, the opposite wall illuminated by moonlight.

Shutting his eyes, he tried to get himself comfortable. It took a few moments. His mind was still running in circles. Sometimes there was so much going on that he couldn't figure out where to start. That alone forced him to inaction which helped increase the burdens he put on himself forcing himself to still further inaction.

On the one hand there was so much left for him to do, more training, more people to talk with. He wanted to hang out with Noe and go to the arcade. His mental itinerary jam packed with obligations. On the other hand, what did it all have to do with being a Channeler? Why did he have to learn to fight? Where Channelers only good for fighting?

Since he arrived at the airport he'd been trying to justify it to himself by trying to believe that something special was going to happen on this trip. That he was going to learn what it was to be a Channeler. He might as well have been searching for the meaning of life.

Did meeting these other Channelers mean anything? He could have showed up in this small town and not met anyone with his abilities, wasted a month and a half of his life then headed home empty handed. Would that have been any more productive?

In desperation he grabbed a pillow from under his head and pressed it over his face. Even if he liked the people he'd met, most of them anyway, how would he feel in a year? No, he hadn't expected it, but he had hoped for so much more.

Anxiously he expanded his thoughts, feeling out the radio waves for comfort. He had been doing it less and less lately except he was training. Afraid that Alden might track him down, it wasn't as fun any more. Far from the relaxing past time that it had been.

For awhile he laid there, eyes open, starring at the ceiling. Finally he settled his tuning. He dropped the stress from his mind, feeling so much like a physical wall crumbling away. Jazz, it felt nice; he didn't get much of it in Japan.

He smiled. He couldn't see himself fighting to it, but it felt nice. The deep bellow of the saxophone overlaid with the sharp notes of the trumpet. It was a roller coaster ride for his senses.

Slowly he became aware that he wasn't the only one on the station. Who was it? Quickly he gave up on the idea of probing deeper. If they were willing to share he wasn't going to rock the boat. Over time he got the feeling, through from what he wasn't sure, that it was Elli with him. He started to drift off to sleep, he would have to ask her about it the next time he saw her.

The sun was shining radiantly above, giving just the prefect amount of light to make its way through the overhead branches. Kazuki enjoyed the air coming off the lake for a moment. It had been some time since he had last been down by the beach, or even just wandering around town for the heck of it.

It wasn't just coincidence; there was that feeling again on the stations. He wasn't sure exactly but he had a hunch who he might find nearby. He reached the end of the path, the asphalt melting away under the sand as the lake rolled out before him.

Looking around he scanned the beach. A moment later he had his new heading. "Hello." He greeted as he approached. On the beach in front of him a woman was sunning herself in a two piece green bikini, a book lying over her face as if she had fallen asleep that way. It was the scar leading along her shoulder and down her arm that gave her away. That and her long brown hair that was splayed out behind her more fully than the blanket she was laying on.

Unfortunately, the salutation wasn't enough to stir her from her nap. Kazuki made a face before looking around one more time, trying to find any sign of her companion. He tried to rack his brain. It had been some time, Casey and... Julie.

There were two men nearby on their own towels, face down. He was less sure which of them would be Casey so he decided to test his luck, "Julie?" He tried again. Instead of getting her attention though one of the men turned his head to the side form his prone position.

"Oh... hey." Casey squinted into the sun. "Long time..." He pushed himself up from his blanket, the fabric leaving impressions against his chest where it had bunched up.

"Nice to see you again." Kazuki replied back, squatting down to match Casey in height as he didn't seem inclined to get up from the ground.

"How've you been enjoying America so far?" Casey asked, rolling more onto his butt and wiping the sand off his arms and face.

"It has been nice." Kazuki noticed Julie stirring out of the corner of his eye, "I have been learning things from the other Channelers."

"Were you the one...? I heard something about someone fighting Alden." Julie asked, her face still covered by the book. With her face covered that just left other inappropriate parts on which to focus, so he kept his eyes on Casey.

"Yes, Alden beat me up." Kazuki admitted, it was hardly something he would consider a fight, especially the more he dwelt on it.

"Couldn't of been too bad." Casey offered quickly, "You look like you're all healed up now."

"Apparently I am a quick healer." Kazuki countered bluntly.

"So, what else have you been up to?" Casey asked.

Kazuki looked around to Julie for a moment, wondering if she had fallen back asleep. "Hanging out, eating hot dogs." He tried to make the last bit come out jokingly but didn't get much of a smile in response. "Learning more about being a Channeler."

"How's that working out for you?" Casey asked with a laugh.

"It is mostly fighting I found out." He said regretting it, he wished there was more to it.

Julie spoke up, "If you want to look at it that way." She moved her book off her face and rolled onto her side, sitting up on her scarred arm, "Alden could have just as much fun with it if he played baseball, or did track and field." She signed, "He's the one that's always fighting." Julie dropped onto her back again and lifted her book back up, this time keeping it some distance away from her face as she started to read it.

"I fight just for fun…" Casey spoke up again, "To relax, you know the feeling." His smile widened, "But it is a blast to really go at it as a Channeler." For a moment he turned his attention to his girlfriend, "We used to train all the time, but thankfully Alden never wanted to fight the two of us."

Kazuki wanted to mention her scar but didn't. Still, he wanted to keep up the current direction of their conversation, "Why do you not train any more?"

"It got too dangerous." Casey answered succinctly. "When you get really good at Channeling, it starts to feel like second nature. That's when things can go wrong. There are things your powers can do that your body just isn't meant to do. And when you cross that line…"

Out of the corner of his eye Kazuki caught Julie turn further away, provoked to speaking again, "We were training by the lake last fall." She started out, again rolling onto her side and propping herself up on her arm, "The two of us were trading off as quick as ever."

Casey took a moment to explain, "When we trained, we shared a station. I mean, you know two Channelers can't use the same station at the same time, so we'd share it by giving up control of it just for an instant then take it back when we needed it." He gave a laugh, "It was kind of like two people trying to fight each other with only one sword between them."

"Casey could throw a punch and trade off the station to me in time to block it. It was all second nature." Julie flopped onto her belly, holding her head between her two hands, thinking a moment before changing the direction of the conversation, "You know, when a song ends, you still have that power for a second or two, right? Not just the usual bit of power from the station either, but the good stuff."

Kazuki nodded his head, knowing the feeling of it fading away quickly.

"You've got all that power, and it takes a second to dissipate." Julie looked up to meet Kazuki's eyes, "What we were learning to do was store that power for a few seconds each time so that one of us could still use it to fight and the other could use it to block." Julie sighed deeply, shifting her eyes toward the ground, "This is what happens..." She moved her arm from beneath her, holding it out, "When you store too much power for too long."

Kazuki looked her arm up and down, the scar wasn't just superficial, the skin was raised nearly a centimeter along its length, even higher in some spots, though it was fairly uniform in tone.

"And that's after the plastic surgery and the two weeks in the hospital." She continued somberly, pulling her hand back and propping her head back up.

Casey picked up where Julie had left off, "That's why we gave up on fighting. It was fun, but we decided that we didn't want to risk something like that ever happening again."

Kazuki was still trying to process the information, her body had acted like a battery, no, a capacitor. She'd absorbed the energy and then discharged it through her arm. The scar had been ragged but he could see where the energy had branched out down her arm, trails that split again and again to the smaller strands that feathered out into her tanned skin, only visible as indistinct shadowing.

"I am sorry." Kazuki offered, it was all he could think of to say.

"Why would you apologize?" Julie replied, again rolling onto her side, her hand digging into the sand slightly. "I figured you were curious about the scart." She perked up slightly.

Kazuki turned, hearing something over his

shoulder about 'Japan'. The feeling in his heart was suddenly cold. "Ano...." Quickly he turned to Casey who caught his gaze and followed when he turned his head.

Standing just at the edge of the beach Alden and his two cronies, Jayson and Bailey were starring him down. Kazuki couldn't match their gaze but for a moment before turning away. He kept looking back though as they made their way across the beach.

Julie pushed herself into a sitting position her previous expression crumbling. Casey likewise dropped any friendly feelings.

"Hey, if it isn't Mr. Japan himself!" Jayson called out, moving a few steps ahead of the other two, even in the light of the full sun he looked disheveled, his scruffy sideburns meeting in the middle of his chin in a scraggly patch of hair.

Kazuki pushed himself to his feet but held his ground. He looked down and to his sides, seeing that both Julie and Casey were there if he needed them. He was hoping though that Alden wouldn't want the trouble.

"Hey." Alden called out, kicking some sand up and onto Kazuki's legs, "How ya' holding up after that beating? Ready for round two yet?" He gave a little hop bringing his fits up to his face leaving no question about what he was asking.

"I will not fight." Kazuki said firmly.

"Doesn't matter." Alden laughed, "You said the same thing last time and I kicked your ass anyway, so why don't you just bend over and take it?"

Bailey laughed, "After the beating Alden gave you, I'm surprised you're stupid enough to go walking around town."

Playing off his energy, Jayson continued, "Yeah, what are you, some kind of retard."

Casey stood suddenly, hardly looking intimidating shirtless and wearing shorts that Kazuki himself would have thought to be too short, "Hey, we were in the middle of something, so unless you're here to enjoy the beach I'd get out of here while you have the chance."

Kazuki caught the look that Casey was shooting to Bailey and Jayson which caused the two of them to shift backward. Meanwhile Julie had stood from her towel. Although he was trying not to pay attention to the stations, Kazuki could feel them shifting, someone, maybe all three of them were already searching. He might already be at a disadvantage. Still, Alden didn't want to start something the last time until he'd been able to give him an honest to goodness fight as a Channeler.

"Forget you." Alden huffed, "If you need these two to protect you, you're a bigger pussy than I thought." He laughed which proved infectious between his cohorts. Briefly he paused, looking Julie over without a trace of modesty, "I've got other things on my 'to do' list today, but maybe if you'd be willing to teach me that lightning trick I'd give you the time of day."

"I'm sorry," Julie started, "I'd show it to you but you'd never see it with my fist up your ass." She smiled through clenched teeth as she lifted herself up from the towel. Casey gave a sharp intake of breath he too tensed up.

"I hope you're getting ready for our next rumble." Alden mocked, ignoring Casey and Julie for the moment, "Because the next time I see you... it's on." He raised his eyebrows and smirked before turning on his heel and walking away. Jayson huffed before heading off and Bailey gave the three of them the finger.

The tense situation lingered beyond the trio leaving. "I fucking hate those guys." Casey cursed, drawing a reprimanding look from Julie that immediately softened.

"Thank you both, I am not fully better yet from

before." Kazuki bowed slightly as Julie dropped back onto her blanket.

"No problem. Whatever we can do to help."

Casey echoed the statement, "Yeah, no big deal." It didn't look that way to Kazuki though; both of them looked stressed.

Kazuki protested, "No, it is important. I am very grateful." He bowed even deeper to each of them, "Thank you Casey, thank you Julie." It was a good feeling; they'd made him feel safe. After all of his training, his confidence was still not up to muster, that was until they were there to back him up. And he couldn't thank them enough for that.

"I think I'm going to go take a swim." Julie said after a moment, pushing herself onto her feet.

"Have fun." Casey nodded, giving another look in Alden's direction before giving her another nod of approval. It was easy to tell they were straining to act normal in the face of what just happened.

Casey and Kazuki sat there in silence as Julie rubbed the sand off her body before heading off into the water, swimming out into the lake a little but remaining within earshot.

"You know..." Casey started, his voice dropping a few decibels, "I was just thinking about back when me and Julie first met." His smile had that earnest nostalgic quality to it that put Kazuki at ease, "I used to use my powers to sing Karaoke to her... kind of."

"What?" Kazuki probed.

Casey gave a reserved laugh, looking out toward the lake, his eyes no doubt on Julie, "I'd sing to her, whatever I could find on the radio. She used to think it was so romantic. She'd never sing to me, she insisted she didn't have the voice. Really, I don't either, but she seemed to love it..." He trailed off a moment, "I don't know man, I just... there are other things you can do with channeling besides fighting."

111

Kazuki nodded his head, it was a sweet story, "I will remember that…"

"Kazuki?"

Taking a moment to swallow his mouth full of mashed potatoes, Kazuki looked up to meet Miranda's eyes, "Hummm?" He offered, emptying his mouth. Kazuki looked between Miranda and Satoshi, noticing for the first time the worry on Satoshi's features.

"I was watching you work out today with your friends…" She paused, leaving Kazuki to wonder about her point, "How is it you can do those things…" She trailed off yet again, "I saw you and that other guy Noe fighting, he's got to be at least 6 feet tall and you *jumped* over him." She watched him for a moment to gauge his reaction, "And it's not just that, you slam each other into the ground so hard the windows shake, you move faster than I can follow, and even with the hits you take you're up and about laughing afterwards." Miranda shook her head, "And before you say anything, don't expect me to fall for that stereotype that everyone from Japan is just that good at martial arts."

Kazuki looked to his brother, wondering what he had already told her. He gave his broth an exaggerated puzzled expression, obviously he'd played dumb. Kazuki struggled, why his brother hadn't given him a little warning. They'd agreed not to tell Miranda because they didn't want to have to explain things, or maybe make her treat him differently. Now Kazuki found himself staring her down from across the table unsure as to what kind of move he should make.

"Have you ever been thinking about song, or humming song, and you turn on the radio and that song is playing?" Kazuki started off, deciding that his standard explanation was in order; it had after all been honed by use.

Miranda nodded, "Yeah."

"It is like that all the time with me, it is like I have a radio in my head." For a moment his eyes met with his brother's. "I can hear all of the stations right now if I liked." Kazuki turned back to Miranda, "It's called tuning, and the people that can do it are called Channelers."

"So what? It's like a Walkman or something?" Miranda offered dismissively, it made him want to give up.

"There are more people like me… here. That was one of the reasons I came here. To talk to them." Kazuki swallowed dryly, "There are not others like that in Japan so I came here." Taking a deep breath he looked down at his plate.

"Okay…." Miranda drew it out, forcing him to continue.

"When I am tuning I get stronger, faster. I can… jump higher." He added trying to make it clear that he was trying to explain what she had seen earlier in the day.

"Well, that at least makes some sense…" Kazuki could hear the breath she took from across the table. "No, it doesn't," She laughed, "but I guess it doesn't matter." She shook her head, "It doesn't make sense to me but I don't know what you could tell me that I would believe."

Miranda looked between the two of them, "I guess seeing is believing, but somethings take even a bit more than that." She looked between Satoshi and Kazuki, "Don't give me that look; I've been paying attention since you two showed up. It wasn't the first time I watched you guys go at it in the back yard. And after that night when Kazuki got beat up I knew something must have been going on." She gave an exasperated sigh, "But why didn't either of you tell me, you just left me worrying and wondering." Roughly she rubbed her hands across her face, "Can you do this stuff too

113

Satoshi?" She asked sounding more hurt than anything.

Satoshi was quick to reply, "No, no, it's only Kazuki, I can't do any of it, I'm just a normal guy." Kazuki saw the hurt look his brother gave him, he hadn't meant to offend, but Kazuki didn't feel offended, he tried to show his brother with a smile.

Trying to diffuse the situation Kazuki broke back into the conversation, "We did not want you to think differently of me, I… we… were afraid you might be afraid." Kazuki paused, not sure if he had chosen the right words to get his point across.

"I can see where you're coming from." Her eyes locked with Satoshi's, "But please don't keep me in the dark any more. I need to know what's going on if you're going to staying here with me Kazuki." Despite the direction of her words her gaze was fixed on Satoshi.

"We can do that." Satoshi offered back, sounding breathless.

"So, it's you, Noe… who else?" Miranda asked.

"Everyone." Kazuki offered, not wanting to have to struggle over their names at the dinner table, he'd never been good at names. "All the people that have come over, even Elli that brought me back the night I was beat up."

"That many? They can all do this? But if there aren't any in Japan, why here? What's special about this place?" Miranda pressed.

"We don't know." Satoshi answered for his brother, "It just turned out that way."

"That other night, when you were beat up, was that another one of these radio people that did it?" A bit of worry made its way into her voice.

"Yeah." Satoshi answered for Kazuki, "That's why he didn't want to explain it to the cops, and that's why he's been training so much lately, so he doesn't have a repeat."

The table went silent before Miranda spoke up again, "I guess, that at least gives me something to go on." She shook her head, "Just don't keep me in the dark for so long. Please." She stood from the table, pausing a second to look at Kazuki before heading up stairs, "I don't want to be blind-sided with someone breaking into my house in the middle of the night or something."

Satoshi watched her leave the kitchen and climb the staircase. *"Sorry about that, she caught me when I got home and I couldn't think of anything to say."* His brother said at last once Miranda was out of earshot.

Kazuki nodded, *"Don't worry about it, it seems like she took it okay. I guess we should have told her sooner though."*

"Really…" Satoshi started, getting his brother's attention, *"How are things looking? You think you're going to have to fight again?"*

Kazuki sighed, *"Well…"* He saw no reason to lie, *"Probably…"* So he told his brother about the encounter at the beach with Alden.

His brother sat there silently as he told him how Alden had threatened him again. He did smile though when he told him about how Casey and Julie had stood up for him.

Satoshi let out the breath he'd been holding, *"I just… I worry about you buddy. I know I can't just hang around in case something happens. And if something did happen, I know there wouldn't be much I could do."* Satoshi shook his head, *"Just take it easy out there."*

"Yeah." Kazuki looked away slightly, *"Don't worry about it."* He felt embarrassed that his brother was actually telling him these things. *"I'll be okay, I've got friends here now."* He admitted, knowing it was true but still bashful of the bond they shared.

"Okay, but just remember, you can always talk to me if things get too heavy."

Kazuki nodded and Satoshi pushed himself from the table, *"Good, I'm going to call it a night."* Satoshi started heading out of the room, ruffling his brother's hair as he walked by, *"See you in the morning."*

"Good night big brother."

Sometimes the shower was undeniably the best place to think. Rubbing the soap between his hands he looked down at his bare chest, the water running down his face and streaming off his chin as he pitched forward to keep the stream out of his eyes. It was impossible to even tell that he had been so badly injured. The last of the bruises had finally disappeared.

Honestly, he had been expecting to have to explain all of those injuries once he got home. Now his body didn't show a trace of what happened, which left him with only a smashed cell phone as evidence of that night. Tilting his face up he rinsed the soap out of his eyes and grabbed blindly for the shampoo, adding a dollop to his hand he started working it into lather in his hair.

Through the door he heard the faint sounds of his brother and Miranda talking. It was hard to make much of anything out over the sound of the water and the plugging in his ears. He hadn't meant to upset her.

She really was a good woman, and had tried so hard to make him feel welcome during the stay. Rinsing the suds out of his hair he found himself tapping his foot along to a beat in his head. Instead of stopping himself he kept with it as he finished up his shower. The sound came in clearer as he focused on the instruments and lyrics.

Another quick rinse and Kazuki was toweling off his short brown hair, leaving it spiked and shining. A few moments later and he had the towel wrapped around his waist, brushing his teeth. He thought back to earlier in the day near the beach. Another encounter

116

with Alden. He shook his head.

He was still thankful that the others had been there to back him up. But it didn't bode well. He was convinced something was on the horizon. Worse yet, this time he wondered if he was the catalyst for this behavior. Alden didn't mess with Noe or his group, didn't try to antagonize Casey and Julie any more, and apparently left Elli alone except for the occasional snide remark.

Now with him on the scene, it felt like he was bringing these violent streaks to the forefront. The stalemate that things had settled into before his arrival was disturbed.

Kazuki at least would be back in Japan one day soon, but would that be the end of it? Or would he go back to picking on everyone else, maybe even Elli.

Hanging the damp towel back on the rack he tossed on some loose fitting pants and shirt to match before opening the door. The temperature in the room was several degrees cooler and encompassed him as if he had jumped into water. It was just as refreshing as the initial blast from the faucet had been.

His thoughts went to Elli. He hadn't seen her today. He remembered the feeling as he had been drifting off to sleep the night before sharing a station. The more he thought about it the more certain he was that it was her there with him. She was better at these things than he was, so she must have realized the same thing.

Walking into his bedroom, it was even cooler in his room; the window was still open from the morning. He took a moment to pull it shut before moving back the comforter. He gave his laptop a look; he'd e-mailed his parents earlier but no one else. He wasn't in the mood to boot it back up so he shut off the lights in the room and crawled beneath the covers.

He wished that he had a cell phone still. He

wished that he had Elli's number. He didn't know what he wanted to talk about, but he wanted to hear her voice. He was sure she would talk to him, but looking back he'd have wagered his current role was that of the hurt puppy, hardly a prelude to romance.

Satoshi on the other hand... Kazuki settled into the pillow. He'd come back to America to be back with the woman that he'd fallen for. And the longer he stayed here the more Kazuki was sure that Satoshi was considering making it permanent. The two of them hadn't spoken about it seriously yet, but he was sure the conversation was coming. Certainly his brother would come back with him to Japan, but he wondered how long it would last.

It was true that channeling had been the most unique aspect of the trip so far, but watching his brother's relationship grow had been almost as interesting. From the mixed emotions he had seen at the airport that gave way to a suppressed bitterness for the first week or so. That bitterness eventually fading, slowly replaced by friendliness and companionship as they again found their reasons to care for one another.

It was the first time Kazuki had seen his brother honestly happy since before he had joined the army in the first place.

Too much thinking. Kazuki slowed his breathing and tried to let his mind unwind. He found that he was still slightly tuned in, his foot tapping beneath the sheet of its own accord in time with the music. Concentrating more on the action he sifted through the stations, eventually finding his way back to the Jazz station. This time though he was curious. It was a commercial. Commercials were never a good thing when tuning. Because a Channeler could chase their way through the stations so quickly and smoothly there was never any incentive to stay on a commercial, it was like reading a newspaper. You saw the ads but you never had to read them, your eyes would just find their way to another interesting headline.

He stayed with it though, the annoying pitchman trying to sell his snake oil straight to Kazuki's brain. One commercial traded for another, then another, and just when Kazuki was actually straining to stay with the annoying channel, the music again started. Letting out a sigh of relief Kazuki rolled onto his side, bunching up a pillow in his arms. The music relaxing him, then, a moment later, he felt it. The same presence from earlier. Elli was there again, and shortly thereafter he found sleep for the night.

Chapter 7

The phone rang once. Another ring sounded, and then another and finally a 'click', a groggy voice on the other end of the line, "Yeah?"

Kazuki took a breath to steady himself, "Hello, it is Kazuki." He started, "Did I wake you up?"

On the other end of the line he heard Elli shuffling around, "Yeah, but I should have been up awhile ago." She paused a moment and Kazuki could picture her trying to get her bearings, "So, what's up?" She asked, sounding more like herself.

"I wanted to invite you to the mall." Kazuki paused for a moment before adding, "With Noe and his group, we're all going." He held his breath in anticipation.

"Oh, well... I guess. I've got nothing else going on today." She paused and Kazuki imagined her looking around her room or checking her closet for something to wear, "What time?"

Kazuki looked at the clock; it was still early, "About in an hour."

"Meet you at your house?"

"Yes." Kazuki smiled as she agreed, "I was wondering one thing..." He paused trying to figure out the best way to ask, "Last night I was tuning a Jazz station and there was someone else on it... was it you?" He decided to be forthright.

"Well, yeah, I mean, there's only one Jazz station around here and I'm usually on it." He heard her laugh, "Couldn't you tell it was me? I knew it was you."

Kazuki felt himself flush, "I thought but I was not sure."

"Oh, yeah, I love Jazz. The station actually went away for a while, it turned into a Gospel station but I guess the ratings tanked so they changed the format back a few months ago." She'd found her wakeful voice somewhere in the conversation, "I didn't know you liked that kind of music, do you even have Jazz in Japan?"

"Yes, but not much, I think it is good, I like the station a lot. I listen when I am trying to sleep." Kazuki thought for a moment but couldn't find a good segue into another topic.

"That's my fighting station you know. I mean, I know you don't see me fight, but when I want to show off..." She sounded excited. "Anyway, I've got to get up and get showered, see you in an hour?"

"Yes, please."

"See you then, bye."

"Good bye." Kazuki hung up the phone. It was amazing how much her voice could pick up his spirits, he was glad Noe had her number. He pushed himself up from the bed; he still had to take a shower himself. There was bound to be a long day ahead.

As they walked, Irvin gave a quick laugh, turning toward Kazuki, "I guess WRFK got their exemption to broadcast at a higher wattage."

Noe laughed along with her from up ahead, "Yeah that station is out at least an hour a day from someone, if only they knew what was really going on."

Kazuki chuckled along with the rest of them. Obviously none of the higher ups in the company knew about Channelers. Kazuki turned slightly toward Tommie just behind him. She was dressed in an over-sized pair of pajama pants and a matching red and blue striped shirt and as usual she was jamming along to her MP3 player.

Another glance to his side and he looked over Elli. It was strange to have her hanging around in this group, but it was nice. He was glad that she decided to join them. Even though she didn't have to wear her uniform she still wore a short skirt to compliment her azure shirt.

Noe lead the group toward the fountain in the

mall, sitting down at the edge of it. Was it a Channeler thing to keep close to water? He couldn't figure out a reason for it, but Noe always seemed to be hanging around a fountain, and Casey and Julie were always by the lake.

Irvin and Mike sat down next to Noe, with Tommie taking a set next to Mike. Kazuki found his own seat next to Irvin with Elli sitting at his side. Kazuki looked along the group; Allene was missing, she had a dentist appointment. It made things a little out of place. Elli was a nice addition but she didn't make much of a replacement, each of them had their own place in the group that was not readily filled.

Noe leaned forward looking over to Kazuki, "So, you think you're ready for the big rumble?"

Irvin smiled, "We've taught him just about everything we can, he'd better be ready."

Kazuki nodded, "Yes, I think so." He was still holding out hope that this 'rumble' wasn't going to happen.

"Don't worry about it." Tommie started from the other end, "Alden isn't some invincible monster, the only reason he got the best of you was because you didn't have much experience. He's not all that." She laughed as she leaned backward.

It was true, when Kazuki had first fought him, he'd been training, but it had been in the wrong areas. Grappling wasn't worth a damn unless he could take him down, and taking down a Channeler was a different matter entirely than sparring in the back yard with his brother.

"He doesn't have a chance." Elli boasted, rubbing Kazuki's head and earning a strange look from him in return, "You've been training too hard to get beat by that punk again."

"I'm going to try really hard to fight my best." He nodded in her direction. "But I hope you are all there with me so that he doesn't get carried away like last time." It was Kazuki's only consolation, if he was going to fight Alden, he hardly ever traveled alone any more. Someone was bound to be there to help him out and if things went awry.

"You'll win it." Noe called out, pushing himself to his feet and fishing around in his pocket. A moment later he pulled out a quarter and gave it to Kazuki, "For luck, throw it in the fountain and make a wish."

Kazuki looked at it, for a moment before standing up from the barrier surrounding the fountain and looking down into the waters. There were a number of pennies and other change at the bottom already beneath the swirling waters. He focused on the quarter, "I wish I win the fight." Tossing the quarter end over end it landed in the water with an inaudible splash before sinking to the water.

"Well, that clinches it." Mike said from down next to Tommie, breaking from whatever conversation he was privately having with her.

"Come on; let's go get a pretzel." Noe offered, motioning for everyone to come along with him.

The six of them wandered away from the center of the mall and out toward one of the arms. The mall shaped like a giant cross with the fountain located at the intersection. For a Saturday the foot traffic was light so in no time, Noe was taking orders from everyone and money was changing hands.

The best thing about the mall it turned out was the variety of food. Compared to the rest of the mall, the food court was disproportionately large. Add to that the small stands dotting the mall just to pick up the random pretzel or hot dog and there was a smorgasbord of options. Between them being young and being Channelers they somehow avoided the pitfalls of a high-fat life style. By all logic they should have all been large as sumo.

"So, how is it like to hang out with Noe and his friends?" Kazuki asked as Elli sat down next to him at the table.

"We've hung out before; I'm usually just too busy studying and things." She rushed out the explanation as if Kazuki were suggesting something scandalous.

"Oh, good." Kazuki offered back at a loss.

Mike and Tommie had taken seats on the other side of the table with Irvin next to Mike. Irvin moved closer to the middle of the table, coming in toward Kazuki and resting on his elbows, "So, do you really think you've got this thing with Alden on lockdown?" He asked in a hushed voice.

"I hope." Kazuki smiled.

"Good, good, yeah, good luck man, you're a nice guy, I'd hate to see something bad happen to you again." With a few quick nods Irvin leaned back into his seat, leaving Kazuki wondering about the exchange.

"This one's yours." Noe set down a box with a pretzel in it in front of Kazuki, "And this one is yours... I think..." Another box was set down next to Elli. The trend continued around the table as Kazuki started to rip his pretzel apart, alternating between dipping pieces in cheese and chocolate.

It really was a whole different set of friends from his companions back in Japan. He smiled at the thought; he would have never seen himself here a year ago. It only took a short while for their snacks to find their way into their stomachs.

"Any other place we wanna stop at?" Noe asked.

A series of head shakes was the general consensus.

"Maybe there's something going on in town?" Tommie offered.

"Meh." Noe shrugged, "Probably not, but whatever. We can check it out."

It was still plenty early in the day, for them to be

struggling to find something to do. Kazuki had a feeling that they were going to be returning to the standby of the arcade or the library soon enough. If that was the case he'd probably head back home.

As one they rose from the table and started to head toward the door. More training? Kazuki thought about it, he was about burned out on training. He could mess around on the laptop for awhile. But then again, this was the first time he got to hang out with Elli in some time. He wondered if maybe she would come with him if he offered. She'd accepted his offer to come to the mall after all. But that was with other people. The worst she could say was no.

Tommie walked out of the mall ahead of him and Kazuki caught the door, holding it open as Elli made up the rear of the group. As they were walking across the parking lot Noe stopped, then Irvin, then Elli, then finally Kazuki froze.

Further ahead, where the parking lot met with the road, Alden, Bailey, and Jayson where skateboarding, a single skateboard between the three of them. Kazuki and his group were spotted before they had time to react.

"Ummm..." Noe started, not turning back, "You still feeling confident Kazuki." The irony was that Noe had lost the confident air he normally had.

Kazuki forced himself to take in the situation. Pressing past the cold feeling in his stomach, the overwhelming indecision. "I'm ready." He nodded, everyone now looking in his direction.

"You sure?" Elli asked, taking a step closer to him.

"Yes, I would like to do this while everyone here." It was the best he could hope for.

Kazuki knew he wouldn't have to instigate things; just showing enough backbone to step to the front of the others would be enough. Walking past Noe he grounded himself steadily on the asphalt.

"We'll be rooting for you." Tommie spoke up, her hushed voice nearly drowned out by the far-off traffic.

"Don't worry," Irvin started, "We'll make sure those two don't get involved." He nodded toward Alden's cohorts.

Kazuki felt his confidence bolstered and started boldly scanning the stations as Alden and the others approached.

"Well, lookie lookie, Mr. Japan is back with the rest of the misfit crew." Alden taunted, taking a few sidelong steps.

Noe chuckled, "You're one to talk, still hanging out with those same two stooges." No one laughed at the joke but it still irked Alden visibly.

"Whatever. So, it looks like you want to do this for real this time. You have enough time to get nursed back to health?" Alden leered at Elli who starred him down strong enough that Kazuki felt uncomfortable from proximity.

"This is it, I fight you, it's the last time. Never again." Kazuki stated firmly.

"Whatever helps you sleep at night" Alden answered cryptically, Bailey and Jayson flanking him, each with a shit-eating grin. "I'm not an idiot though; I won't take you all on even if I do have a good chance of winning."

"Look-" Noe stepped forward between Kazuki and Alden, "Just think of us as referees. We're here to make this a fair fight, if someone gives up, this fight is over. If not… we'll have to break it up…" He added the last bit in a deeper more threatening voice.

"So, you're actually going to man up on this one." Alden laughed, "Well, if you guys are done polishing each others boners…" Alden began, making a mockery of a respectful tone, "I think we're ready to fight here." He gestured back with his hands and Bailey and Jayson backed up a few steps.

Kazuki stood motionless; Alden was before him, hands up in front of his face. He didn't know how he wanted to start things. It was on, the fight was on. But he couldn't just charge in, he didn't want to throw the first punch, but he didn't want to take the first punch either. Yet again he found himself froze by his indecision.

"Kick his ass Kazuki!" Elli yelled from behind him.

Alden yelled at him, "Just pick a station already!"

Barely Kazuki resisted the urge to smack himself. He hadn't even been tuning, he was out of it. Alternative, rap, punk, lots of commercials, he went through a lot of crap before he forced himself to settle on some classic rock. It wasn't the best, but it was certainly better than the other options.

"Okay then, are we ready to get things on?" Alden asked mockingly, taking a half-step forward.

Kazuki in turn took a half step back; it was hard to believe he was trying to put himself up to this. Desperately he tried to pull his station together, fully take control of it. It was just distracting that there was a pit in the airwaves nearby where Alden had so fully consumed his own station. "I'm ready when you are." He offered reluctantly, steeling himself.

"Well then…" Alden gave a half-grin, "Let's go!" Alden rushed forward in the blink of an eye; Kazuki recognized the attack, the kickstand right off. Kazuki sidestepped, leaving Alden off-balance. He put everything into the attack and his momentum carried him a few extra steps after missing.

Kazuki retaliated with a rapid low kick that caught Alden in the back of the knee. He didn't even stumble. Alden brought his own foot around, trying a more elaborate kick aimed at Kazuki's jaw.

Bending backward he avoided the brunt of the kick, but Alden brought his foot down hard, scraping the sole of the shoe sharply against Kazuki's chest. Kazuki let out a pained noise from the rubber digging against his shirt so roughly it tore against the skin beneath it. Kazuki fell onto his butt but quickly rolled, pushing himself to his feet and into a quick few steps to gain some distance.

His adrenaline was starting to kick in, that feeling of actually fighting. The fears of a quick beating were fading. Kazuki concentrated on the station, trying to feel the music, Alden rushed him and Kazuki threw out a kick on reflex. It missed but kept Alden at bay, Kazuki followed it up with a kickstand punch, it landed solidly against Alden's shoulder, spinning him in place. Connecting almost hurt though, Alden had completely tensed up, and his body was like fresh clay.

Without even looking he knew Alden was coming at him. Kazuki let the momentum carry him to the ground, catching himself painfully with his hands. He kicked out behind himself with the sole of his foot like a mule, it didn't connect but he heard the surprise from Alden.

Dropping his hands out from under him, Kazuki rolled onto his shoulder and back onto his feet. He struggled past the momentary disorientation. The kick to his back came as a surprise; it shoved him forward several staggering steps. He staggered sideways on impulse in case Alden was just behind him before turning in place.

Alden hadn't moved, he was smirking, "I bet you think you're hot shit." He raised his eyebrows, "But you ain't got nothing on me."

Kazuki looked toward his friends, nods of encouragement, shouts, Elli was louder than all of them, "Come on! You can do it, get it together!"

Rubbing his palms together, the small pieces of gravel that had embedded themselves in his skin fell to the ground. Tentatively Kazuki flexed his hands, it was that moment that he felt ready.

Alden rushed; Kazuki back peddled toward the mall. There was the sound of a car horn and Kazuki jumped to the side, avoiding the slow moving vehicle. Alden snaked around the other side of the car, hidden behind it. Kazuki barely managed to block the surprise punch to the face, the next few kicks drove him back, and every block caused the bones in his body to creek, the power behind each hit... incredible.

He was losing ground; Kazuki retook control of the station, embracing it fully. He brought his foot back, chambering the kick, but not for long. It shot out along the parallel of the leg and narrowly missed Alden's head. Instantly he hooked his foot around and twisted, for a sudden flashing moment realizing how vulnerable he was. His worry was unfounded; he brought his foot back around, connecting solidly with the hinge of Alden's jaw, rocking his head to the side. Without missing a beat Kazuki brought his foot back down, planting it firmly on the ground.

"Bitch!" Alden yelled, his hand coming to his face.

From the crowd there were shouts but nothing coherent. Kazuki kept with it, already Alden had regained his footing, and he was starring him down. The kick did some damage but aside from the initial outburst, Alden was a rock.

The next few punches came even faster; Kazuki stepped away, forcing Alden to extend himself. Kazuki felt a hand slip around his wrist, he twisted his own hand in response, reversing the grip, holding onto Alden's wrist he pulled them together and using the momentum threw out his fist full force towards Alden's head.

With his dominant hand immobilized Alden contorted and brought his shoulder up to block the attack, but couldn't avoid the raw power of it. Kazuki was sure he felt something give when the hit landed.

Alden's body spun free and he dropped to the ground flopping into his side for a moment before pushing himself, obviously in pain, to his feet.

"Bitch... bitch... son of a bitch..." Kazuki could hear his deep breathing as he wiped his face roughly.

"Do you give up?" Kazuki asked, his bloodlust quickly waning. He realized how strange it was but he was actually worried that he had hurt Alden.

"Fuck you!" Alden cursed, stepping back a few steps and rubbing his shoulder. Already there was a deep bruise on his face from when Kazuki's kick connected.

Kazuki took a few deep breaths, his song was almost over. He took the opportunity to quickly check some of the other frequencies. He caught something just starting and settled on it as quick as he could, claiming it for his own before Alden could take it away. A moment later he felt the same thing happening on a different station. Alden's song had ended. He had been buying time to get another. Being injured had just been a convenient excuse.

The move was hardly telegraphed as Alden lashed out and kicked one of the parking lot stop signs dead in the middle. The steel bent nearly in half and the cement base lifted from the ground. Faster than he could follow the whole mess of it took flight directly at Kazuki. He dodged but the iron and concrete mess crashed into a nearby minivan, embedding itself in the frame and lifting two of the wheels off the ground amidst a shower of glass.

Kazuki spun to the ground from the sucker punch. His face felt like it was already swelling and his vision was shaken. Thankfully he rolled to the side, the kick aimed at him just grazing his body instead of landing full-force. Another kick came dangerously close to his head, the next was aimed lower and Kazuki reached out, snagging Alden's foot and twisting.

The fighter flipped to the pavement hard, a solid thud accompanying the impact. Kazuki continued to twist, forcing Alden onto his face. "Gahh! Bitch!" Alden cursed but Kazuki didn't let up, moving up along his back, if he could get him into a submission hold it would all be over. He sat up fully on Alden's back and torqued his foot, pressed his own foot into the back of Alden's knee to give him leverage.

"Give up!" Kazuki yelled, realizing the others were yelling the same thing. He pressed his hold harder, he felt Alden's knee separating at the fragile intersection of cartilage and tendon.

The yell startled Kazuki enough, but it was the sudden force that took him even more by surprise. Kazuki felt like his arms were going to rip out of their sockets as Alden yanked his foot away, taking Kazuki with it.

Thrown to the ground face first, Kazuki felt the bits of rock and glass dig deep into his skin. He didn't have time to think, Alden pushed himself back up, throwing himself to where Kazuki had fallen he grabbed him by the head and slammed him into a car door. Kazuki felt himself being pulled to his feet, felt his head being pulled back, then thrust forward.

He wasn't sure what Alden was going to bounce his head off this time but he dropped his legs out from under himself, taking the ground instead of taking the hit. The song was building to its crescendo in his head, the third of three choruses. He focused on that instead, clenching his fist he brought it straight up blindly into Alden's solar plexus.

He heard the wind disappear from his lungs. Kazuki pushed himself to his feet. Grabbing Alden's shirt roughly he pulled his whole body down and connected his jaw with his knee, he changed his grip to Alden's shoulders, stomped his instep, and threw him down to the ground with enough force to cause him to bounce.

Alden recovered in less than a second, moving onto all fours, skidding to a halt a few feet away. Bracing against the ground, Alden raced forward, catching Kazuki in the chest and lifting him off the ground. Struggling Kazuki kicked down as hard as he could, driving his foot into Alden's quads and knee causing him to cry out. The two of them toppled to the ground and Kazuki tried to separate hastily but Alden grabbed onto his shirt, it gave a ripping sound but held.

Kazuki saw stars from the punch to the face "Faku!" Kazuki cursed, pulling back as hard as he could and leaving a handful of shirt with Alden. Kazuki pushed back on his butt to get some distance and reached up to his nose, it was bleeding heavily. He felt sick, the asphalt was almost painfully hot, uncomfortable, it was humid. Alden leapt at him from his prone position; Kazuki struck out and managed to land a punch squarely in the middle of Alden's forehead. He went down, Kazuki's fist hurt.

Pushing himself to his feet, Kazuki tried to get further away, he focused but used too much of his strength, nearly tripping over his own feet as he lost traction. His song was almost over but Alden was still going strong.

"So, is that good." Kazuki struggled to regain his breath. That was it, his song was over. He suddenly felt the exhaustion weigh on him like never before.

Alden pushed himself to his feet as well, that damndable smile back on his face despite the bruising, "Already done?" He laughed and spit out some blood, "Is that it?"

Noe yelled from the sidelines, "Give it up loser, it's over, you lost!"

Kazuki wished that he felt the same confidence, instead he felt like every moment brought him a step closer to a merciless beating. Every time he felt like things were coming out to his advantage, Alden did something to one-up him. "That is it." Kazuki said in tune with Noe, "You need to give up." Kazuki pulled in a few deep breaths, still searching the stations, hopeful that Alden was too distracted to notice.

"Me give up!?" Alden gave an unhinged laugh, "You're ready to keel over and you want me to give up!?"

"Unh huh." Kazuki muttered out, finally feeling the light-headedness fade away.

"Kick his ass Alden!"

Kazuki couldn't tell if it was Bailey or Jayson but he turned toward the both of them anyway. His eyes suddenly widened. Kazuki felt the familiar beat of one of his favorites. He tuned as fully and as fast as he could, making a vacuum in the stations around that that could be felt by the other Channelers there.

"Just buying some time I guess." Alden laughed at him, "That's what I'd expect from an underhanded Jap."

Kazuki ignored him, focusing instead on the song, "One more time." Kazuki said carefully, offering for Alden to bring on his attack by motioning for him to come forward.

"You're an idiot!" Alden leapt forward with another kickstand. Kazuki tried to avoid but Alden had expected and pivoted enough to catch Kazuki in the middle of the chest. He felt something tear deep inside.

The momentary victory of the attack was short lived; Kazuki brought his fist down from above and pegged Alden in the back of the head. He pulled back and Kazuki threw out three quick punches, they all landed. Another two punches landed solidly against Alden's chest. He jerked around as he was pushed back. Kazuki let out another volley of punches, realizing that they were in time to the music in his head, and that he was humming along with.

"Cops!"

Alden had taken too many hits too fast and was too out of it to fight back. Kazuki pressed his advantage, pummeling him with kicks mixed with the punches. Kazuki reached out and grabbed Alden tight by the shoulders and brought him forward, kneeing him in the stomach again and again.

"Cops! Come on Kazuki!"

Kazuki turned on a dime when he felt someone pull at his shirt from behind; he hardly had time to decipher who it was before stopping himself.

"We've gotta go!" Elli yelled at him, pulling at his shirt with a pleading look in her eyes.

"I… what?" Kazuki asked confused, his body hot, on fire.

"Cops!" Elli pointed; they were turning into the parking lot. Kazuki also noticed that Jayson and Bailey were helping Alden away from the scene, leaving just the smears of blood on the asphalt where they had been fighting. "Come on!" She pulled at his shirt again.

The two of them started running, Kazuki looked around, he couldn't see any of the others, they must have gone ahead. He kept running, Elli didn't seem to have trouble keeping pace. The thought crossed his mind that she must have been tuning too. He pushed harder, moving faster and Elli matched him step for step, leaping over concrete dividers and dodging between the traffic of a nearby highway. Finally they jumped the divider on the other side of the road and dodged around a store. When they were far enough away, Elli motioned for him to stop.

There was forest all around. Elli slumped to the ground, leaning up against the tree and breathing heavily. Kazuki had to force himself to breath, force his hold loose on the frequency. It was painful. As he let it go the injuries came rushing to him, the pain, and exhaustion. His legs gave out when he was only tuned slightly. He kept it that way, not wanting to completely give up the station with his injuries.

"You... were really... going at it..." Elli managed out between breaths. "I don't think... you heard anything we said." She said with a smile, but it was lost on Kazuki, his gaze was fixed upward from his prone position on his back.

"Are they... going to come after us?" Kazuki asked, feeling the dread in the pit of his stomach.

"Unh uh." Elli shook her head, "They know better than that." She took a few deep breaths, sounding more like herself, "They've watched us enough to know what we can do, and know that no one will believe them." Kazuki felt her put a hand on his knee, "They just show up to break the fights up when we're in public, after that we're free to go again..."

The way she trailed off though made Kazuki press further, "Are you sure..."

"Well... you guys did trash a mini-van, at least Alden did. But hey... they'll probably go back to the tapes and just pin it on him and let you off the hook. You're going back to Japan anyway so it's not like it matters." She joked with a windless laugh.

Kazuki kept on his back sucking air. His mouth full of steel wool and batteries. His chest burned with every breath, he couldn't remember from what but there was a raw wound stretching from top to bottom that throbbed where the sweat was seeping into it.

Most of all though, more than his injuries, his muscles protested with every movement by a cascade of sharp pains that stole his breath. He tried to lift his arm but the shaking stopped him from lifting it above his chest. "I... I can't move." Kazuki mumbled as he struggled.

"It'll wear off." Elli said dismissively, "You just overexerted yourself, give it a half hour." She rubbed his knee, reminding him that she had put her hand there, "Then we'll all go out for victory buffet."

Wincing, Kazuki brought his hand behind his head to use as a cushion. He gave a pained laugh; it was always the 'all you can eat' restaurant even if he only ate one plate. It had to be an American thing. Finally, his song faded completely from the radio waves. Kazuki took a breath through clenched teeth, the pain was worse, but... it wasn't as bad as when he had been beat by Alden, the time Elli had to come to help him before.

Turning his head slightly he caught the worry in her piercing green eyes before she turned away just enough to break the eye contact. He swallowed hard, wondering if he was really feeling better already or if he was just imagining it. Slowly he let himself relax against the cold ground, his eyes closing as he watched Elli smooth out her skirt.

The ringing of a cell phone brought Kazuki back to attention, his eyes opening immediately. Had he been asleep? He wasn't sure but the pain was definitely lessened.

"Hello?" Elli spoke into the receiver.

"Yeah, I've got him right here, he's fine." She looked down at Kazuki and gave him a nod.

"Okay, cool, that sounds good." She paused listening and Kazuki strained to hear the other side of the conversation but failed, "Okay, yeah... probably not till tomorrow though." She smiled widely, "Okay, see you then."

Elli nodded to Kazuki, "Buffet's been rescheduled for tomorrow." She smiled, "You feeling up to walking yet?"

"I don't know." Experimentally he rolled onto his side and pushed himself up. With a grimace and a grunt he made it to a sitting position. His nose was numb but that was probably for the best.

"You still seem a little stiff." She laughed, "Just give it a minute." She added, halting Kazuki from further effort.

"Did I fall asleep?" Kazuki asked, scooting back on his butt to lean against a tree.

"I think so... it was hard to tell." Elli answered after a moment.

Silence settled over the duo again, but Kazuki knew from experience that it wasn't a bad thing. Elli just wasn't the type of person to make conversation for the sake of maintaining background noise. Kazuki wondered if that was one of the reasons she didn't have her own circle of friends. It was nice though, the sun was nearly hidden but it was certainly past noon. He was thankful for the overhead cover, without it the heat would have been stifling.

"Do you like hanging out with me." Kazuki asked before he could lose his nerve. The question was simple enough but it still embarrassed him.

"Yeah. I wouldn't be doing it otherwise."

Kazuki kept starring upward into the canopy; he decided not to point out that she just might have been bored. "I just did not know, with the culture thing, I wanted sure to make." He covered for his embarrassment quickly.

For the moment Kazuki decided that words were not the best course of action. In the distance he could hear the cars tearing by on the highway, but the sound was muted, almost a part of nature. His chest was hurting less so he allowed himself the pleasure of a deep breath, which turned out to be the wrong thing to do. The subsequent round of coughing hurting even more.

Reaching behind himself and pressing against the tree, Kazuki steadily brought himself to his feet, his legs didn't so much hurt as feel completely useless.

"About ready to go?" Elli asked, pushing herself to her own feet with only slightly less effort than Kazuki.

"Yes." Kazuki nodded, feeling the way his weight hung on his frame after the injuries.

"Here." Elli reached into her hand bag and pulled out a travel sized box of tissues. She handed the tissues off, "How's your nose feeling?"

"I can't feel it." He answered honestly, accepting the tissues and taking out a few. Timidly he reached up and used them to wipe his nostrils. They were caked with blood which flaked off and large chunks. He rubbed harder, the solidified blood peeling from his skin.

"Is it broken?" Elli asked, moving a step forward.

Kazuki experimentally tried to move the bridge of the nose, it didn't budge but hurt. "I don't think so." It was his best guess but he didn't know better. He took out another tissue and blew his nose, loosening a large chunk that he quickly balled up in the tissue, refusing to look at it and amazed that Elli would watch without flinching.

"You're going to have to lick it or something; you've still got red all over." She offered after a cursory inspection of Kazuki's features.

Kazuki licked his finger tips and rubbed under his nose then used the tissue.

"Looks like you got most of it." Elli gave a nod of approval as Kazuki threw down the last tissue and offered Elli back the remainder of the box.

"Keep it, in case it starts bleeding again later."

"Thank you." Kazuki jammed the cardboard box into his back pocket.

"So," Ellie started out, turning away slightly, looking down the trail, "Are you going to go home and rest after all this excitement?"

"I was going to go home, but... would you like to come with me?" Kazuki asked, immediately feeling flustered.

"How about I just walk you home and figure it out from there? You know, just to be there for you if you need it."

Kazuki nodded, "That sounds good."

Chapter 8

It was a little too early for a buffet. On a normal day Kazuki would have still been shaking the sleep from his bones, let alone on the day after a massive fight. However, when it came down to it, the buffet wasn't about food; it was a place of bonding.

Kazuki tried to hide the wince as he sat down at the table. His nose hurt when he touched it, he could ignore that. It was the pain in his chest that radiated outward to every extremity that was crippling him. Deep breaths, twisting, bending, everything aggravated it. Something was cracked; it hurt much worse than the night before. It gave another shot of pain as he scooted toward the table, and yet again in retaliation for being ignored, begging for his attention.

"Come on man!" Kazuki looked over, the comment clearly directed at him. Irvin had a big smile on his face, "You know it's the skinny Japanese guy that always wins the eating contest!" Noe laughed with him, the two of them had been trying to goad him into an eating contest all morning. He blanched at the idea, too early, too much pain, and besides, he'd seen the two of them eat before.

"No thanks." Kazuki shook his head, looking down at his food.

Tommie, across the table, pulled out one of her earbuds, "Alli, you should have been there, Kazuki really gave him a beat down." She started from nowhere.

"Huh?" Obviously Allene hadn't been paying attention.

Tommie reached up and pulled out the other earbud, letting the two of them dangle over her shoulders, "It was so awesome watching Alden get beat like that." She smiled widely, smacking her hand on the table causing everything to shake.

Allene turned to look at Kazuki, grimacing at his swollen nose, "I wish I could have been there, but it sucks that you got so messed up."

Kazuki gave a terse reply, "You should see the other guy."

Allene gave a half-nod, "I'm sure he'll crawl back soon enough."

Kazuki started eating slowly, the pain from his nose pulsing with every clench of his jaws. He wished that Elli had been able to make it. At the end of the table, Noe and Irvin were going at it. Vaguely he felt the stations shift slightly. Curious, he tried to feel out what was going on. "They're tuning for the eating contest?" He asked somewhat incredulous and hopeful that Allene might try to explain away the comment.

In return she lifted her hands slightly, shrugging her shoulders. He smirked and went back to his food. Chewing a mouth full he looked across the table at Mike and Tommie talking, she seemed to only be half-listening, though that could have been because she had re-inserted one of her earbuds. Out of everyone in the group Mike got along with Tommie the best.

"Aghh, gonna die!" Kazuki turned to the sound of Noe kicking back in his chair and wiping the real or imaginary sweat from his forehead.

"Whooo! Ain't got nothin' on me." Irvin laughed, polishing off the remaining bread roll in one bite.

"Whatever, you always win." Noe mumbled loud enough for everyone to hear causing Irvin to smile.

Kazuki looked between them, thinking about the amount of food they had both just packed away and how skinny they remained.

"To the victor." Noe dropped his chair back down onto all four legs and pushed a plate forward with a slice of French silk pie. Kazuki had been wondering about that singular slice of pie that had somehow escaped the frenzy.

Irvin grabbed a fork and started eating the pie and in no time it was gone. Kazuki had never seen this spectacle before; he wondered if it was an older tradition for the group.

"You know-" Allene spoke up in Kazuki's direction, "-Alden might keep messing with you, but he probably won't fight you again even if he got you alone." She flipped a tendril of blond hair out of her face, "He's too much of a coward, he won't want to lose, he tries to always play the first one off as a fluke or whatever." She let out a breath and gave a quirky smile, "Pisses me right off."

"Yeah, you shouldn't have to worry about Alden again after yesterday." Tommie spoke up from across the table.

Meanwhile Noe and Irvin had scooted their own chairs closer. "We need a toast." Noe grabbed up his glass. "Come on, grab your glass." He quickly added when Kazuki didn't move.

"To Kazuki beating the snot out of that punk." Six glasses clinked together. "Hold on." Noe called out as people started to sit back in their chairs, "One more." The glasses came back together once more, Kazuki wincing at the movement, "To us for helping him too."

Kazuki gave a big smile as he set back into his chair, "Thank you all so much." He saw smiles all around. Sometimes he wondered why they were all so nice to him, but they were, and without a hint of cynicism. Maybe it was the novelty of helping someone from another country, or maybe it was as Allene mentioned, they just liked his accent.

Noe spoke up again once the celebratory mood had settled, "So, did you tell your brother."

Kazuki shook his head, "Yes, I had to in order to explain why my nose looked mashed." Kazuki turned his gaze downward before continuing, "He was glad that I had won but was upset that he could not be there."

"What was he going to do?" Irvin spoke up, "He's seen what a Channeler can do, no doubt."

"Yes, he knows, he just wanted to be there in case I needed him." Kazuki turned back up from the table, "But he was still happy I think."

Tommie spoke up again. "Well, you did win."

"Man, right at the end, you must have found something really jamm'in on the stations." Noe laughed, "I mean, there was just a black hole where you were tuning the airwaves."

Kazuki remembered the end of the fight, the dominating feeling he had while punch after punch was landing. "It was one of my favorites." He smiled, "I got lucky."

Noe spoke up again, "Sometimes you get lucky, sometimes you don't, I mean, you went through at least two other songs before that one came up." He cracked his knuckles, "Sometimes you just hold out for something good. Even that's a strategy."

Kazuki understood it wasn't all skill; there was a degree of chance there. Still, the win had been a large boon. He'd woken up that morning feeling relieved, eager to get out and face the day. For the first time since his beating, not afraid of a chance meeting with Alden. For the first time he was certain that the trip to America had been worth it.

Noe stopped, Irvin and Kazuki following his lead, "From here the radio tower looks pretty big, doesn't it?"

Kazuki turned slightly, far ahead the tower stood atop a large hill, it was just visible over top the evergreens that encircled the forest.

"Yes, it does look large." Kazuki agreed, turning to look across the pond. "Noe, this place was here, I did not even know." Kazuki continued, looking around.

"It's kind of hard to find." Noe explained, "I mean, it's got forest all around it, you probably wouldn't think there was anything here if it wasn't for the signs."

Kazuki nodded. It was the same place that Elli had rushed off with him after his fight with Alden. It felt like they had been deep in the woods but they had just been at the edge of this park on one of the nature walks. From what he had seen so far, most of the park was just nature walks going through the bit of undisturbed forest surrounding this large pond.

Allene had told him that at one time they rented paddle boats but the running the stand hadn't shown up in the last few years. Straining his eyes and looking across the pond he could make out Allene, and Tommie sitting on a large tire with Mike on a set of swings at the edge of the pond.

"Irvin, how did you start hanging out with Noe and the rest?" Kazuki ventured suddenly curious.

"I'm a Channeler. It just kind of happened." He smiled and ran a hand over his black, buzz-cut hair.

"Actually... he started then paused again, letting out a deep breath, "I used to get a kick out of bullying people. I think I was one of the first to figure out that channeling and fighting went together better than peanut butter and jelly." Irvin stopped, realizing that Kazuki didn't get the reference but continued anyway. "But back then I don't think we had a name for it, channeling I mean." Irvin put his hands in his pockets, "Then one day I picked a fight with Noe." Irvin gave a little laugh that Noe followed with his own.

"Long story short, he kicked my ass. But the funny thing was, after that we started hanging out." Irvin took on a more serious look, "I stopped picking on people, started trying to help other people that could do this shit, you know. That's where Tommie and Mike came in, they were getting messed with when they first got into middle school because they where Channelers, not that anyone else understands what it is, but we could tell they were different. It started out with just me

144

and Noe, now look at us…"

"What about Allene?" Kazuki felt compelled to ask as she seemed the odd person out.

"Actually-" Noe started out, "She kind of comes and goes." Noe turned to look across the pond, "She used to be really popular, never would have associated with us, but then people found out that something was different about her. I mean, there are a lot of things Channelers do that seem odd to everyone else, spacing out when good songs come on, songs that no one else can hear, singing along to them, it's kind of like you're delusional, hearing things… After that her popularity went… pthhh…" Noe gave a thumbs down, "Right down the crapper. She started hanging out with us once in a while, she still tries to get invited to parties and regain her popularity but she always ends up back with here."

Irvin spoke up, "But don't go tellin' her we told you any of this. She's pretty sensitive about it."

Kazuki nodded his head, where he came from things were no different. He wasn't planning on dredging up her past.

The trio stood in silence a moment longer, looking out across the pond until Noe again spoke up, "I guess that just leaves me…" Kazuki heard him take a deep breath, in turn Kazuki focused his attention on Noe. His face creased with worry for a moment before smoothing out, "My dad passed away when I was little…"

"I am sorry." Kazuki answered on reflex.

"S'okay. It was a long time ago." Noe nodded his head, "After that I kind of became the man of the house, doing the chores, helping with my brothers. I guess I held things together okay for awhile." Noe shook his head, "But things kept getting tougher, more responsibilities, you know what I mean?"

Kazuki nodded, "Yeah."

"It was just too much. That's when I started being

able to tune. And somehow that was enough to bring my mom out of it. She thought that I was going crazy, some kind of cry for help. She made me go to a psychiatrist, but really, it helped her focus and... she ended up landing on her feet again." Finally Kazuki saw a smile again on Noe's face, "After that I couldn't stand my family, I mean, I love them, but they suck the life right out of me." He finished sounding light hearted.

Kazuki didn't know what to make of the admission so he laughed.

"Think we should head over to the playground Irvie?" Noe asked at last. Leaving Irvin to nod before moving ahead.

With Irvin taking up the lead, Noe matched pace with Kazuki, "Remember when you were talking to us about those forums you used to visit?"

"Yes?" I'd been a while since he had mentioned them but that had been the whole reason for his trip.

"I got your e-mail..." Noe admitted, sounding a little ashamed, "I didn't answer back though because... well, I wasn't sure who you were, or what you wanted. I just figured you were some stranger thousands of miles away." Noe let out a sigh, "Sorry I ignored you man."

For a few moments Kazuki thought on it, "I came anyway." He decided with a smile. "Were you the one that put all the dots on the map?"

Noe nodded solemnly, "Yeah, that was me. I thought it was pretty cool at the time, I think I added a few too many though. You know how it is with the internet and exaggerating."

"Yes." Kazuki agreed, "I do."

Even at night, it was still almost bright enough to read outside. Satoshi set back in one of the wicker rocking chairs that flanked the back door of Miranda's house. A moment later the screen door closed and Miranda walked to the other chair, dragging it the few

146

feet to put herself next to Satoshi before sitting down.

The wooden flooring creaked in time with the slotted wood seat as Miranda experimentally rocked back and fourth a few times, pushing off the banister. A moment later she slowed, Satoshi taking to rocking as well and for some time the two of them rocked wordlessly.

"You know…" Miranda began, stopping her rocking momentarily, "It's almost like it was before you left."

Satoshi didn't immediately pick up the conversation, instead content for a moment to continue rocking. Eventually however the pregnancy of the silence had gone on too long, "Yeah, almost." He replied sounding somewhat cautious. "Except for Kazuki I guess."

Miranda let out a deep breath, "Does that help or hurt things?"

"Helps…"

"Yeah…"

"Before when I was here I missed home, now, it's different than before."

Miranda waited a moment before replying, "I like Kazuki, he's a nice kid."

"I'm glad." Satoshi answered, his smile warming his words, "This would have been a pain in the ass if you two hadn't of gotten along."

"I bet." Miranda started before copying Satoshi's tone from before, "But he can still be a pain with his stubbornness and his fighting."

"Yeah, I guess he's like me in that way."

"The moon is really bright out tonight." Miranda changed the course of the conversation.

"Yeah, it is." Satoshi let out a sigh, "I haven't seen a moon this bright in a long time."

Again, the conversation was modulated by rocking between the two of them. Finally Miranda picked up the mantle, "Have you thought about staying this time?"

After some time Satoshi answered, "Yeah, thought about it."

"Kazuki told me that you haven't been up to much since you got back."

"I've been doing things."

"He said you didn't even have a job."

Satoshi let out an exasperated breath, "Well, I was working on that."

"You've been back over a year."

"The economy's slow right now." He insisted defensively, picking up his rocking.

"You remember," Miranda swallowed audibly, "They did offer to let you keep working at the base in a permanent position if you kept with the service."

"I know... I just..." Satoshi let out a sigh and trailed off.

"Satoshi, the last time you were here... I felt like I was grasping at straws. That if I fought to keep you then I would have just made myself look like an ass. But, it's more than that now, I haven't been with anyone else since you left, even though I was sure you were never coming back. There's something here for sure."

"I- my life, my family and friends are all back in Japan." Satoshi stated sounding steadfast, "It's not some half-hour drive, it's not just around the corner, it's on the other side of the planet." His voice raised but there wasn't a hint of anger.

"You can visit them; they can come visit us here. And you've got friends here too, and, you've got me." She finished with her voice growing weaker.

Satoshi sighed, "I know, I know, I've thought all of this through before."

"Then, just keep thinking on it." Miranda said with a hint of finality.

"You know, you were part of the reason I came

here." Satoshi admitted, "Kazuki wanted to come here because of his thing, but there was no way I was going to travel to America just for that. But when he showed me where, I mean, coincidence, fate, whatever you want to call it... I wanted to help him, and I wanted to see you again."

"Really, what can Kazuki do with his trick? You guys explained it to me and all, but how strong is he? What you guys come all the way to America?"

"Before I promised to take him, he'd been bugging me for weeks. I'd seen some of the things he could do; I mean it was impressive but nothing that I would write off as impossible." The melancholy from the previous conversation faded away as he continued, "Then one day I told him basically that if he really impressed me then I would take him."

"What'd he do?"

"There were these stacks of paver stones in the backyard, like this big... by this big..." He gestured with his hands, "... and I told him that if he could show me how many he could lift then maybe..."

"How many did he lift?" Miranda asked in a hushed voice.

"He lifted the whole stack; it must have weighted over five hundred keys."

"Five hundred kilograms?"

"At least a thousand pounds."

"On his own?!"

"Yeah.. heh, I told him he should try out for the World's Strongest Man." Satoshi laughed, "He was lumbering around and stumbling but he lifted them, left a set of footprints in the ground along the way too."

"But he's not that big of a kid." She continued incredulous.

"I know, that's what really impressed me, I don't think he's ever done weight training or anything."

"Wow." Miranda sounded honestly impressed.

"And that was before the training." Satoshi stated succinctly.

"That's more than I would have imagined."

"After that, I didn't know what it would accomplish, but I wanted to help him out, take him to America, and help him find other people here like him. When he told me it was in Wisconsin, we went inside right away and got out the map, and when I found out it was near the base... He found something on the internet or something pointing to this area. That's when I knew it was something that was meant to be."

Miranda spoke up, "Maybe both of you were meant to come here, but maybe one of you is meant to stay." She said in a voice that went contrary to the smug smile it came from.

Satoshi laughed again, "You know... I am thinking about it." He finished on a more serious tone, "Are you getting as eaten up by mosquitoes as I am?"

"Yeah, but I'm trying to ignore them." The sentence followed by an audible smack.

"We can talk just as good inside."

"Good idea."

The chairs were re-shuffled and the screen door creaked open, slamming a moment later. Kazuki rolled over in his bed, pulling his pillow close to his chest. If his brother did stay, he was going to miss him for sure, but he seemed so much happier here, he wanted him to stay. He wondered if it even crossed their mind that his window was only a few feet away.

Kazuki buried his head in his pillow, his cheeks still burning; it was always embarrassing to eavesdrop on someone talking about him, no matter the outcome of the conversation.

Stepping out of the shower, Kazuki grabbed a towel and immediately retreated to standing in the tub. It was easier that way; he didn't drip all over the floor while drying off. He looked down at his chest, the seeping red mark from his fight had faded away completely, and it had stopped hurting to breathe the day before.

When he looked back on it, he'd undeniably healed much faster than he had from the first encounter with Alden. It had only taken a few days and already he was back in peak form. He stepped out onto the bathroom rug, fully dry. Efficiently he threw on his night shirt and shorts and wiped down the mirror before picking up his other clothes and leaving the bathroom.

Walking into his own room he tossed down his clothes in the pile by the door. He'd wanted to get a hamper but decided that it wasn't worthwhile, his time in America was nearly gone and he had a feeling that Miranda didn't need the guest room very often.

Flopping down on the bed he didn't bother to pull back the covers, too hot outside. Already he was sweating; he'd have to take another shower in the morning. With a grunt he hefted himself from bed, setting up against the headboard and stretching across the night stand to get his laptop off the dresser.

The bottom was still hot from the last time he'd used it. It was uncomfortable on his legs but he ignored it. Opening the hinge the screen instantly booted to his background, he smiled at the faces of his mother and father while his computer searched for a connection to the internet.

A moment later and he was loading up his browser, checking the weather, and checking his mail. Looking over the subject lines he dismissed most of them as spam. There was however a single message that stuck out. The subject in English wasn't that uncommon, though it did look odd among the kanji. He clicked on it and opened the message in a separate window.

"*Another Channeler?*" He mumbled to himself as

he read through the message. Apparently one of the forums that he had posted to about his trip to America was not as dead as he had thought. This person living in the area had read it and decided to contact him to see if he was still in the area and if he wanted to meet.

Kazuki tried to control his excitement as the opened the widow for a reply. Composing his message he asked if he knew any of the others, surprised he hadn't met them yet.

It took a few moments more for Kazuki to compose the message to his parents. Finally though he was powering down the portable computer for the night, pushing himself from the bed with a grunt he laid the laptop on the dresser and shut off the lights for the room, laying back down on the bed he watched the curtains for the room blow in the moonlight. As he drifted off to sleep he tuned slightly to the jazz station, it was empty.

Waking up the next morning, Kazuki laid in bed for a few moments enjoying the warmth around his body which contrasted well with the chill that had finally settled in sometime during the night. A few breaths later he pushed himself from the mattress only to grab his laptop and drop back down onto the bed, pulling a sheet over himself to savor the sleep aura a few moments longer.

The computer booted slowly, as groggy as he was. In reality it wasn't long until he was checking his e-mail again. He smiled, he'd gotten a reply. They wanted to meet, the far end of the park, eight o'clock at night. A little late but that wasn't the issue. He was thankful that he had found out the location of that particular park in the days previous, otherwise he would have been lost. Regarding Noe and the others though, the new Channeler said he'd never met them or tried to contact anyone else.

Eventually Kazuki got himself up from the computer and dressed. He wandered out of his room, the bleary feeling of sleep absent from his movements as he rounded the staircase and headed into the kitchen. He stopped at the refrigerator to pour himself a glass of orange juice. It was the weekend; he figured that Miranda and Satoshi were still sleeping in, so he headed out onto the porch, taking a seat in the rocking chair.

He used the porch banister to push himself backward slightly, letting the chair do the rest of the work, swinging him forward, and then back again once that momentum ran out. Looking out at the yard a few landmarks caught his eye, specifically the circle that he and his brother had wore in the grass with the help of Noe's group. He was sure the grass would grow back, but it would take some time.

Kicking back in the chair fully, Kazuki stopped rocking and sipped his juice. The wind felt nice. Even though he had just woken up he felt like taking a nap again, or maybe it was because he had just woken up. Either way he closed his eyes and relaxed. Slowly at first he expanded his senses, feeling out the stations, tuning them in one at a time, wrapping his mind around each in turn, finding their limits. It was strange, the sensation that it aroused.

It was another dimension entirely; there was an up and down. After talking with some of the others he figured that was just the way that he visualized it, everyone saw it differently in their minds eye. But still they could all tune. It was strange, but the feeling was like walking down a dark hallway with balloons hanging from the ceiling.

Occasionally one of the 'balloons' would hit him in the face, then he would stop and take the time to reach out, feel the proportions of the station, go further, tune the station, feel that electric impulse as he pulled power from it into himself.

Kazuki shook himself out of his thoughts, he'd nearly fallen asleep. With a grunt he rocked back and pushed himself to his feet as the chair pivoted forward. He moved back into the kitchen, the door shutting unintentionally forcefully behind him. Dumping the remainder of the orange juice down the sink he rinsed out the glass and headed back to his room.

Going through his suitcase he pulled out a loose fitting pair of pants and a t-shirt with the words "Prune Candy" emblazoned across the front in a gothic font. He'd bought it because it seemed so strange, but as many odd looks it brought in Japan, it brought twice as many in America.

Heading back to the kitchen table, Kazuki bent over, scribbling a message in kanji on the notepad there:

> *Going into town, be back before dark.*
> *-Kazuki*

Satisfied with his message Kazuki headed outside. First he'd try to find Elli, or maybe Casey, or Julie. Someone that he could talk to about the fight. Now that his body was healed, he was starting to feel really good about it.

It was getting late. Just below the tree line the sun was setting. The sky itself was lit by the familiar orange hue, criss-crossed by the vapor trails of airplanes landing at the military base. After the heat of the day it was starting to feel chilly with the sun sinking out of sight. Kazuki chided himself at the thought, if it were winter he'd be sweltering.

As he headed down the path, he checked his watch, ten minutes. He trailed his eyes up the trees ahead of them, focusing beyond them, over their tops.

The radio tower was just ahead, plenty of time. Keeping his pace he avoided a bunch of roots that had erupted from beneath the Earth. He stuck his hands in his pockets for the slightest of added warmth.

With the sun dipping, the path was taking on an eerie feeling. The light filtered through the leaves and limbs above and ahead causing shadows to form in unusual places. When he had been here during the daytime everything had been in stark contrast from the summer sun, now it seemed uncertain in the unfamiliar area.

Kazuki ignored the atmosphere as best he could by focusing on the day he'd had. Unable to find anyone else to hang out with, he'd settled at the library. It had been some time since he had indulged his brain and not his body and it had been an unexpected relief.

The radio tower came into sharp focus as he left the forest behind, ending at the roadside he turned and started following along the gravel up the hillside. Kazuki pulled his hands out of his pockets and picked up his pace after looking at his watch, he had thought that it had been closer. Curious, he wondered if the hill itself was a product of some kind of glacial influence. Despite having occurred thousands of years previous there was significant talk of the last ice age in the area.

Kazuki glanced over his shoulder, no cars as far as the eye could see. It wasn't so much a road as a driveway to the radio tower. That would certainly account for the lack of traffic. The grade started to get steeper as he approached the top of the hill, a small building with a stylized WRFK was positioned just to the side of the steel tower. Beside it was a sizable concrete parking lot dotted with the occasional car that each looked years older than the station building itself.

Kazuki wiped his brow, half-expecting to find sweat despite the evening chill. A few more steps and he found himself standing next to the abandoned phone booth, just like the e-mail had said. He took a few moments to look it over; it looked like it was out of a movie. The door was stuck, rusted to the tracks, but it was ajar enough to allow him a peak inside.

The plastic panels along the top had become faded and warped from the sun, and the glass sheet that had served as the roof was shattered, laying all about the floor. The telephone itself was missing, a significant rectangle on the wall off-colored indicating where it had once been situated, now just a piece of steel conduit terminating in its place.

It was somewhat interesting. Kazuki looked down at his watch again, it was time. He turned and looked back down the road he had followed up, he couldn't see anyone. "Hummm…" He mumbled to himself, taking a moment to sit on the curb next to the phone booth. Carefully he looked over the parking lot as if it might reveal something. Nothing. Minutes passed before he started to wonder if he was squatting on private property, he wondered if someone would say something if they saw him sitting here. What would they think?

Kazuki dismissed the idea but noted the sinking sun. The light was fading faster now, nearly twenty minutes had passed. He sighed, he'd give them another ten minutes then he was going home. He hated staying out so late when it left him to find his way home in the dark.

"Yo!"

Kazuki turned to the voice coming from the forest. "Hello…" His stomach felt like it was full of lead. His face was drawn; someone had effectively splashed him with a pail of ice water.

"Looks like you're all better." Alden stepped out of the trees as Kazuki got to his feet.

"You e-mail the sent?" Kazuki stumbled, both literally and metaphorically.

"Yeah, I thought it would be a good way to get you

out here, you know, so we could talk." Alden said with a half-smile that seemed earnest but effectively doubled his paranoia.

"What would you like to talk about?" Kazuki asked cautiously, taking his time to speak more eloquently.

Alden continued to come forward, there was a little hobble in his walk and he stopped just a few steps from Kazuki. Alden up on the grass, Kazuki back in the parking lot, "You, fighting, you know, Channeler stuff." He answered in a dismissive tone.

Kazuki frowned, he wasn't buying it, and he took another step back and could have sworn he saw Alden tense as if he was going to suddenly leap forward, but he held his ground. "Why not with the others? Where is Jayson, where is Bailey?"

"Those two? I left them behind; this is just you, and me." Alden extended both of his hands away from his body, showing he had nothing to hide.

Kazuki looked Alden over, superficially he looked fine, but the way he was moving, he still had some deep injuries. "How are you feeling?" Kazuki asked, curious and at the same time worried that he would make him angry. Mostly Kazuki was just stalling for time as he tried to come up with an exit strategy.

"You know how it is when you overwork yourself. It hurts a little here." Alden pointed at his thigh, "And here." Alden pointed at his chest where Kazuki had landed one of his solid punches, "And, well, it hurts a little everywhere." Alden gave a light laugh that actually helped the mood, "Anything else you're wondering?"

"Why here, why so late?" Kazuki stumbled, taking another step back; he couldn't shake the uneasy feeling.

"Well, there is a couple good reasons for that..." Alden paused, closing his eyes momentarily, a few seconds passed. At the very edge of Kazuki's senses

157

he realized that Alden was tuning just the tinniest bit. "First, I thought it would be appropriate since this is a radio station, and we are both Channelers." He smiled, "I mean, that makes sense to you, right?" Again he paused, "Did you know that the closer a Channeler is to a radio station the stronger their powers from that station become?" Alden explained off-handedly.

"No, I didn't." Kazuki admitted, trying not to sound surprised at that information being divulged.

"It's true." Alden nodded his head, gesturing toward the tower, "It makes sense right? The signal doesn't have to travel as for so there is less loss of overall power." Kazuki looked toward the tower but then back to Alden, his face shadowed by the fading sun, "And second, as for the time…" Alden gave an unnerving laugh, "It's their all request hour, and wouldn't you know they decided to play my favorite song?"

"Really-" Kazuki felt the station pull away so quickly that it ceased to exist. He had never felt a station so thoroughly tuned, it was gone. Quickly Kazuki took a few more steps back, just as Alden lifted his head, revealing his malicious smile.

Kazuki took another step back, then another, on the verge of running. Alden had been stalling for time, he saw that now. Quickly Kazuki turned to look at the radio tower and did a double-take. They were almost beneath it, what Alden had said before… the power of the station being proportional to the distance from the transmitter…

Alden laughed, his voice sounding amplified as if coming from a boom box, "Payback's a bitch!" And with that he rushed forward.

Chapter 9

Kazuki tried to steady himself with a deep breath. If he ran, Alden would run him down. He had to find a song and quick. Ride out for however long Alden's song lasted and then disappear into the forest. Kazuki flashed a look longingly past Alden at the trees. Even if that was his plan, it focused fleetingly little on the here and now.

Still, Alden was injured, that much he was sure of, if he could just find something on the stations. Kazuki threw himself into the æther, the darkness, pushing himself into one station then through another. Running blindly down the hallway and grasping for help.

He couldn't find anything. Too distracted he realized by the presence of Alden and the hole he left in the stations to take the time to find something properly. There had to be something, anything. Not a commercial, not another, he cursed to himself as he tuned.

"Screw this!" Alden yelled out, coming forward in just shy of a run.

Kazuki back peddled as fast as he could, "Shimatta... shimatta..." Kazuki mumbled, hoping against hope to find something, anything. "Ah!" Kazuki nearly tumbled onto his butt as he finally came across something, tuning past it then backtracking to find it again. He'd burned himself out on the song shortly after coming to America but that didn't matter now, didn't matter at all.

"You finally found something?" Alden laughed with a dangerous inflection, "Sure took you long enough."

Alden rushed forward in the blink of an eye. Kazuki tried to dodge backward but Alden just took the extra step and landed a punch right in Kazuki's stomach. He tensed up as best he could but it still partially winded him. His shoes made scraping sounds as they lifted off the ground with him.

Bringing his fist down, Alden replaced it with another fist, juggling Kazuki in the air for a moment, his body taking flight off the second blow, arcing away from Alden and toward the ground. Things moved in slow motion as Alden took a step forward, again catching Kazuki in the air, this time with a high kick that added to his momentum.

Kazuki's head snapped back as he felt his body take on a ballistic shape. Weightless for a moment Kazuki knew that he had come to the apex of his flight but he couldn't do anything to break himself out of it, the landing was going to hurt, at least he knew that much. He focused on his song, tensed his muscles, braced for the impact.

It was horrible, a sharp pain in his back, his whole body snapping in the opposite direction, inverting as he slammed against a parked vehicle. His left hand flung out uncontrollably, carried by the momentum, and smashed through the window. His right hand instead hit the frame of the car and hurt considerably worse. He felt the car shift, push down on the side where it had taken the impact as the shocks compressed.

A moment later, his body not yet at rest, he felt the car rock back up, repulsing its original movement and shoving him aside weightlessly. Falling to the ground he tried to catch himself on his feet but failed, his shoes slipping out from beneath him on the glass and his arm catching in the hole by the break, preventing him from completely falling onto his butt.

"Aughh!" Kazuki looked up more at the thunder of feet than the angry cry. Alden was rushing at him.

As fast as he could, Kazuki braced himself against the ground and lifted, shifting his arm out of the window. Alden was already on top of him. Kazuki let his foot drop out from beneath him; he fell quickly, that along with shifting his head to the side was barely enough to avoid a knife-hand attack. He pushed himself away on his butt. Watching Alden pull his hand out of the hole it punched in the sheet metal. The steel had blossomed inward from the impact, when he pulled his hand out it cut into the skin, leaving it dripping blood.

Kazuki knew the attack would have at least maimed him. It had been aimed where his head had been; there were not enough muscles there, even with channeling, to steel them to take that sort of impact. Frantic he managed to get a foothold strong enough to push himself to his feet. He continued his momentum back a few steps as Alden pivoted in his direction.

"Oh no, get back here..." Alden growled, stalking toward Kazuki.

Stopping for a moment Kazuki went for the offense, if only for a moment, if he could daze Alden he could get away. He took a strong stance readying himself for attack, it backfired, leaving him suddenly more aware of the shooting pain in his spine.

Alden wasted no time, covering the distance between the two of them. Too fast, Kazuki was nowhere near ready. Alden came in with a kickstand punch. The speed was greater than Kazuki had ever seen from that move, but it was still slower than a regular punch. Seizing the opportunity he reached out and grabbed hold of Alden's hand, and shifting his weight he attempted to gain control of the fighter.

Nonplused, Alden twisted his hand effortlessly in Kazuki's grip, and he turned the move around, gripping Kazuki around the wrist. He gave a grunt and suddenly Kazuki again felt himself spinning free of gravity. His feet were in his field of vision as he felt himself wrenched backward by his arm. "Gahh! Maitta!" His teeth slammed together as he collided with the bumper of the car. There was a bang as the airbags inside deployed and the trunk popped open from the sudden structural deformity.

There wasn't time to contemplate the situation though as he felt himself hauled up by the same arm, pulled from his dent in the bumper and tossed harshly to the ground, the pavement digging into his face, his nose. He rolled onto his back, feeling his face, his hand coming back red, almost black, with blood.

He was still looking at his hand when Alden's strong hand reached forward and grabbed his shirt, yanking Kazuki off the ground. "You didn't beat me, and if you mess with me again, you're dead, got that!?" Alden spat in his face.

Kazuki's barely managed to get a hand up in time to block the swing, but Alden's fist hardly slowed as it threw Kazuki's arm out of the way. His vision swam, it wasn't so much the pain of impact as Alden slammed the back of his fist into his head, it was a wave of heat, nausea, the feeling that his neck was going to tear from its base and his head was going to go flying. Then again, the same as the first time. Kazuki let himself drop down to the ground, looking up at Alden. Kazuki was losing it, he could tell, it was harder to keep the song in tune, even though he was singing along to it under his breath. At least he thought he was he was hardly even sure he was tuning it all aside from the fact that he was still alive.

"No… more…" Kazuki muttered, lifting his arm he had used to block. It was broke and already swollen, trying to twist itself in odd directions. He focused on the muscles, willing it to hold together. He tried to tell himself that the muscles could be stronger than bones.

"Whatever." Alden snorted, pulling his sleeves back down as he got to his feet. He took a step before stopping and turning, "See ya later." Kazuki could barely grunt as Alden gave a half-hearted kick to Kazuki's side.

He'd barely heard Alden's departing words, the

ringing was too loud. The heat, Kazuki turned his head slightly toward the radio station. There were people outside watching, one person on their cell phone. Kazuki hoped that they were calling for help. The stations felt normal again, Alden had stopped tuning wherever he was. At least that was one good thing.

Kazuki reached to his side and tried to push himself up with his good arm. It was only then that he realized that shoulder had been dislocated. He grunted as he allowed the arm to drop back to his side.   It weighed a ton. *"Damn…"* Kazuki muttered to himself, how long had they been fighting. It felt like forever.

Like the first one.

But this one he knew it had lasted only two or three minutes. That was it. The only thing faster would have been being hit by a train or a car. Kazuki sighed pitifully, his eyes tearing up. He was mad, but more than that, he hated Alden. Hated him for taking his win away. And he hated him for ruining his trip to America. Another shaky breath, then another. He fought against the tears, but it was hard to hold them in.

"Are you okay?" Kazuki turned, looking up starting at the tennis shoes to the blue jeans. Past the polo shirt and finally to his skinny face.

"No… please call ambulance." Kazuki croaked out despite his best efforts.

"Don't worry, one's on its way." The man assured Kazuki as he knelt down by the Japanese teen.

"Thank … you…" Kazuki mumbled with a little nod. Slowly he allowed the stations to fill his thoughts, moving from one to the other methodically, unable to go straight to his target. Moments later though he was feeling out the dimensions of the Jazz station. Subtly he could tell Elli was there. Now all he had to do was find something to get her attention.

He took the station as far as he could without dropping her out of it. Then he let go, then he took it again. Then released his hold. He waited a moment and she took it more fully, then he took it slightly, they struggled half-heartedly for it. Kazuki hoped she wouldn't just think it was a game though; he hoped that she would have felt what had just happened and realize that something was wrong. He needed her now more than the others.

Through the process he started to feel better, the energy of the stations flowing into his body. Relaxing him, and lulling him to close his eyes.

Bit by bit, painfully, Kazuki opened his eyes. He looked around slowly; his eyes moving in their orbital caused him pain. He tried to move his head but failed, it was immobilized. Letting out a ragged breath he suddenly realized how quiet it was. When he thought of hospitals he thought of ventilators, whiling machinery, pulsing beeps in time with his heart.

There was none of that, just the sound of himself breathing. The silence was pervasive; sound was so absent that it seemed loud. He swallowed dryly, turning his eyes as much as he could he looked out the window, it was dark. Was it even the same day he wondered, or was it like the movies? Had he been out for days, weeks?

He tried to move, his left arm coming up quickly, but his right arm, he focused on it better once it cleared the sheets, two IVs dangled from the appendage and there was a cast to just above the wrist. He tried to trace the IVs to their source but it was outside his field of vision.

Reluctantly he leaned back into the bed as much as his body would allow him. He would just have to sit and wait; eventually he was sure someone would explain things to him.

But... he felt the wetness in the corners of his eyes again, he had tried so hard. The sudden welling of depression caught him off guard. Everyone had helped him get into condition to fight Alden, and he had done it. Now that was overturned and he felt as weak as ever. No, weaker, weaker because he knew that despite the training he was still unable to do anything to defend himself.

Regret at having gone to the radio tower alone. He felt something was off, why did he let himself do it? He sniffled, the mucus going to the back of his throat causing him to gag. His back, chest, neck, face, it all hurt so much.

The sound of the door knob turning crushed the silence. Kazuki turned his head as far as the immobilizer would allow and ended up wincing for all of his effort.

"*Hey...*" Satoshi greeted him as he walked into the room, rushing over to a seat next to the bed and sitting down his coffee cup on the end table. "*How are you feeling?*" Satoshi reached out and put a hand over Kazuki's hand with the IVs and cast.

Kazuki forced a ghost of a smile, "*I've been better.*" Kazuki swallowed dryly, "*Do you think you could get me a drink of water?*"

"*Oh, yeah, sure!*" Satoshi lifted out of the seat and rushed out of Kazuki's field of vision with a cup. He heard water running, there must have been a bathroom to his far left.

"*Sorry if it's a little warm, I don't know where they keep the ice around here.*"

Satoshi tried to bring the glass to Kazuki's lips but Kazuki reached up with his good hand and grabbed the cup from him. His hand shakily gripping the waxed paper he brought it to his lips as his brother took a step back. The water felt nice, plenty cool, but hardly enough to quench his thirst. "*Thanks.*" Kazuki offered the cup back to Satoshi.

"*No problem little brother.*"

Kazuki's smile was genuine this time; he hadn't been called 'little brother' since before Satoshi had left for the service. *"What time is it?"* Kazuki asked, feeling slightly more like himself.

"I don't know, 'bout two or three I'd guess." Satoshi looked around for a clock before continuing, *"We've been here for awhile, I got a call around eight thirty from Elli saying that she was worried about you."* Satoshi let out a sigh, *"By the time I got a hold of the hospital they were trying to call mom and dad but no one here knew how to dial an international number."*

"Where's Elli?" Kazuki asked, immediately feeling stupid when there were more pressing matters.

"I called her back when I found out where they were keeping you. She said she'd come and visit tomorrow if you were still here." Satoshi cleared his throat, *"What the hell happened to you?"*

So, Kazuki told him about the fight. The ambush. How helpless he'd felt. How he'd feared for his life. He finished with tears in his eyes. As much as he tried to stop them he couldn't.

"It's okay…" Satoshi offered from his seat, *"That's about how everyone said it happened."* Seeing the questioning look from Kazuki he continued, *"Yeah, apparently that car belonged to the station manager, as soon as you slammed into it everyone went outside to see what the commotion was."* Satoshi gave a laugh to lighten the atmosphere, *"At first they thought someone was filming a movie but then they realized that you were really getting hurt. In the end I guess they even broke into the broadcast and asked for the cops and an ambulance over the radio."*

Kazuki's eyes widened. He wondered if that was the reason that last kick from Alden was so weak. The radio station must have disrupted his tuning when they stopped his song.

Satoshi continued, *"But I guess you were lucky, I*

mean real lucky... I saw the car..." Satoshi trailed off for a second, *"Despite everything there's nothing life threatening. You'll be out of here in a week, and then it'll be about time to head back to Japan. You won't have to worry about any of this shit any more."*

"How bad is it?" Kazuki wondered aloud, he had a rough idea of the injuries but wasn't sure.

"Uhh..." Satoshi paused, thinking on it for a moment, *"Broken nose... cracked orbital, cracked skull, broken ribs..."* Satoshi took an audible breath, *"Blew out some blood vessels in your eyes or something, tore everything up in your back, pinched some nerves, whatever, the MRI said you were a mess back there but nothing was broken. You broke your arm in like three places and I think you dislocated you shoulder."* Satoshi said, moving from Kazuki's bedside. *"There was some other stuff too but I can't remember, they were going through it too fast."*

Kazuki lifted his arm, looked at the cast, the IVs. That was when he had blocked the punch aimed at his head at the end of the fight. If that had hit... it had been a close one. *"So, that's it..."*

Satoshi sat up fully in his chair again, this time with the clipboard from the foot of the bed, "Contusion on the head... lacerations... oh, you blew out your knee, and tore a bunch of the muscles in your neck too." Satoshi switched off to English as he read before adding, "Looks like that's the big stuff at least."

Taking a deep breath he realized the ache was from his ribs, from his back, even from his neck and nose. No surprises there.

"Don't worry man, you'll be up and running in no time." Satoshi assured him, this time bending over to put his hand on Kazuki's knee causing Kazuki to wince.

"I know it will be fine." Kazuki agreed, starring ahead at the ceiling.

"You should try to get some sleep buddy, and I'll

be back by in the morning." Satoshi pushed himself from the chair in exaggerated pain, "You know these chairs weren't designed for sleeping."

"Yes." Kazuki agreed as Satoshi walked to the door, but he stopped there; hand on the knob, just barely in Kazuki's field of vision. Waiting.

"I'll see you tomorrow then." Satoshi offered at last.

"I'll look forward to it." Kazuki replied, starting to feel weak after the interaction. A moment later the door closed, his brother disappearing. Kazuki tried to relax, despite all of the injuries; he was going to be okay. At least that would be the case if he gave himself time to heal.

"Hey."

Kazuki looked toward the door, "Noe!" Kazuki gave a wave, "I was wondering when you guys would show up." I'd been three days since he'd been admitted to the hospital without a word from Noe or his group.

"Actually, it's just me, but I'm here on behalf of everyone else too." Noe admitted, standing awkwardly at the foot of the bed.

"Come over to sit down." Kazuki offered, gesturing to the chair with his good hand.

"No, I'm good." Noe insisted, holding his ground. "I just wanted to wish you the best; you know... do you got a place for cards?" He asked, holding out the envelope to Kazuki.

"Over there." Kazuki pointed with a grunt at a table in the far corner, "But just hand it to me. Could you open it first, I have a hard time with just one hand."

"Sure thing." Noe nodded and ripped open the seal, handing it off to Kazuki. Kazuki accepted with a smile and fished out the card by pinning the envelope to this chest with his thumb and using his middle and forefinger to extract the card. He looked at the front then folded it open. The words were pretty generic, but the signatures, and the notes, he appreciated them the most. "Thank you."

"No problem, I wish I could have made it here earlier, but we just found out that you were in here."

"Who told you?"

"Alden of all people." Noe looked downcast, "He told us he got carried away and that he wondered if any of us had checked on you."

"He said that?" Kazuki asked shocked.

"Not so apologetically, but that was the feeling I got. Whether it was worry over you pressing charges or not is another matter." Noe explained with a hint of anger.

"Oh." Kazuki leaned back onto his good arm; he hadn't realized that he had been holding himself so far forward.

"So, how did this happen? You beat him the other day." Noe asked sounding worried.

Kazuki looked him over for a moment, "Did you know about... that if you are closer to the radio tower you get more power from it?"

"Humm... it makes sense." Noe reached down and gave the chain hanging from his wallet a spin. "But I never thought about it."

"Neither had I." Kazuki sighed, "Alden sent me an e-mail pretending someone else to be. Some different Channeler who wanted to meet me in private." He let out a deep breath, "And he asked me to meet him by the radio tower at the edge of park."

"Ohhh..." Noe acknowledged knowing where things were heading.

"He made a request, his favorite song I guess, and the tower was right there... I never felt anything like it..." Kazuki shuddered, "He was strong, stronger than I was, I-- I had no chance."

"Ahh man, that bites."

"He punched me and knocked the wind out of me, then kicked me into a car, slammed me into the bumper, and threw me into the concrete like I was weightless." Kazuki picked up his good hand and dragged it over his face, his nose aching from the action, "He took me apart in less than two minutes there was nothing I could do. This-" Kazuki lifted his arm in a cast, "-is from the good block I managed."

"Woah."

"I thought that I was going to die."

"Jeeze." Noe went silent a moment. "Don't worry, the next time we see Alden, he won't know what's coming either." Noe promised solemnly.

"It is okay, I will be back in Japan soon. You have to live with him, just let it go."

"What he did was wrong, it was a freaking setup!" Noe argued, taking a sidelong step toward Kazuki around the bed.

"I should have been able to defend myself." Kazuki brooded, shifting his eyes from Noe whenever the taller teen attempted to make eye contact.

"You can't just let this go."

"That is what everyone told me the last time, and look what it did to me." Kazuki wheezed he overexerted himself; his ribs were suddenly on fire.

"You didn't come all the way to America for something like this to happen." Noe insisted.

"It's okay, I am through with this."

"No, you're not. You can't let him do this to you." Noe raged, "You're better than this, better than him. I saw it." He insisted, referring to their fight at the mall, "I know you can beat the guy when you're on even footing. It's not your fault that he's an asshole who can't stand to lose a fight."

"It does not matter, look at me." Kazuki rocked his head in his neck brace for emphasis, "There is nothing I can do."

"Are you even trying to get better?" Noe asked with an accusatory tone.

"Yes." Kazuki mumbled.

"No, you're not. You know by now that if you tune you heal faster. You'll be out of here in no time if you gave it half the effort you're devoting toward being hard on yourself." Noe insisted exasperated.

Kazuki tried to look down, away from Noe. He'd suspected that, "I... know, I just don't want to have to worry about this any more."

"About Alden you mean." Noe said frustrated, "Forget about that son of a bitch." He spat, "Look, you just focus on feeling better, and we'll take care of Alden."

"I said do not worry about it." Kazuki raised his voice painfully.

"Look, I don't think you understand. Even if you're going back to Japan, you're still a member of our group. You're still a Channeler. It doesn't matter if it's Tommie, Irvin, even Casey, if something like this happens, we're gonna fight." Noe insisted.

"But…" Kazuki muttered defeated.

"You're one of us. You came to America to find other Channelers… but we're all your friends. We're all glad that you found us. After you're gone, you're still going to be our friend, and what he did is still going to be wrong. He's not going to get away with this."

Kazuki woke from his nap to the sound of knocking. He looked up to the television to make sure that the noise hadn't come from there. On the screen an overweight man dressed in a business suit gestured to a map showing clouds sweeping across the state. "Come in." Kazuki called out.

Elli walked in a moment later, the door slamming behind her from the pressure differential. "How are you doing?" She asked as she ushered herself into the room and took a seat next to Kazuki's bed.

"Better." Kazuki admitted, the last time he had seen Elli had been the day after the ambush, and at the time he hadn't been much for talking, as a matter of fact he hurt more then than immediately after the fight.

"That's good. I heard that Noe came by to visit?"

"Yes, he was here earlier."

"It's nice that he stopped by..." Elli trailed off.

Kazuki propped himself up on his good arm and pushed himself back further onto the bed, he could have used the electronic controls but they made him feel infantile. "He said that he and the others were going to beat up Alden..."

"Doesn't surprise me." Elli said dismissively, "I wouldn't mind taking a swing at him myself."

"Elli, don't do it."

"I wasn't going to, it just sounds like fun." She laughed at the suggestion.

Kazuki could think of nothing to say to fill the silence so he pretended to stare at the television. Watching the rendered clouds pass across the state over and over...

"You know, I knew something was wrong... that night." Elli started, turning from Kazuki and looking out the window, "There was something in the stations, I couldn't put my finger on it, but it worried me."

"You mean that when I was taking the Jazz station?"

"No, even before that something felt off. And of course I felt it when Alden basically ripped that station out of existence." Elli sighed, "I was worried, and then I felt you on my station..." She stopped, blushing slightly, "I mean, the Jazz station, and well, that's when I knew it wasn't just my imagination."

"I was worried that you wouldn't figure it out." Kazuki admitted.

"You should know better than to underestimate

me like that."

"You will not have to worry about me much longer. The doctor says I will be out of here in two or three days, then I'll be heading back to Japan after that." He finished with his voice dropping an octave or two.

"It's weird to think you'll be leaving..." She sighed, "You're a good fit here." She turned back for a moment, "Don't you like it here?"

"Yes." Kazuki stopped for a moment, thinking, it had been a good trip except for Alden, "I can not stay."

"I know that, I wasn't asking you to stay, just... do you think you might come back someday?"

"It is a long trip." Kazuki stumbled, "I mean, and it costs a lot of money, I do not know." Kazuki trailed off.

"Well, I'm gonna miss you." Elli admitted after a pause.

Kazuki locked his eyes with her green eyes for a moment, "I am going to miss you too, but I'm not leaving yet." He added it felt too much like a goodbye.

"What if I came to visit you, in Japan?"

"What?" He'd heard her but the suggestion was outrageous.

"You know, just over summer break or something."

"I guess..." Absently he wondered not only how she would come up with the money but how she would work things out with school in the mix.

"You don't sound enthusiastic." She answered slightly peeved.

"I-- I just do not know, I would not want you to--" Kazuki struggled to find the word, "-inconvenience yourself like that."

Elli let out a huff, "Sometimes you can be so sweet. And sometimes you can be so thoughtless." She pushed herself from her seat, reaching out she handed him an envelope, "I hope you get well soon."

Kazuki took it, "I will try." He answered, unsure of

himself.

Elli gave him a nod then hurried to the door, without another word. That had been odd; Elli had been all over the place. Her, coming to Japan? He was the only Channeler that he knew of, though when he got home he at least knew how to track down others if they existed.

He looked over the envelope. "Carmela?" He said aloud, he had forgotten that was her first name. Carefully he opened the envelope, holding it in his teeth as he worked his finger along the seam. Expertly he pulled out the card, "Get well soon, and do it before you have to go back so we can hang out, Elli." Kazuki read the card aloud before reaching out with his good hand and putting it on his night stand.

He grabbed the remote while he was reaching out and turned off the television. He was sure that he had the ten day forecast memorized by now. He settled back and tried to relax. He was starting to feel bad for himself again, as dense as he tried to act he knew that Elli had some sort of feelings for him, at least he couldn't deny it after her offering to visit him in Japan. But, he'd never had a girlfriend before, let alone one overseas. It was a scary thought.

There was no reason to lead her on. Or start something that he would be unable to finish. No, it was for the best for both of them that he just play stupid.

"Hey man."

Kazuki opened his eyes slowly, expecting to see his brother. He hated that people walked in and out of his hospital room without so much as a knock. It was creepy. "Casey?" Kazuki asked, his hair looking browner in the artificial light. He had hardly recognized him. Julie was there as well to complete the pair. His neck gave a little throb of pain but nothing more, regardless, he was glad to have the immobilizer off.

Julie took the seat next to his bed without any prompting. He looked her over, blue jean shorts that were cut too short, a sleeveless t-shirt that showed her belly button, he had forgotten how hot it must be outside. Still, it all served to show off her scar even more, one thing was true he'd never noticed her try to hide it.

She was the first one to speak up, "We thought we should visit you before you got out of the hospital." She started, kicking one of her feet up on the railing of his bed.

Casey walked around to stand next to his girlfriend. "I can't believe Alden pulled a stunt like that."

Kazuki sighed, he was sick of hearing that, he did it. End of story, "Yes, a lot of people have said that."

"That guy's always been a punk." Julie mumbled, "At least you'll be okay though, or, at least that's what Elli said."

"Broke my nose, and ribs, and arm but said I am healing quickly." Actually, with all the tuning that he had been doing the pain had subsided, and he was pretty sure his injuries were completely healed. That's why he had been insisting on a second x-ray of his arm before he was to be discharged, if only to get his cast off for the plane ride.

"Roughed you up pretty good it sounds like." Casey commented, looking over Kazuki as he lay in bed. "He's been bragging that you didn't even last one song you know."

Kazuki frowned, "I didn't…"

Casey nodded, "I know, but I also know about the radio tower and everything, word gets round."

The room descended into silence. Kazuki wondered, it seemed like before when Noe had come that Alden was a little worried about how he was doing. Now that word got around that he was doing okay he was up to the same old cocky attitude. Kazuki hated it.

It made that want for revenge well up in him.

"You know-" Julie started, sitting up and moving closer to Kazuki, "-we hope this doesn't mess up your image of America. I- You know by now we're not all as screwed up as that guy, right?"

"Yes." Kazuki tried to lighten his mood for their benefit, "And I think I have learned a lot coming here."

"Sorry that we couldn't teach you to fight better." Casey answered quickly.

"No, not that." Kazuki thought on it for a moment, "I met you two, and Noe and his friends, I made a lot of friends while I was here." Kazuki smiled, it was as Noe had said, it was more than just the Channeling. He had friends now that seemed even more steadfast than the friends he had known for a lifetime back home.

Whether they were training or doing anything together, he always had fun with all of them. He gave a chuckle at the memory of him and the rest of Noe's crew singing along to American pop songs at the top of their lungs outside the library. They had been eerily harmonious with one another to anyone else, but right in time in their heads. It was one of his favorite memories.

"It's been great having you around." Julie replied.

"Yeah, you're a pretty cool guy." Casey backed her up, putting a hand on her shoulder.

"When I get out of here..." Kazuki trailed off, making sure he had their attention, "Will I see either of you after I get out of here... before I go back to Japan?"

Julie spoke up, "Oh yeah, sure, we'll make a point of it." She answered assuredly.

"It will be strange going back to Japan." Kazuki lamented, "I think I am the only Channeler in my area."

"Must be strange." Julie agreed. "If I didn't find out there were other people that could do this kind of stuff, I probably would have probably gone crazy."

"That reminds me." Casey spoke up.

"Me going crazy?" Julie wondered aloud.

Casey made a face, "No, there was this kid down by the lake, really looked like he needed a shower." He made the motion as if wafting away a bad smell, "Anyway, I tried to talk to him but he never responded, just kept walking away, but I think he was a Channeler, he had that feeling about him, you know…"

Julie nodded her head, "Yeah, I kind of remember you saying something about that, wasn't he pretty tall."

"Yeah, but he was all hunched over." Casey shrugged his shoulders, "It was just strange, I mean, I never saw the guy before and he was stalking around."

Kazuki thought about it for a moment, wondering if he had felt someone else on the stations recently. He had gotten fairly good at figuring out who it was on any given station just by how they held onto it. It was a fingerprint of sorts.

Julie pushed herself up from her chair, "Anyway, we'll have to have some kind of going away party, you know, you, your brother. He seems like a nice guy."

Casey put his hand on her shoulder, rubbing it as she got to her feet. "Maybe we could have it down by the beach, a cookout or something." Casey suggested.

Kazuki spoke up, "Why do you both always hang out at the beach?" He had to ask.

"Never really thought about it? There's really not much else to do around here…" Casey answered semi-serious.

"A cookout at the lake, that sounds doable." Julie smiled, adjusting the purse on her shoulder.

"Well, anyway, we'll talk to you once you get out of here and see how things are going." Casey offered.

"That sounds like a plan." Kazuki answered back with one of the phrases he'd heard a lot in the area.

"See ya then." Casey pulled Julie alone with him, "Come on, let's go." He said between the two of them as they headed out of the room.

As they walked out Kazuki closed his eyes, focusing on the stations. Noe was right; he hadn't been trying to heal before, but now he was.

Chapter 10

Satoshi moved forward, pushing Kazuki out of the way, "Let me get that for you." He gripped the door knob and turned it, pulling the door wide as Kazuki hobbled forward. It still hurt a little to stand fully upright but that he was managing to get around at all was what his doctors insisted was a miracle.

"Thank you." Kazuki smiled as he made his way inside, Miranda and Satoshi taking up the rear.

"Here, let's get you to your room." Miranda offered, toting along the majority of Kazuki's things from the hospital.

Kazuki waited as Miranda took the lead and followed her to his room with is brother at his side. It wasn't that his legs were hurt, just that he hadn't been out of bed in over a week. Sometimes it was hard to keep his balance but that was passing rapidly with each step.

Soon enough the three of them were in Kazuki's room. It felt strange; everything was just as he'd left it that morning. The laptop on the dresser, his clothes from his shower draped at the foot of the bed, his night clothes folded atop his suitcase.

"If you need anything…" Miranda started, moving toward the door, "I'll be in the kitchen doing some dishes, I should be able to hear you through the back window."

"Thank you again." Kazuki replied with a stiff smile, setting himself down on the bed, his body groaned like a decrepit wooden floor.

Miranda walked out of the room a moment later, leaving Kazuki with his brother. Satoshi sat down on the corner of the bed, "I'll be back in a minute, okay?"

Kazuki nodded as Satoshi headed out of the room. Kazuki kicked off his shoes, feeling odd for wearing them all the way into the house. A moment later he took off his shirt, socks, and slid down to lay on the bed fully. The pain was gone but he felt so weak. Timidly he rubbed his bare arm; it felt strange without the cast. There were a lot of strange feelings being out of the hospital, almost as many as he had when he had first been admitted.

Satoshi moved into the room with purpose, brandishing the cordless phone in front of him and dialing fluidly. Kazuki watched as his brother stopped and held the receiver to his ear, "It's ringing."

Kazuki reached out and took the phone curiously. He paused a moment before putting it to his ear.

"Moshi moshi."

Kazuki narrowed his eyes, "*Mom?*" Kazuki looked to his brother; he would have expected at least a warning. He looked to the clock; she was probably just waking up.

"*Son? Your brother said you would be getting out of the hospital today. How are you feeling?*"

Kazuki swallowed hard, he hadn't had a real conversation with his mom since before the incident at the radio station, "*I'm doing okay. I feel a little stiff though.*"

"*That'll happen; I remember it being like that when your brother was born. I was in the hospital for almost two weeks.*"

"*I'm already starting to feel better from getting up and walking around.*" Kazuki insisted, feeling that his mother was a little uneasy.

"*I just…*" Harumi trailed off, even over the phone and despite her best efforts to hide it, Kazuki could tell his mother was crying, "*I just want you home, with me, where I can protect you…*"

"*Don't worry mom, I'll be home soon. Besides, I've got big brother here with me.*" Kazuki offered, he wasn't exactly sure what she wanted him to say.

"*I know… I know, I just miss you.*"

"I miss you too, I love you." Kazuki was starting to feel a little choked up. His eyes were burning at the corners.

"I love you too and I hope you have a safe trip back."

"I'll talk to you before then." Kazuki insisted.

"That doesn't change things." Harumi replied, *"Just like you being there doesn't mean I love you any less. I'll have your father call you when he gets home so be sure to leave your phone on."*

Kazuki was going to remind her that his cell was destroyed but he figured that he had reminded her enough. Between the two of them they would remember. *"I hope you have a good day."*

"And I hope you have a good night, say hello to your brother for me too."

"I will." There was a click and the line went silent. Kazuki pulled the receiver away from his ear and turned it off before sitting it down on the nightstand. With a groan he reached over across the nightstand and grabbed his laptop.

Flipping it open and powering it on he thought about what he was doing for a moment. It felt like things had changed since the last time he had turned on the laptop. But really they hadn't, he and Alden had gone around before this, and that time too he was sure that Alden had been trying to kill him. He wondered if that had truly been the case this time as well.

With other thoughts on his mind he moved his cursor around the desktop, bringing up his e-mail. There were a number of new messages. There were a few from his friends and several from his mother and father. He was sure most of them were those horrible internet 'get well' cards with dancing penguins. Instead of focusing on the new messages though he scrolled down and looked at the read messages.

Sighing he opened the last message that he had

gotten from Alden. He looked it over, re-read it, his cursor hovering over the 'delete' button. Then it was gone. He went back to the main screen and deleted the second message, this time without even looking at it. The overwhelming feeling of idiocy got even stronger.

From the front of the house Kazuki heard banging on the door. He gave it a few minutes and it managed a repeat performance, but this time he heard someone coming down the stairs. He breathed a sigh of relief.

"Kazuki, your friend is here!" Miranda yelled from the front door.

Seconds later there was a knock at his bedroom door. "Hey man, you got a minute."

"Yes, come in." Kazuki offered, moving his legs off the side of the bed to sit on the edge.

The knob turned and Noe walked into the room, "Man, how are you doing?" He asked with his voice muted.

"I am doing better." Kazuki answered honestly.

"Well, I'm glad you're feeling better." He paused then changed his tone, starting off almost jokingly, "You know, you almost had to pay a visit to all of us in the hospital? Wouldn't that have been an ironic going away present?"

Even though some nuances were lost on him, Kazuki could tell that Noe was leading him on. "What do you mean?" He asked, giving Noe the opening he needed.

"Well, earlier today we were hanging out at the library, and there was this guy…"

Noe was moving back, sitting down atop the concrete wall surrounding the fountain. He looked up, his eyes trailing over some of the taller buildings. It really was beautiful out, and with the wind blowing off the lake the weather was just about perfect. "Hey Irvie, what should we do today?"

With a smile Irvin turned toward Noe, even his dark skin shining in the sun, "Don't know man, gets too hot though we could rent some moves and head back to my house and hang in the AC."

"That sounds like a plan." Noe agreed, rocking his head. Out of the corner of his eye he noticed that Tommie had shifted, lying down on her back, her hands behind her head and sunning herself as she listed to her MP3 player. Sitting on the ground, his back against the concrete was Mike.

"Be right back; I'm gonna get a soda." Noe turned to Allene on the opposite side of the fountain as she scavenged a few dimes out of the water before heading off.

Noe gave a wave and set back slightly, using his hands to brace against the seating.

"Did you catch the news last night?" Irvin asked, pulling Noe out of trailing after Allene with his eyes.

"No, didn't watch it." He mumbled, closing his eyes and feeling the sun on his face.

"Meh, wasn't anything good, just some crap about tearing down the old school building." Irvin trailed off.

For a moment Noe thought about it before he realized which building. It was the old elementary school, he looked to his side slightly, Tommie and definitely Mike never even saw the inside of the place. Allene was probably old enough to where she spent a few grades there. "Hum, could have seen that one coming." It had sat abandoned for quite a while; it was surprising that it hadn't been tore down earlier.

"Hey..." Allene walked up to Noe, bending down slightly so she could talk in a lower voice, "What's up with that guy?" She whispered loud enough for Noe and Irvin to hear.

Turning on his butt, Noe watched the newcomer. The person had turned off the sidewalk and was crossing the brick courtyard of the library. Noe squinted, trying to see in the sun. He was slouched over, and even from a distance he could tell his clothes were wrecked. Noe wondered if it was a new look, "Don't know." He responded dismissively.

Allene took a sip of her soda and re-capped it, "Something weird about that guy." She said squinting at him in the distance.

Whoever it was, they were heading right for the fountain, "Heads up." Noe directed at the two relaxing members of the group.

Tommie opened an eye, "What is it?" She asked, with the lethargy of a lizard on a hot rock.

"Don't know..." Noe started, something definitely felt off now, it was putting him on edge, "Sit up, and get on your feet Mike."

"What?" Mike asked, turning up toward Noe, "He's just a Channeler."

"Channeler?" Noe repeated, looking across the courtyard, he was closing the distance nonplused. Now Noe could tell that his clothes were tore, shredded in parts, sweat stained, grass stained, and stained from who knew what else. "Whatever, I don't like the look of him." Expertly Noe expanded his mind, feeling out the stations. Yes, this person was definitely a Channeler, but it felt wrong. He was tuning but he couldn't find the station, he tried to go through them one at a time to find the one that was missing, but didn't have time, if they were tuning right now, they must have been fully in tune to make a station completely disappear like that.

"Hey man!" Noe called out, stepping away from the fountain to meet the new guy half-way. Noe stood his ground as the guy didn't slow, didn't say a word, "How's it going?" He asked. The gap between the two of them halved then halved again and finally the new guy stepped right past Noe, leaving behind only a smell.

"Hey-" Noe started as the same guy that had just

passed him by jumped into the air, over the fountain, and landed next to Mike. "Watch out!" Noe called out breaking into a run, his heart sinking in his chest.

Reaching into the nothingness Noe grabbed his station, it was weak, someone else had been using it, he wrestled it away from them. A heartbeat later he was next to the soiled newcomer, he didn't have time to take in Irvin or Tommie's shocked looks. He could feel the sudden malice in the air; he had to get between Mike and this guy.

As quickly as Noe made it there, the guy had changed his target, spinning on his heel he was face to face with Noe. "Khsssss!" He sprayed, lashing out with more of a claw than a fist.

Noe danced away but just barely, the attack was a complete surprise, the only reason he'd dodged it at all was sheer luck. Instantly he jumped back a few steps, turning to Irvin he made eye contact and nodded. Noe turned his attention back ahead, "What was that man?" He yelled out, but the question didn't garner a linguistic response, another snarl, maybe a yell, Noe wasn't sure. "Calm down, what are you so pissed about? You don't go attacking people for no reason!"

The hunched kid groaned out as he broke into a run, his body stooping over even more.

Noe dodged to the side and brought his foot up aimed at where he expected the guy's head to be. At the last moment though he changed direction, shadowing each movement of Noe's dodge and slammed into Noe's midsection.

Noe huffed as he toppled into the brickwork and skidded along with the stranger's unwashed hands around his waist. "Irvie!" Noe called out, he released his hold on the station for a moment, passing it off to Irvin.

Immediately Irvin was rushing the two of them, but just as quickly Noe felt the hands release from around his waist. The element of surprise was gone as the stranger threw himself to his feet to meet Irvin head on. The two of them literally smashed into each other, Irvin forced to take a few steps back from the hollow impact, "Noe!"

The station changed hands again, Noe ran forward just as the stranger was turning. He leapt forward and grabbed the stranger around the waist, Noe tried to ignore the smell, the slick feeling of his unwashed skin beneath his layers of unwashed clothes, "Irvie, get him!"

With his station gone, all Noe could add was dead weight, if he took a hit he was done for. Thankfully he wasn't the focus of attention any longer. Irvin rushed forward and slammed his fist into the guy's stomach, dangerously close to Noe's arms. Noe let go as the stranger doubled over, quickly scrambling to his feet.

The victory was short lived, without even resuming his slumped posture he rushed Irvin, "A little help here!" Noe yelled out at Allene, Tommie, and Mike who had scattered further away. "You guys try to find something good while me and Irvie hold him off!" He called out as the three of them started to converge back on the action.

Noe looked around; people on the sidewalk had stopped what they were doing. Their destinations forgotten, they were looking at something considerably more interesting now. Noe sighed; he really liked hanging out at the library but doubted that would be a possibility in the future if this continued to escalate.

"Damn it! Just stop what you're doing and get out of here!" Noe yelled at the stranger. His comment didn't even earn a sidelong glance. Noe gritted his teeth; if that was the way he wanted it.

A few attacks landed on Irvin, forcing him back, "Damn, this guy hits like a frigg'in potato gun!" Irvin yelled out, trying to move out of his reach for even a moment, he just kept coming.

Looking around, Noe tried to take stock of the situation. Even though this guy wasn't backing off, he seemed to understand the situation. Whoever they were, they kept glancing at Tommie, Allene, and Mike on the sidelines, they knew that they were tuning. That didn't seem to scare them however; as a matter of fact they were fighting harder.

"I got something!" Tommie called out just as Irvin dodged a kick that knocked a dozen or so bricks in the wall to pieces.

"Anyone else?" Noe called out, noticing that the guy had decided to focus his attention directly on Tommie.

"There's nothing good on!" Mike yelled frustrated.

"I got something that will work." Allene said nodding.

"Okay... okay..." Noe took a deep breath, "I'll take over for Irvie. Tommie, you and Mike share, and Allene... just be there if we need you." They all nodded, watching the fight between the stranger and Irvin, there was no doubt about it, he was losing. Irvin was being beaten back, hardly able to hold his own with his back literally against the wall. Even the attacks he was blocking were doing a number on him. Especially the open-handed attacks that the stranger threw out consistently, knocking Irvin to one knee.

"Mike, Tommie, distract him." Despite the stranger not paying attention to their conversation, Noe still kept his voice hushed.

Noe watched Mike and Tommie run forward, one sprinting ahead, then the other catching up, trading off the station without a word exchanged between them. Noe nodded then rushed forward as well. The two leading Channelers made it within a few strides of the stranger when he turned suddenly. Forgetting about Irvin, his movements were erratic, rushing toward one, then the other, and then back.

Running around the commotion, Noe passed the three of them, "Irvin!" He yelled, kneeling down next to his friend.

"Dude that sucked." Irvin mumbled, pushing himself to his feet with the aid of the wall. He had gashes on his forearms where he had blocked some of the outsider's attacks, his body was shaking, he'd overexerted himself but the other guy was still going strong.

"Don't worry man-" Noe reached out, offering a hand and clasping it with his friend, "-we've got it from here."

"Thanks." Irvin gave a grimace as he released his hold on the station.

Turning, Noe watched Mike and Tommie go at it. The way they traded off the station... The stranger could tell which one was tuning, which was a threat, but they were changing off so quickly that he always seemed to be caught with his back turned. One hit, then another. Tommie came in with a powerful kick to the back of his knee, switching immediately to Mike, whose kick landed right under his chin.

For a moment, Noe stood there watching, it looked like things were under control. The station he was tuning went to a commercial break and he allowed himself a moment to relax. If they could take this guy...

The tables turned faster than Noe could have imagined, the stranger reached out and smacked Mike with a wide open hand across the face, but instead of following through he grabbed the younger man firmly, lifted him off his feet, and smashed his head into the ground. Noe's eyes widened, Tommie was slack-jawed, frozen, and took the complete brunt of the kick that was aimed at her stomach, sending her flying up and into the fountain, impacting strongly against the center of it causing the pedestal to rock and the pipes inside to cry out as they bent.

"Allene!" Noe yelled panicked.

She was some distance away but Noe could see her confusion, she looked between Tommie in the fountain, between Mike bleeding and on the ground, and between the stranger. Her dilemma was decided for her however when the stranger again broke into a run. He dodged her kick, he dodged her punch, she yelled out in frustration, anger, Noe wasn't sure.

Running across the battlefield to the fountain he fished out Tommie. She was conscious, on her knees and draped over the inside edge, the water running over her face. She sputtered some out as Noe put a hand on her shoulder, "I had the station... I had the station..." She yelled hysterically, "Go check on Mike, I think he's really hurt." She winced as she pushed herself to her feet.

Noe nodded, jogging over to where the youth lay on the ground. "Mike!" Noe called out, kneeling down at his side.

In response the younger kid lifted his arm from his side shakily and planted it next to his face, flipping himself over on his back. There was a pool of blood, but it wasn't as bad as it had appeared, it was more of a spatter. "You okay?" Noe asked worried.

"M-my head hurts..." He cried, weak and drained.

"We'll get you out of here; can you walk?" Noe asked, helping Mike to his feet.

"Yeah, don't worry..." Mike wiped the blood from his forehead but the cut immediately started dumping blood again, "How's Tommie?"

"She's fine, just a little banged up..." Noe rushed out, turning back to Allene for a moment. She didn't so much fight as lead the stranger along and stay out of his way. She was faster, not stronger but quick enough to keep him playing without getting hurt. Noe was afraid though that her luck was gong to run out as suddenly as it had for these two.

Mike vomited over the brickwork, "I feel sick..." He finished weakly.

"We're getting out of here..." Noe looked around at the scene again, things were looking worse by the second, "You're going to have to man up and help Tommie and Irvie..." Noe swallowed hard, Mike probably had a concussion, "I'm going to go help Allene."

"My song's just about over!!!" Allene yelled out as soon as she noticed Noe closing in.

Noe broke into a half-jog, trying to sort through the stations as he went. If he couldn't find anything he would be just about useless. He watched as Allene tried to keep a tree between herself and the outsider, the two of them circling at an ever increasing pace. Finally the stranger stopped and bobbed his head from side to side before yelling out and bashing the tree from the side with the palm of his hand.

The tree, thicker than Irvin's quad muscles immediately bent at a ninety degree angle, a mash of bark and wood pulped where the plant had been held together in the middle. "Shit!" Allene yelled out, breaking from her hiding spot and sprinting toward the library with all the speed of a Channeler.

Noe took a deep breath, he had something. Drive; move forward, you're faster than this... Noe repeated in his head, his body felt like it was flying he was moving at such a rate, he had to slow his run or risk wiping out. He planted himself between the stranger in pursuit of Allene and held his ground.

The stranger tumbled into Noe, sending both of them to the ground, sliding, painful brickwork digging into his flesh, Noe lashed out a hand to stop his movement, the flesh on the tips of his fingers quickly wearing down to the nails. He was back on his feet in a heartbeat, throwing himself in the air, for the first time he felt like he was moving faster than his opponent.

Despite the kick landing firmly Noe might as well have been kicking the ground for all the good it did. His body stopped in midair and he lost his balance as he suddenly found himself hanging there with his foot pressed against the stranger's shoulder. He fell to the ground but managed to catch himself on his feet, sinking to his knees. His eyes widened as he saw the kick aimed for his face, dodging caused him to fall backwards, he turned it into a roll, trying to put some distance between the two of them.

Rolling onto his feet he realized he had the distance he needed, he didn't have time for subtlety, "Get ready!" Running forward Noe waited for the opening and sure enough the stranger shot out his hand. Instead of dodging though, Noe reached out and grabbed his hand, then changed his trajectory, inverting it and circling around the stranger. He grunted, pulled down, and the stranger's body followed his arm, arching down over Noe's shoulder, then down toward the ground. At the last moment Noe continued the circle, the strangers' shoes catching the pavement as he was again pulled up into the air, and finally, mercifully, slammed into the ground with enough force to lift the bricks for several feet around the two of them.

Noe didn't take the time to see if his opponent was still in the mood to fight, "Come on you guys!" He yelled out. Ignoring the crowd that had gathered the five of them ran off away from the library as best they could down toward the lake.

"You don't even know who it was?" Kazuki asked, still in shock from the story.

Noe shook his head, "He didn't give a name..." He trailed off, picking at the band aids that he had bundled around his finger tips.

"We ran off into the woods after that. Then he

started to follow us." Noe let out a sigh, "He never got close enough for us to see him but we knew he was there. We figured he was able to follow us because we were all tuning to some extent so we hid in the bushes and completely cut it out." Noe rubbed his hand over his face heavily, "You should have seen us..." He sighed, "After a while I think he gave up, I came here to warn you."

"Thank you." Kazuki couldn't really think of what else to say.

"I think it was actually the tuning that irritated the guy. It was like fighting a monster." Noe shook his head hopelessly.

Kazuki shuddered, remembering his beating at the hands of Alden, "What about you, you have to live here..." Kazuki asked after a moment.

"We'll figure something out, maybe they'll arrest him. It should definitely be on the news tonight."

Kazuki frowned, that didn't sound like a good thing, and he wondered if his beating had made the news and hoped that it hadn't. The less the average person knew about Channelers the better as far as he was concerned.

"There were a few people there with camera phones; I bet it's already on the internet." Noe said with a smile, nodding in the direction of the laptop.

Kazuki eyed the laptop as well but decided to save the search for later, "So, how is everyone..."

Noe frowned, "Allene is fine, Irvie's got some cuts on his arm and he's whining about being sore, Tommie... Tommie's hurt, but I don't know how bad because she just keeps insisting Mike go to the hospital. And, well, Mike's hurt but he keeps insisting Tommie go to the hospital." Noe laughed it off, "Don't worry though, I've got Allene taking care of the both of them right now."

Kazuki knitted his brow, "Do you feel that?" All of

the talk of tuning had made Kazuki more aware of the stations, there was something strange there.

Noe closed his eyes, keeping them open just a hairs width. "That's him." He said with certainly, "At least he feels far away... I think, I can't figure out what he's tuning exactly."

"There's someone else too?" Kazuki asked, wondering if Noe could feel it as well. There was a large disturbance, unsettling all the stations, and then another smaller disturbance, almost completely hidden by the first.

"Yeah..." Noe started, trying to focus on the feelings.

"I think-" Kazuki started before stopping himself short, "I think it might be Alden?"

Noe nodded, "Yeah, that's definitely Alden."

"You think they're going to fight?" Kazuki asked, both of the presences seemed to be about the same distance away but that didn't mean they were in the same area.

"Do you even have to ask?"

Shaking his head, Alden looked on amused as Jayson spun a penny on its side across the table. Looking around the restaurant to make sure no one was looking; Bailey picked up the salt shaker and slammed it down on the spinning penny.

Bailey snickered, "Let's get out of here."

Alden gave a smile in return, "Yeah, forget this place." The three of them stood from the table and headed outside without a glance back. Although Alden really wanted to see the look on the waitress' face when she picked up the salt shaker and all the salt came pouring out.

People on the sidewalk cleared the way as the three of them walked down the street, purposely spreading out to take up as much room as possible.

"Ooops!" Alden casually kicked Jayson in the back of the knee causing him to stagger and almost fall.

"Dick!" He laughed, catching himself and turning around he gave Alden a shove.

Alden laughed, joining Bailey before the three of them resumed their walking. At the edge of the main drag, Alden stopped, "Bailey, get your thin arms over here." He called out jokingly, beating his hand against the side of the vending machine.

Bailey walked over and got down on his knees, plunging his arm up to his shoulder into the outlet of the vending machine. A few minutes later he pulled out his hand accompanied by a banging sound. With a smile on his face he handed Alden a soda.

"Cool." Alden took the soda and popped the top, taking a drink as Bailey got to work on getting more freebies.

Off the main street the three of them crossed by the park, following the tracks. Alden stopped a moment after stepping onto a rusted steel bridge crossing over the river. He held out his hand as a signal to his crew that they needed to hold it for a moment.

"Channeler stuff." Alden insisted, holding his hand still as he tuned the stations. "There's someone around here..." He trailed off as he looked from one end of the bridge to the other, holding his ground.

"What's the hold up man?" Jayson asked after a few minutes, sounding slightly irritated.

"Just hold on!" Alden insisted, needing the silence to concentrate. There was the sound of the water rushing over the pieces of steel that had fallen from the ailing bridge. The wind blowing between the girders and cross sections, and eventually dragging footsteps.

Alden focused his attention on the newcomer at the far end of the bridge. "You guys stay back." Alden motioned to his buddies behind him with his hands, "Get off the bridge."

"Got it man." Bailey mumbled, taking a few steps back as Alden started walking forward. The bridge was quite a piece of work, built nearly a hundred years previous, it had been taken out of service decades ago. But through lack of interest, nothing had ever been done with it, no upkeep, and no demolition. It had sat there for years crumbling into the river. Topping the surface of the bridge had been a facsimile of what one would see on the land, wooden railroad ties and gravel. But over the years as the surface had failed, holes had appeared beneath the gravel, leaving sink holes, and rotted broken ties all about.

Alden turned around for a moment to look back at his buddies before going to the task at hand. He concentrated, focused. "You know this is my turf, right?" Alden boasted, "You should just walk away with your tail between your legs while you've got a tail."

The stranger continued to come forward without hesitation. Alden looked him over, unimpressed by his tattered clothes, unruly hair, and generally unwashed appearance. Though if he hadn't been bent over the way he was he would have been the taller of the two of them by far.

"And what's up with that shirt, it looks like you stole it from a corpse in a car wreck." Alden joked, laughing as the two of them closed the gap. "God you look like shit." He laughed again, the hairs rising up on the back of his neck as he sent his consciousness into the void.

The action though spurred the stranger on; he picked up his pace to a jog. Alden hardly had time to find something, let alone brace himself before the two met. But it was the look in this newcomer's eyes that unnerved Alden the most. Made his breath catch in his throat, he had to end this fast or there might be trouble.

Noe shifted uncomfortably sitting at the foot of Kazuki's bed, "I hate to say it, but I hope Alden wins this one."

Kazuki nodded weakly, he understood where Noe was coming from, the thought made him look again to Noe's bandaged hand.   But, that didn't matter, if anything he wanted Alden to lose more than ever, and suffer.   He tried to think of something else.   Revenge was never justified he had been taught.   Before he had explained it to himself as training, bettering himself, but now he couldn't apply that same rationale.   He just wanted to see Alden get hurt.

"They're not that far away." Noe commented to fill the silence.

"I am in no shape to do much of anything." Kazuki lied despite feeling much better throughout the day.

"I guess…" Noe looked out the window, "Maybe Alden will be able to handle this guy." Noe folded his hands in his lap, "I mean, we were all out of practice, and Alden's always fighting…"

Kazuki nodded in agreement, at least that much was true.   Even if it didn't change what outcome he was wishing to happen.

Chapter 11

Hearing the stranger cry out, Alden braced himself. His eyes widened as Alden locked on the signal fully, creating a vacuum in the radio waves where the signal had been. The impact forced him back, causing his feet to drag into the gravel until he halted instantly, his momentum absorbed by one of the railroad ties.

"You trying to hug me or fight me." Alden grunted through clenched teeth. He was holding his ground. Gripped around the waist Alden felt the pressure change, this guy was trying to pick him up. Bringing his hands in front of him, Alden laced them together and slammed them into the stranger's back.

"Tsthhhh!" He expelled the air in his lungs causing Alden to redouble his efforts, slamming his fists again and again into his back until he let loose his hold, lurching forward, off to Alden's side, stumbling and catching himself against the lattice of rusty metal.

Alden ran forward, seizing the opportunity. The opening didn't last long enough as the outsider spun toward him mid-stride. Alden swung at his face. A fist came up to block his; there wasn't enough time to change the trajectory.

"Ahhh! Bitch!" Alden yelled out stumbling back holding his throbbing hand, "Ufff!" The wind was knocked out of him; he looked up to see the stranger moving in again. Alden fought through it and brought his hands up to block the next attack, a sweeping blow from above that dug into his arm, the cut was superficial but the muscle hurt the whole way through. "Bitch! Son of a bitch!"

It barely registered the strange grunting and hissing noises of his attacker. Alden jumped back trying to get some distance between the two of them. It didn't make a difference, the guy was relentless. Every step

Alden took back was in time with each step the stranger took forward. "Just give me a second!" Alden yelled in frustration, bringing up his right hand for a haymaker. He sucker-punched the stranger with his left. As the new comer was doubling over, Alden struck with his right hand, clobbering him in the back of the head and staggering him.

Alden's song was coming to an end; he'd caught just the final chorus. Anxiously he looked off toward the end of the bridge, afraid of drawing attention. Bailey and Jayson were still there. He wanted to tell them to get away but thought better of it. Instead he focused on finding a new song, searching the stations. "Hummm?" He led on as the stranger was left sucking air. "I can't seem to find the station you're using ..." Something was fundamentally wrong with the situation.

"Woah!" Alden tried to dodge backward but just slammed himself into the lattice work. He'd been earnestly distracted by the situation while his opponent had recovered. Frantically he reached to the radio waves but found himself just as quickly being thrown through the air. He hadn't even felt the impact, and the next thing he knew he was toppling into the gravel, skidding, finally coming to rest with his hand hanging through one of the sink holes to the river below.

It wasn't great but it would do. Alden tuned the new song as best he could as he pushed himself to his feet, his hands and chest bloody from the impact and subsequent skidding. He knew he had to end this, the longer this went on the surer he was that something was wrong.

"All right, it's on now." Alden yelled out, focusing as best he could on the song, even lip synching to eek that extra little bit of power out of it. He sprinted forward, one foot in front of the other atop the railroad track, it was faster that way without his feet sinking and spreading out the gravel.

Alden yelled out as he crossed paths with the stranger, snapping out his foot. The stranger took it full on, hardly staggering him; instead the stranger brought up his hands and tried to catch the appendage. Alden yanked it back, sacrificing his balance in the process, but he couldn't afford to turn this into a grappling match. Rebounding forward by bracing his foot against the second track of the pair he brought up his fist in a hook, this time the stranger managed a dodge.

Alden had exaggerated the movement on purpose; he turned the fist into a knife-hand and brought it around back toward the stranger's neck. The attack never connected, again Alden found himself slicing through the air. This time he impacted painfully against the tangle of iron works bordering the tracks. His face was killing him, his nose was numb and wrecked. The one consolation was that he managed to land on his feet.

He didn't have time to dwell on it; instead he surged forward again, meeting the stranger who was already rushing at him. They collided, body to body, impacting savagely. Alden pushed out his chest, hoping to give himself that little extra boost and succeeded in pushing the outsider back, stunning him. His blood was rushing, his limbs were shaking, Alden felt the same as he had those nights before when he had fought Kazuki.

"Come on bitch!" Alden yelled out, blood flying out of his mouth from his busted lip, "I'm gonna beat the-" The attack came out of nowhere, a kick to the chest; more than enough to send Alden back a few steps. They were too fast to block, his movements... they were hard to read, he was fighting entirely on instinct. Each moment was independent of the one before. Chained together by chance and speed alone.

Alden coughed terribly, his chest feeling empty, "How the hell are you so fast..." He trailed off, he wanted to limit the talking, it cooled the blood flowing through his veins.

This time when the stranger came in low, Alden knew what was coming; instead of trying to dodge he brought up his knee full force. His knee caught the stranger in the face, causing him to stumble backward and leaving him wide open for when Alden's follow-up punch, full on in the face. It wasn't enough to slow him, barely enough to faze him even though his nose was just as bloody as Alden's was now.

"I've got you now." Alden rumbled, moving forward he grabbed the stranger by the shirt and hefted, grunting. The stranger lashed out, pegging Alden in the shoulder, kicking him in the solar plexus, the inner thigh. Alden clenched, going defensive but kept the stranger lifted. Open to attacks he took the full brunt of them as he endured the unsteady steps on the crumbling surface to the edge of the bridge, throwing the outsider over the edge.

At least that had been the plan. Instead Alden found his hand held in a death grip, holding the stranger hissing over the rushing waters below. Alden grunted, swinging the stranger in an arc, slamming him into the railing. Again, and again, "Damn you, let go!"

The weight suddenly disappeared as the stranger lost his grip, tumbling down into the water below, barely missing the I-beam jutting up from the water. "Damn..." He said breathlessly, he didn't want to go to jail for murder but he was sure he would have been able to justify it.

He felt hot, his body quivering. Alden let out a shaky breath and let his station loose, feeling the sudden weight of his injuries he hobbled down the bridge. "Hey man, awesome!" Bailey called out once he was in ear shot.

Alden waved it off, "He was a chump."

Jayson spoke up, "You took that guy to cripple

town."

"Yeah…" Alden huffed tired, he was hurting all over his chest and face but it wasn't anything major. He felt lucky; the guy had been out for blood.

There was a scream from behind him. Alden turned, looking back down the bridge. It was silent for a minute, just the sound of rushing water, and then there was another. It was his opponent; hung up on the debris below the bridge. The sound wasn't sad, or hurt, it was simply angry.

"You guys better just head home." Alden said at last, feeling his blood cool suddenly, his tunnel vision clearing up.

"You sure man…" Jayson wondered aloud, unsure of himself.

Bailey nodded, "See you later man, good luck." Agreeing quickly as he realized the severity of the situation.

Alden took a deep breath, "Thanks…" Slowly Alden went back to the stations, he didn't want to fight that guy again, he was going to cut out of there as soon as his friends were gone, but he had to be sure he had something to fall back on if the guy caught up to him.

The sun had long ago set, leaving Alden to wander the woods alone. It was cold, and he was wet after spending almost a half an hour hiding in the river along the bank. Eventually he had come to realize that he was being tracked through his tuning. But even after he pulled away from the stations, he knew he was still being followed.

For a moment he leaned up against one of the many trees along the path. He was soaked to the bone, his face hurt, he felt like he'd been awake for days. He was being hunted. Alden took a deep breath but muted the exhale. If he was still being followed he didn't want to tip off his location. He'd been walking for too long, one of the kicks to his leg had left him limping.

The moon was high into the sky. He was tired, running for hours. Slowly he stared moving again, his body cramping from the moment of inactivity. He heard his foot dragging more than he felt it. Grudgingly he tried to rectify it; he couldn't afford the extra noise. A moment later he found himself pushing against his nose again. He couldn't tell if he was trying to straighten it or what but he kept messing with it.

He hated doing it but gingerly he extended his senses, and immediately retracted them. That guy was still around, not too close but he couldn't give him the option of closing in. He had to get home, someplace that he could relax. But he couldn't afford to be followed. That would just beat all. Could he call the cops? They were still looking for him after the incident at the mall… after what happened at the radio station…

Hearing something in the woods, Alden moved behind a tree, crouching down. The movement caused his leg to throb again. He was afraid to even breathe. The guy was relentless, single minded. Alden forced another breath to calm himself. If it came to it he hoped that he could find a station quick enough to put up a defense. And if it came to that, he would have to go for the kill.

The silence of the forest was only punctuated by the occasional chirping of crickets. The fireflies that had been out along the pathway had called it a night. When he dwelt on it, it seemed creepy, but he hadn't had the luxury of thinking of something so frivolous. Instead, wondered about the guy that was stalking him.

What had he done to get this guy against him… Maybe Kazuki had set it up, or one of his friends. He didn't see them as that vindictive; then again he had gone a little overboard in the last match. Fiddling with the damp fabric of his shirt his thoughts wandered.

It had taken him the better part of the night to

figure out how the guy was following him so persistently. Never once did it seem like he was taking a break, no commercials. Either he was tuning even the commercials fully or there was something else at play. Then he noticed that when he was looking for a song that the spaces between the stations were vacant. Like someone had turned off the ambient music in a department store.

The bastard was tuning the noise, static, it was non-stop. There were no commercial breaks, and as far as Alden could tell, he was tuning every bit of it in the spectrum. That's why he never got weak, took breaks. And the way he acted… Alden thought back to how in tune he became with a song when tuning. Singing it, getting it stuck in his head.

If this guy only heard the static, day in and day out, even when he slept, well, it was no wonder he seemed untamed.

There was another noise off in the distance. Alden pulled his knees in toward his chest, he couldn't shake the chill in his bones, and with every passing minute it got worse. Alden held is breath and waited.

Kazuki sat down at the picnic table. The sun was out, the wind was just right. It was the prefect day to get out of the house. "So… Noe was telling me about what happened yesterday…" Kazuki started out, looking between Noe's crew sitting at the table.

His statement earned him a round of nods so he continued, "Mike, Tommie, how are you two?" He looked between them; aside from being unable to meet his gaze they seemed fine.

"I'm okay." Mike spoke up first, "Mom took me to the hospital last night when I got home and they said it I might have a little concussion but based on the other tests it wasn't anything to worry about."

Kazuki nodded, with the side of his head all

wrapped up in bandages it looked worse than road rash.

Tommie shifted in her seat, "My back hurts, but it felt better after I put some ice on it."

"That's good." Kazuki agreed, looking between the lot of them, Irvin messing with the bandages covering his arms. For a moment Kazuki looked out across the beach, across the lake before he pulled himself back to the situation at hand.

"Long time no see."

Kazuki turned to the voice, Julie and Casey heading toward them along the path, with Elli following behind the two of them. "Hello." Kazuki greeted the three, looking down at his watch, he'd been a little early but they were right on time.

"Hey you guys." Noe waved, Irvin and Allene greeted them likewise with little waves and head nods.

Casey walked up along side Kazuki, giving him a playful tap on the shoulder, "How you feeling?"

Kazuki smiled at the attention, "I am doing okay."

"That's good, first time you been out since the hospital?" Casey asked, putting his arm around Julie's shoulder.

"Yes."

"Well, that's good. In case I don't see you again, good luck in Japan, you can bet we're going to miss having you around here." Casey replied somberly.

"Yeah." Julie agreed before changing the subject, "So, what's the deal, what's going on?" Julie asked, moving to the end of the table and bracing herself against it with her hand, Elli squeezing in between Kazuki and Allene.

Noe, being the leader of the group spoke up, "You guys got my message about trying not to tune right?" He asked, getting straight to the point.

"Yeah." Julie answered for the both of them.

"I have, but it's so hard, I mean, it's like the only

way I can sleep." Elli pouted.

"Well, give it a try, real quick then stop, feel how different the stations are." Noe offered, pausing as he too started the process.

For a moment the group was in silence save a side conversation between Tommie, Mike, and Irvin. Casey spoke up first, "Something feels funky."

Noe nodded his head, "That's this guy, whoever he is." He let out a sigh, "If you tune for too long he tracks you down." Noe glanced between the other members of his group, "We tried to talk to him… nothing. He just came at us ready to fight."

Julie shook her head, "Yeah, we heard about it."

"We didn't have a chance." Noe replied, "Even with all of us going at it he took us apart." Taking a moment to swallow he continued, "He was fighting for real, even after we ran he was trying to track us down."

Noe pointed down the table, "He smacked us around like we were action figures." Noe ran his hand over his face heavily.

Continuing, Noe placed his hands solidly on the table, "I know it's only been a day, but I don't think this guy is going to leave on his own." Noe sighed heavily, "He took the five of us out, and last night he tracked down Alden too." Noe stopped himself, before starting again more impassioned, "Look, we're Channelers, it's what we do. I do it all the time too, it's not even conscious any more. But if you're tuning around this guy, he comes and he finds you and he will try to kill you for it. And… we need to do something."

"Look." Casey started, gaining the attention of the group, "There's like nine of us, there's no way he could stand up to that."

"And I thought five would do the trick the last time." Noe replied with a bitter edge, "I'd like something more to go on than just superior numbers." He admitted sounding a little more downcast, "We need something radical, you know, a plan." He answered with a hint of sarcasm.

The group descended into silence. "You said that Alden fought this guy last night?" Casey started, "Has anyone talked to him?"

"I don't think so." Noe replied.

"Alden is the most underhanded guy I know, but he's pretty damn good at strategy. Maybe he figured something out while fighting with this guy that we could use." All eyes turned to Kazuki.

Kazuki swallowed hard, "We should check with Alden then." The thought made him sick to his stomach, his injuries may have healed, but he felt just as weak at Alden's hands as Noe and his group had felt fighting against the stranger.

"Are you sure?" Elli asked her voice barely above a whisper and her breath hot on Kazuki's ear.

"Yes, it will be fine." He shook his head, forcing his worry aside. With everyone else there he was sure of his safety.

"Come on." Noe pushed himself from the table, "Let's get this over with."

Noe moved to the head of the group, everyone else taking up positions behind him as he knocked on the heavy wooden door. Kazuki took a deep breath; it was surprising the house that Alden lived in. It was huge, beautiful; it left him wondering how he could be such an asshole.

Giving three hard knocks, Noe took a step back and waited. Then he saw the buzzer and rang that as well. With the sound of chiming coming from beyond the door, Kazuki felt his nervousness swell. Elli must have noticed because he felt her hand encircling his own.

There was the sound of the deadbolt disengaging before the door opened slightly, "Can I help you." A meek woman's voice came from inside.

"Yeah, we need to talk to Alden." Noe stated outright with an authoritative voice.

"Oh, I don't think you can do that. He got home late and said that I shouldn't wake him for anything." She answered with a voice so low that Kazuki could hardly hear it from the back.

"Could you wake him up for us, please? He's going to really want to talk to us." Noe changed tactics, dropping the aggressive edge and instead trying to sound understanding. "I guarantee it, like one-hundred percent."

"I could…" She paused looking over the group, "I guess can you wait here for a moment?" She asked at last.

"Not a problem." Noe nodded his head as the door closed silently in front of him. Noe looked back to the group and gave a victory nod before turning back to the wooden door.

The wait started to drag on after a few minutes. "How you holding up?" Elli asked finally; just low enough for Kazuki to hear.

"I am fine. Do not worry." He insisted.

The footsteps approaching the door were heavy enough to be heard clearly on the other side. Kazuki's breath caught in his throat as the door came open. "Oh, it's you guys." Alden said deadpan. "If you're here to kick my ass, could you give it a shot some other time?" He said smoothly with a hint of malice.

Kazuki looked him over, he had dark circles under his eyes, and his hair was all over the place. He lacked the aura of dominance that he usually possessed. That was what Kazuki noticed most. The way he moved, the swelling in his nose, he'd been afraid.

Noe was the first to speak up, "It looks like you got in a fight or something…" Noe commented.

"Or something…" He paused a moment before

shouting out, "No shit Sherlock, next time just come right out and say it and stop beating around the bush!" He shot back, sounding more like himself. "I know you guys were out there on the airwaves just laughing, picturing me struggling with that guy. Just who the hell is he?" He yelled the last bit irritated.

"We don't know." Noe replied after a moment of hesitation. "We were hoping you might have figured something out."

"Pthhh…" Alden made a noise with his tongue, "Not likely, he didn't say a word the whole time we were fighting."

"It was the same with us." Noe motioned over his shoulder with a jerk of his head, "He just came at us and wouldn't stop."

"That son of a bitch tracked me until the sun came up." Alden growled before he suddenly took on a curious look, "Hey, are you guys planning on taking that guy out or somethin'?" Alden asked suddenly excited.

"We can't just wait for him to come after us." Noe confirmed.

"Hell yeah. I want a piece of that. Just tell me where the party is and I'm there."

"We don't know, we're trying to make some kind of plan."

"A plan?" Alden laughed, "Step one; Let's all of us get together. Step two; kick his ass. That's enough for me." Alden laughed, unnerving Kazuki.

Noe sighed, "Was there anything you noticed while you were fighting with him that might help." He asked frustrated.

"I think I figured out a few things over the twelve hours this guy was stalking me. But… I want a piece of the action, you tell me when, you tell me where. You make me a part of the plan, you got that."

Noe looked back to the group and Kazuki nodded his head slightly. He didn't like the idea but if Alden had some useful information it could really help things. It was the whole reason they were there.

"I guess we agree it's going to be the ten of us." Noe agreed at last.

"Great…" Alden trailed off a moment before moving his fist forward and extending the pointer finger, "Well, first, he's a Channeler, but not like any of us. The guy tunes static. All the crap between the channels, that's why the stations feel like someone slicked em' up with Vaseline."

"What-" Noe started before Alden cut him off.

"What that means is that he doesn't have to stop, he's always at full power, and he's always got something good in his head. And it also means he's batshit crazy." Alden added the last bit sans his usual cocky attitude.

"Second-" Alden extended another finger on his hand, "-if you tune, he will find you. He will track you down and keep finding you no matter how well you hide until you completely stop." Alden continued, stressing the last part. "Even if it's only a little, something that no one here would even be able to notice, he will find you…"

"And third-" Alden extended his thumb to match the other two fingers, "-we have to figure out something to call the bastard."

"A name?" Kazuki asked, drawing Alden's attention and a wicked smile.

"Yeah, I'm sick of calling him 'that guy'. I say we call him Noise, like the stuff you find between the stations. Noise fits the son of a bitch like a glove."

"I thought the stuff between the stations was static." Tommie mumbled, it was still loud enough though to draw Alden's attention.

"Yeah, but Static sounds gay. And by the time we're done with him he'll be crying like a baby. Unless any of you have a better idea… Didn't think so." He answered decisively, "And besides the name there's all the other shit you've already figured out for yourselves. Like the fact that he never talks, follows you relentlessly, and punching him feels like you're digging holes in the ground with a sledge hammer." Alden enumerated the remaining points quickly on his fingers before moving his hand back to his side.

The group went silent as they processed the information leaving Alden to be the first to speak up, "Just drop me an e-mail when you figure out the plan. Mr. Japan's got my e-mail addy." He laughed as Kazuki winced. The e-mail was deleted but he could still get it out of his trash. "Until then I'm going to take a nap, see ya." And with that Alden walked back into his house, slamming his door behind him. Faintly through the wood Kazuki heard Alden yell out, "Mom, breakfast!" before everything went silent.

Unfazed by the door slamming in his face, Noe turned on his heel, "So what's the plan?" He asked to no one in particular as everyone started to head away from the home.

"He tunes static." Irvin started, "He's always tuned in, that's going to make it hard. It won't matter if we catch him off guard."

"Well, what are we going to do anyway?" Elli asked at last, "If we beat him up, then what? We can't kill the guy, cripple the guy, or anything like that." She said exasperated, "Unless we can talk some sense into him he'll just be doing the same thing in a few days once he gets back on his feet, and he'll probably be pretty mad."

The group went silent for a few minutes, just walking along the sidewalk, "We'll have to call the cops." Noe said at last, "We knock him out, tie him up, and call the cops."

Hearing no signs of approval or disapproval Noe continued, "I think that's about the best we can do."

Irvin spoke up, "Why not call them right now, why even fight him?"

"It's not like they'd do anything, they always leave us alone when we fight unless it's in the public then they run us off. If we don't knock the guy out he's just going to run away, or fight back. Maybe if he goes to jail they can get him some help, run his finger prints, something." Noe finished disgusted with the situation.

"I tune all the time." Elli muttered, "I had to stop myself last night a bunch of times when I started doing it without realizing... we have to do something, I can't be worrying about this guy breaking into my house in the middle of the night to smash my skull in..." She trailed off, changing the mood of the group.

"So, that's another vote for killing him." Mike said laughing, and putting a hand to his bandages, trying to break the mood of the group.

"We will figure something out." Kazuki answered sullenly as they walked down the sidewalk. Even though he was going back to Japan, he had to do something. He couldn't just pass this off on his friends, not after all they had done for him. He had to fight.

Kazuki was sitting down on the bed across from Elli. The light outside was fading. The two of them had been sitting together talking about their options since they had made it back to Miranda's home. Starting first on the back porch and working their way into the house as the biting insects began to swarm.

So far the two of them had picked out a potential spot for the conflict. And a few plans of attack. Some of them called for one person to lead the charge, others to attack in pairs. As long as there was some plan it would be better than a ten person free for all with only so many good stations between them all.

"I think I might have it..." Kazuki said at last, an idea forming in his head.

"Yeah?" Elli asked, scooting slightly closer to Kazuki.

He nodded, "When we were walking by there earlier I noticed something that sparked my memory."

"What was that?" She asked, curious as to their first lead in hours.

So, Kazuki told her.

"That's it." Elli said succinctly, "That's what's going to work." She nodded firmly.

"What do you think the others will say?" Kazuki asked, not at all convinced he could get the others to buy into his plan.

"They'll think it's a great idea unless they've come up with something better." She smiled. "Just... As much as I want this to end, I'm worried about going too far. What if this is just because his tuning is messed up...?" She sighed, "What if the same thing could happen to any of us." She went silent for a moment, starring off into the distance.

"I guess I've got some phone calls to make. And an e-mail to send." Kazuki said the last bit with a hint of disgust. He fished around in his pants pocket and pulled out the list of phone numbers that he had taken down earlier. Kazuki pushed himself from the bed and began to excuse himself from the room when Elli interrupted.

"I can make some calls too." She offered, pulling out her cell phone.

"Thank you." And with that Kazuki left the room, to borrow his brother's cellular phone.

He walked back into the room, "I like you offering to help, but it is late. You should be going home probably." Kazuki suggested, sitting down on the mattress.

"I don't have to if you don't want me to." She answered back without missing a beat. Her voice hollow with false bravado.

212

"I-" Kazuki tried to swallow the knot in his throat.

"Don't worry." Elli continued, "My mom and dad won't be mad, and even if they were, you'll be gone before the weekend even gets here." She smiled, "So, what's it gonna be?"

"But..." Kazuki stumbled, unsure what she was getting at but flustered with some of the ideas passing through his head.

Elli looked hurt, or at least pretended to be, "Don't get ahead of yourself. I said it earlier, I tune all the time. Sometimes even when I'm sleeping. I'm worried about being home and suddenly waking up to this lanky foul smelling guy smashing through my window. I-- I want someone there to protect me if I need it." She finished sounding more like herself.

"I... do not mind." He answered back at last.

Elli replied with her cutting smile, her green eyes more piercing than ever, "Well, if you don't *mind*... It's settled then. So, who do you want me to call first?" She asked with a smile.

Kazuki took a deep breath to regain his bearings, "How about you call the girls and I call the guys?" Kazuki offered.

"That's fair." Immediately Elli went to dialing numbers on the keypad. Kazuki slumped slightly, putting his full weight onto the mattress. He looked over to Elli but turned away his gaze before she had time to notice. He listed for a few moments as she talked to Tommie then looked to the bed. It wasn't large by a long shot. Did she expect to share it? Was this something that really had no connotations? He wondered if he could get the laptop to himself before they went to sleep to try and look up American sleeping habits.

"Is this normal?" Kazuki asked, turning his head to stare at the shafts of light playing across the floor.

"Is anything we do normal?" Elli responded, her form hidden in the darkness.

Kazuki took a deep breath, she was dodging the issue. "Can you sleep like that?" He asked, the floor didn't seem to be the most comfortable place. It was hardwood and the comforter that he had given her for padding seemed to be woefully inadequate.

There was a pause, "Yes, I'm fine."

"Oh, okay." He nodded more to himself, the gesture lost on Elli.

"Let's get some sleep." She replied at last.

She had said the same thing thirty minutes earlier but kept talking whenever Kazuki felt like he was on the verge of nodding off. "I have some Jazz on my laptop if that will help." Kazuki offered after a few more moments passed; sure that Elli was still awake.

"No, don't worry about it." She sounded distant. Kazuki laid there silent. It was getting late. "I'm worried." She announced at last.

"Why?" Kazuki asked, there were a number of reasons on his mind but he couldn't know exactly which it was.

"I... I haven't fought in a long time." She answered, her voice sounding weak.

Kazuki thought back to the parking lot where he had fought Alden. Elli had picked him up afterwards, carrying him home as if he were weightless. He had no doubt of her strength, "You will be fine."

"I'm not worried about that." He heard her take a deep breath from his position on the bed, "I'm worried that I won't be able to help you if you need me."

What else could he say? Kazuki slowly closed his eyes, he wondered if she was as confused as he was. He wanted to say not to worry, that she needed to worry about herself and he would take care of himself. But he knew the words would be lost on her. Instead the thought fizzled, the room again silent.

"Good night Kazuki." She said at last.

"Good night Elli." Kazuki mumbled, finally feeling the stress of the conversation fade away as his mind was muddled by sleep.

Chapter 12

Kazuki lay in bed, eyes open, only briefly lifting himself enough to focus on Elli. But even after morning came it was still too early to get up. The sun had hardly risen. Despite that he couldn't force himself back to sleep no matter how hard he tried.

He propped himself up on his elbow and looked Elli over for another moment, her loose fitting T-shirt hanging low over her shoulders, giving him an unprecedented view of her cleavage. He noticed that she must have taken her bra off sometime in the darkness. He shook the thought from his head lest it lead to embarrassment. Still, he had to admit she looked really cute when she was sleeping, her dark brown hair splayed about everywhere but over her striking features.

Kazuki rolled fully onto his back to once again examine the ceiling and sighed. Sleeping in the same room as her was easy; he worried that after waking her things might get awkward. And with the day ahead, he felt just as worried as he had been in the days leading up to his fight with Alden at the mall. That horrible trepidation that festered in the back of his head, making him anxious and worried all at once.

He tried to believe in the certainty that with everyone working together they would undoubtedly come out on top. However, from what Noe had said... every time he thought about it, it made him remember his beating at Alden's hands. Would it be enough?

His mind wandered again to the subject he had been avoiding. He wondered if it would have been any different had he not rejected the proposition of sleeping next to her. He had tried to give her the bed after that but she was insistent that the bed was his and that she just sleep on the floor. She was separated far enough, but he imagined that he could feel her warmth. He refocused, remembering her mentioning coming to Japan. He had scoffed at the idea at the time, but now the idea seemed to have some merit. There were things there that he wanted to show her, share with her.

Kazuki smiled at the thought, showing Elli around the city. Teaching her bits of Japanese just as she had helped him with his English. They could even go to downtown Tokyo together; he'd never been himself but had always wanted to visit.

Carefully Kazuki slid his feet out from beneath the covers. He finally heard Satoshi up and about and was starting to worry that he might be in soon to check on his brother. Slowly Kazuki pushed himself up from the bed, the box spring giving a creek as he got to his feet.

Simultaneously Elli began to stir, lifting her head slightly from the pillow. "Oh…" She muttered, pushing herself up on one elbow, "Kazuki… oh… hey, how'd you sleep." She continued with a little stutter.

"I slept well, how did you sleep?"

"Me? Oh, me. Yeah, I slept pretty good." She answered unevenly as she pushed herself upright stretching awkwardly as she peeled herself off the floor. Getting to her feet she straightened her skirt, occasionally looking at Kazuki with those intense malachite eyes.

The momentary lapse in conversation seemed to drag and Kazuki mentally sighed, Elli seemed somewhat unlike herself. Elli capitalized on the silence, "So, about noon then?"

It took Kazuki a moment to realize she was talking about the plan, "Yes, noon."

"Okay then." She gave a quick nod, running her hands through her hair in the mirror, "I guess I'll see you then, I've got to get home and take a shower." He could tell from her matter-of-fact attitude that there was something else on her mind.

To him it didn't make sense to take a shower

before a fight but he decided against bringing it up with Elli. "Okay, see you later." It was the best he could come up with.

Elli's features momentarily softened as she plucked her bra from underneath the bed. Expertly she laced the underwear through the arm holes of her shirt and fastened it in place. Kazuki felt his heart skip a beat as she opened the window, "Yeah, see you." She finished with an impish smile as she pulled the screen inside and set it on the ground before ducking out the window.

For a few moments Kazuki stood there after she left, just watching the window before he mechanically walked forward and put the screen back in place. No good getting the room all full of bugs. Cracking his back he forced a smile before heading off to talk to his brother.

"So, who wants to kick off this disaster?" Alden mussed, with a snide smile.

Kazuki tried to ignore him, instead watching everyone milling around. There was an expected tension in the air. Still, the worries that he had earlier were fading. Everyone had made it. Toward the edge of the construction site Casey and Julie sat together under the shade of a grove of trees. Nearby Elli kicked a bulldozer half-heartedly before going back to looking it over. She was wearing jeans and a short sleeved shirt, it looked good on her. Kazuki sighed; just a bit further out toward a freight box Jayson and Bailey were messing around with a radio trying to tune it in.

It was the weekend and the site was abandoned for the moment. Thankfully there weren't many homes or businesses to speak of in the immediate area. Lots of open space to fight, that's what Kazuki had been thinking of when he's planned out the battle. In the center of the site was a large rectangular depression where a foundation was to be poured, but it only came up to his knees when he stepped down into the hole.

The far side of the site was lined with the building materials, piles of rebar, and pallets of bricks. High above a basket of tools and a generator hung suspended from a crane. Timidly Kazuki felt out the stations trying to see if their target was nearby. Kazuki couldn't feel him but he was sure he couldn't be too far.

"Did you catch the news last night?"

Kazuki shook himself from his thoughts; it took him a moment to find the source of the voice, "No, I did not see it."

Noe stepped forward a little from the others in his group, Tommie taking a step back shyly to the side with Mike. "They were talking about this guy…" He trailed off but Kazuki didn't have a doubt that he was talking about 'Noise'.

"What happened?" Kazuki asked, looking over the rest of Noe's crew and counting up the rest of the people on the site, including himself there were ten Channelers, that was more than he'd ever seen in one place for sure, he wondered if it was the same for the rest of them.

Noe shook his head, "They didn't have any video of him or anything, but he smashed up a few cars in the parking lot over by where you got beat up." Noe flashed a sidelong glance to Alden before going back to Kazuki, "With the description they gave though I wouldn't doubt for a minute that it's our guy."

"The police ignore the stuff we do for the most part-" Allene spoke up, "-but if this guy keeps going that's going to change for sure." Allene continued uneasily.

"That's why we're here." Alden broke in taking the reins of the conversation, "To kick this guy's ass or put him in a coffin."

"No, not to kill him." Kazuki spoke up, glaring at

Alden, he still felt a hint of fear around him, he was unstable. "We just incapacitate him and turn him over to the police; they will be able to do something."

Alden folded his arms, "That's just going to come back to bite us in the ass later, stop being such a pussy."

"If you want to kill him after we call the cops then go for it." Irvin broke in, "But we'll be long gone, we're not going to be accessories to murder!"

The conversation went silent and Kazuki noticed that even Jayson and Bailey had turned their heads in their direction.

"Fine, whatever." Alden said at last, turning his back on the group.

"So…" Noe rubbed his hands together, "Are we ready to get this show on the road?"

Kazuki looked over Noe's group, "We have to figure out who is going to go first."

"It's your plan." Noe answered back, "Who do you want to go first?"

Kazuki stopped, thinking about it for a moment; he looked across to Casey and Julie, then to Elli. For a moment his eyes settled on Alden, no, they had a different mission. He was an executioner putting a head on the chopping block.

"We'll do it; all you have to do is say it." Noe offered at last.

Half-heartedly Kazuki nodded his head that was the decision that he wanted to make but he didn't want to have to say it. "Yes. You and your group will attack first, and then Casey and Julie-" Kazuki said their names louder, drawing their attention and turning his own attention toward them, "You fight after Noe and his group." The two of them nodded, "Elli, you be ready in case someone needs you, get them out of the way if they get hurt."

Elli stopped her inspection of the machinery but

did not turn to face Kazuki, instead rising up her hand, "Got-cha!" She yelled, going back to looking over some electronics.

"Alden..." Kazuki paused, "You and me are going to finish this."

"I'm going to finish this, you're going to watch." He replied with his usual attitude which Kazuki ignored. Casey, Julie, and Elli took that as a cue that things were about to begin and started to make their way to meet up with the rest of the group.

"Okay you two, get on it." Alden commanded Jayson and Bailey. Within moments they were dialing up the radio stations on their cellular phones.

For a moment Kazuki listed as Jayson started speaking, "Yeah, I'd like to make a request for your all-request lunch hour..."

"Noe, Tommie, Irvin, Allene, start tuning. Mike, you stay on the sidelines in case they need you." Kazuki ordered, leaving Mike out of the fray. Mike insisted that his injuries were healed but it didn't look like that was the case when he was moving around or with the bloody patch of missing hair. It also didn't help that he was naturally frail looking. At once Kazuki felt the stations shift, channels winking out of existence, like the sound of something going out of the pitch of hearing. "Everyone else, off to the sidelines!"

Tense minutes passed. Eventually Tommie complained, "I don't even like this song."

Noe turned to her, "Doesn't matter, we just have to do this until he shows up. Then we can share like normal."

Tommie nodded her head before sneaking a look toward Mike on the sidelines. "Do you think he'll be here soon?"

Noe shook his head, "Should be if we're right about him." Noe took a deep breath, "He could have been anywhere in town, but I don't think it will be long now. I can feel something…" Noe trailed off, his eyes steadily fixed to the forest bordering the construction site.

"Is it him… Noise?" Irvin asked, leaning in slightly to whisper his question to Noe.

"Give it a minute." Noe replied in the same hushed voice.

"He's coming!" Allene yelled out, the first to be certain. Around the edges of the site everyone put themselves on full guard.

Soundlessly a figure stumbled out of the woods, and without pausing he continued forward, making a beeline for Noe's group standing in the middle of the depression. "Hey, you!" Noe yelled, "This is your last chance to talk to us if you don't want your ass kicked!"

Noise gave no inclination of hearing Noe, he sped up, hopping into the depression before rushing forward. "Irvie, Allene, hold him off for a second!" Noe shouted, taking a few steps back with Tommie following, "We're going to share okay?"

Tommie nodded, "Yeah, that'll work."

The two of them were distracted as Irvin clashed with Noise, the sound was hard- concrete and earth colliding, then again as Irvin brought up his hand and slammed it into Noise's midsection, but he held his ground. The vibrations were carried through the packed dirt of the would-be foundation without loss of energy; even the people at the fringes could feel the strength behind the hits.

Allene leapt into the fray literally, jumping high into the air she landed a kick against the back of Noise's neck, snapping his head forward just as Irvin landed a punch into his stomach. For a moment his body hung in the air, suspended by the duel impacts but he still had enough reflex to lash out, slamming one fist then the other into Irvin's unprotected midsection.

Irvin fell back, huffing air just as Allene tumbled to

222

the ground, holding her leg, "Damn, it hurts just to hit him." She rolled out of the way just in time to dodge a stomp aimed at her other leg. She looked up just as Irvin came from behind and grabbed Noise around his neck, wrenching his body back, "Thanks!" She called out, pushing herself back to her feet.

Rushing back in Allene put all of her tuning into her strike, landing a punch straight to Noise's face, busting his lip and loosening his teeth. It hardly even turned his head; he didn't grunt, not a sound. But he did struggle harder, "I can't hold him!" Irvin yelled as he got an elbow to his flank.

"I got 'em Irvie!" Noe tried to help Irvin out with the hold, grabbing one of Noise's free arms and wrestling it behind his body. Irvin used one of his hands to do likewise. "We've got 'em!" Noe yelled, feeling momentarily in control.

Tommie stood back, trying to find a station, but Allene tried to take advantage of the situation, slamming her leg into his midsection twice before he countered with a kick of his own, landing solidly against her quadriceps. She cried out, taking an uneasy step back but Noise pulled forward, dragging Irvin and Noe along with him as he lashed out with kicks directed at Allene.

"I need some help here!" Allene yelled to the sideline, barely staying out of Noise's range and still looking for an opening but not finding it.

Mike started running to help, "I don't have anything!" Elli yelled, keeping her distance while searching for a station forcing her to leave it to Mike.

"Allene!" Mike called out as he closed in and she got the hint, relinquishing her station and taking a few steps back.

Mike watched for a moment as she winced heavily, rubbing her leg where she had taken the hit.

"Let's get him to the ground." Noe grunted, kicking at the back of his legs. Irvin did likewise, each hit caused his knee to buckle forward but he was able to recover each time.

Meanwhile Mike jogged up to Noise and landed a kick directly against his solar plexus. He started gasping for air, and while he was distracted Noe succeeded in forcing him to one knee.

Irvin tried the same maneuver as Mike landed another kick, the power of which caused even Irvin and Noe to lift slightly as they tried to hold Noise down.

"Ahhhhhhhhhh!!!!" Noise screamed out, flailing twice as hard. He pulled out of Irvin's grip suddenly and spun, twisting his arm, Noe held fast as Noise brought his other hand around and got a grip on Noe.

"Oh-!" Noe was cut off as he felt himself lifted, thrown into Mike with ballistic force. Mike crumpled, as he legs fell out from beneath him. The two of them smashed into the ground, Mike taking the brunt of the impact before they tumbled end over end.

"Noe!" Irvin didn't even see it coming, he felt and heard his shirt ripping as he was pulled forward into Noise's punch. Then another slam of Noise's fist into his face. Irvin struggled to get away; he couldn't get his bearings back. This time Noise's body crashed into him fully and the two of them fell to the ground.

There was a yell and Irvin opened his eyes. Allene was breathing heavily standing over him, "I-I-I think I broke it..." She trailed off as Irvin looked up; already her knee was swollen to three times its normal size. Unbelievably, Noise flipped onto his feet, he ran forward, Allene was unable to get out of the way. She let out a scream as he tackled her with all of his mass, lifting her off the ground and sending her skidding across the dirt and gravel until her momentum gave out, leaving her motionless.

"Mike's about had it." Noe said with a wheeze, extending a hand down to Irvin.

Irvin looked up; he hadn't even seen Noe show

up.   Irvin looked across the battle field; Noise had stopped his attack, looking between the people laid out on the ground, Elli dragging Allene away.   It was obvious from the way Elli was moving that either she wasn't tuning at all or it was something useless like a commercial.   Tommie was holding Mike's head in her lap further off in the grass.   His head was bleeding but he seemed coherent.

"Julie, Casey, they need some help!"

Noe turned to Kazuki who was yelling from the sidelines.   A moment later a station winked from existence and Noe turned to the two new fighters. Noise did likewise and Noe seized the opportunity, crashing into him from behind and staggering him.   He didn't give him a moment to catch up.   Pressing his momentary advantage he landed a haymaker against the back of Noise's head, sending him to the ground.

"I got 'em!"   Noe called out, looking off to Julie and Casey who were still getting ready.   Noe looked down just in time to have his perspective changed, his feet swept from beneath him.   Worse yet he'd lost his song, he reached through the stations but couldn't find anything to deaden the impact against the ground. Instead he felt the full force of the hit, his breath stolen from his lungs, his head aching where it had contacted as well.   "Oufff!"

Noise was back on his feet before anyone was able to react.   He was moving faster, not slower.   The plan had been to wear him down, it wasn't working. Irvin hardly had time to block the knife-hand, solid enough to puncture skin.   It was a kill shot if it had hit the soft tissue of his stomach, instead his arm felt like it was useless. He tried to follow up the attack with one of his own, but his attempt at a punch left his side wide open, he felt the kick before he even saw Noise's foot. His arm tore where it was connected to his shoulder; it was then that he realized Noise had a hold on his hand, keeping it raised and kicking him repeatedly in his exposed flank.

Noe muscled his way in; trying for a choke hold, but Noise could sense the attack before it was landed. He let go of Irvin, allowing him to fall to the ground and landed a solid punch against Noe's face, sending him sprawling. Out cold.

A moment later Noise was the one off his feet, a dropkick from Casey sending him into the dirt, and the follow through causing him to bounce. Casey didn't let up as Elli made her way over to drag away Noe. She was able to toss him over her shoulder; at least she was tuning something. "How are you holding up?" Elli asked as she rushed away from the battle scene.

For a moment Noise looked threateningly in her direction but Casey was keeping him occupied. Noise turned suddenly, when the station was handed off there was a change in the air. Noise wasn't fast enough, he still took the brunt of an uppercut. That had been the plan from the start. The station passed fluidly from Julie this time back to Casey who spun in a tight circle, landing a roundhouse against Noise while he was still hanging in the air.

The tempo of the two picked up, the song was almost palatable in the air. Soon they were switching off faster than Kazuki could follow. Faster than Noise could follow. Like the blades of a fan the two fighters blended together.

Casey grabbed Noise's right hand and spun him in a tight circle, whipping him toward Julie who leapt into him, planting a knee in his sternum, then grabbing his shoulders and falling backward, dragging him down with her. At the moment of impact she kicked out with her feet, sending Noise sailing yet again to be juggled in the air by Casey with an uppercut just as his trajectory started to take him down again. He spit blood, weather it was from his busted lip or internal injuries, Kazuki didn't know.

Alden whistled, "You see why I stopped messing with those two?" He gave Kazuki a slight nudge with his elbow. "How are those requests coming?" Alden yelled from across the battle area to Jayson and Bailey.

"They said they'd work on it!" Bailey yelled back.

"Work on it? Call them back; tell them it's a fucking emergency!" Alden yelled. "Damn." He started again to Kazuki, "We're up next and it doesn't look like those other guys slowed him down a bit. But I have to admit Casey and Julie are tearing the son of a bitch up now."

"Yes. It is impressive." Kazuki answered back half-listening as he watched the two of them go at it. Since the two of them started to get serious Noise had spent more time off the ground than on the ground. Kazuki looked down the edge of the construction site; Elli had put Irvin, Noe, and Allene off to the side. Tommie was taking care of Mike, sitting up and petting his hair. At least everyone was conscious again.

Kazuki looked back up at the fight, they were still going at it, but the attacks were getting less frilly. Casey was taking Noise head on. Forcing him to defend himself for once, they were not the type of attacks even he could shake off. Leaving him with only the ability to keep his face blocked and take the hits to the chest. "Just fall down!" Casey yelled, giving another flurry of punches.

Without a word of warning the station was off to Julie, she slammed her leg into the small of Noise's back, sending him stumbling forward and quick as lightning Casey was bringing his knee into his midsection.

"I've got something." Kazuki said low but loud enough for Alden to hear.

"Something good?" Alden asked.

"Yeah, one of my favorites, I do not remember the

227

name though."

"Let me see."

Kazuki let loose the station slightly, enough so that Alden would know what song it was.

"Let me use that, nothing of mine's come up yet." Alden said sounding anxious.

"No, it is my favorite, I will fight better."

"Whatever…"

Kazuki continued to watch the three fighters, he could tell that Casey and Julie were getting worn out, they were slowing down. "Hey! Our song's almost over!" Julie yelled from the battlefield, "We need some backup!" Kazuki had figured as much.

"Give us a few moments!" Kazuki yelled, he had his song, he was hoping that Alden would get his.

Julie nodded and went back into it, taking over for Casey, him and Noise were trading punches now, each one causing the Earth to reverberate. It was impossible to believe that he was that powerful, that either of them were that powerful. Casey jumped back a moment later and Julie rushed from behind.

Noise spun around and punched out, the trick wasn't going to work again, Julie blocked. Her forearm shattered, her body spun, she barely slowed the momentum of his fist as she took the hit to the shoulder and sprawled to the ground. She screamed, screamed loud. Kazuki felt his mouth fall open. They hadn't traded the station in time; he could already hear her crying.

"Julie!" Casey yelled out, trying to run around Noise to Julie, he dropped to his knees, skidding and coming to a stop right next to her.

Noise's kick hit Casey right beneath the chin, rocking his head back and flooring him as well. Elli was there in a flash, leaving a trail of dusty footprints in her wake. She braced herself against the ground and landed an uppercut, threw Noise into the air. Landed a kickstand punch as he fell, she was fighting like a Channeler, using all the tricks to make her force count for the most.

She was running circles around him faster than he could keep up. It was only then that Kazuki noticed her choice of footwear. She was wearing cleats. He whistled he'd never seen someone move so fast in his life. She'd figured out how to use all of her speed without losing the friction necessary to keep her on course.

Tommie scrambled out on the battlefield, leaving Mike behind. She grabbed Julie's hand and Casey's hand and started dragging them both toward the grass. Kazuki rushed over to Julie and Casey, Alden followed close behind.

"Are you okay?" Kazuki asked, knowing it was dumb question.

Casey lifted his head up and let a stream of blood and spit dribble out of his mouth, "He wasn't able to shake it all off… He might not have acted like it but I broke some bones." Casey let his head fall back to the ground, "For the record… I've changed my stance on the plan… it sucks." He said with a laugh before rolling over to Julie. She was on her back seething, her arm swollen as she gently massaged it with her good hand.

Looking back out toward the battlefield Kazuki winced, this was the first time this battle that someone had really gone one on one with Noise. Elli looked like she was doing okay but he couldn't say for how long she could hold it. "I've got to go in!" Kazuki stressed, taking a few purposeful steps forward.

Alden came forward with him, "Me too."

"You don't have a station." Kazuki stated.

"We can share." Alden replied succinctly.

"I don't know how."

"You'll figure it out."

Kazuki paused; it was going to be hard enough

fight to do without trying to do something new, still… "Okay, I guess, but try to find something else."

"You too." Alden gave that bitch of a smile again causing Kazuki's anger to rise.

Kazuki started with a lazy jog that lead into a run, "Elli, get out of the way!" Kazuki yelled, just as he barreled into Noise, checking him with his shoulder and sending the both of them back several steps.

Julie sat up slowly, rubbing her arm, and rocking slightly. Casey looked her over, "How are you feeling?"

"I'm going to take him out." She grunted through clenched teeth.

"No, our part's over." Casey insisted, seeing the determined look in her eyes.

"No, it's not, he's going down." She squeezed her swollen arm tightly, the black and blue bruise looking angrier for it and causing Casey to wince.

"Just… wait, we'll be here in case they need us."

Elli stood back a few steps, trying to keep some distance between herself, Kazuki, Alden, and Noise to prevent herself from becoming collateral damage. Alden and Kazuki however were not doing so well. And Elli had to wince every time one of them took a hit; they were barely getting the station traded off in time for blocking and almost never getting it traded off in time for attacks. Often their punches were landed with no extra force behind them.

Kazuki blocked another ferocious kick from Noise, barely wrestling the station from Alden in time to prevent serious damage.

"You know-" Alden started between breaths, "I'd be able to fight a lot better without you dragging me down."

"And I could fight…" Kazuki barely dodged backward in time, his arms were aching and bruised already, "A lot better with my own station as well."

Kazuki felt the station being absorbed; Alden was trying to steal it entirely for himself. Quickly Kazuki stepped back away from Noise and sunk all of himself into the station, ripping it completely away from Alden.

"Give me back the station!" Alden yelled, no longer the target of Noise.

"No, we cannot share it."

"Then just give it to me!"

Kazuki was forced back as Noise closed the gap, Alden too was moving along with the two of them, "Give it to me dick wad; you know you can't fight worth a shit!"

Kazuki saw the impact more than he felt it as Alden butted his fist against Kazuki's shoulder. He might as well have been assaulted by a toddler. With Kazuki tuning and Alden not, he barely felt it. "Back off!" He yelled, grabbing Alden by the hand and whipping him off to the sidelines.

"Kazuki, I'm here!" Julie shouted, taking up a position at his side.

He looked her over; her arm was incredibly swollen, worse than before. "Go relax, I can handle this." Kazuki looked off toward Elli as well.

"Just think of me as backup. I've got a good song and I don't want to waste it."

Kazuki sighed, "Okay then-"

The two of them were split apart by Noise's next kick, given the option he chose to follow Julie. "This is for Casey!" She yelled, lashing out with her good hand and landing a solid hit in the middle of Noise's face, causing him to stagger. His nose was smashed and blood started to run down his face and spatter with every breath.

Julie ducked low, avoiding his next hit and scored another solid hit against his head, she circled around faster than he could turn and landed another punch, this time against the back of his neck. There was more, kicks, more punches. She was humming the song under her breath, and the tide was turning yet again against a person that had seemed so unstoppable a few moments before. Finally there was weakness, his movements slowing.

But in the midst of it all, Julie lost track of what she had been doing, she landed a backfist against Noise's face… with her bad arm, folding the appendage nearly in half. She screamed, at the top of her lungs, screamed, cried, staggered back, threw up.

Kazuki was there in a heartbeat and took the brunt of Noise's palm strike in her place. "Go!" Kazuki yelled, watching as Julie slinked away, back toward Casey. Tommie rushed up to help her, brandishing a piece of rebar like a sword. The movement attracted Noise's attention, instantly he bypassed Kazuki, snaking around Julie, and closed the gap between Tommie.

Tommie yelled, swinging out with all of her might, the bar struck home, hitting Noise on the shoulder and instantly deforming to his body, the half-inch steel bent like a piece of copper wire. Noise hissed, grabbing hold of the rod, it deformed in his hand as he wrestled it away from Tommie. Immediately she let go, taking a step back as he came forward unabated.

Kazuki circled around Noise, knocking the bar from his hand he grabbed Noise in a mercy hold, dominating him for a moment and bringing their intertwined hands above their heads. Kazuki tried to force him to the ground. To hold him in place for a better attack. He held the movement for as long as he could, giving Tommie the time to help Julie get some distance.

The pain quickly grew to unbearable levels as Noise started to push back "Shimata!" Kazuki yelled out, wrenching his hands away and taking a few steps back, avoiding a kick he didn't know was on the way in the process. Taking a few more steps back he picked a cinder block off the ground and threw it with ballistic accuracy straight at Noise. He smashed it out of the air, cloaking him for a moment in dust and debris.

Elli pounced on the opportunity, barreling in on her cleats with a song no one even knew she had and scored a direct hit on Noise, he recovered dazed. The momentary surprise didn't last. Faster than her eyes could follow, Noise swung around with his hand extended, his fist hitting Elli just as she tried to dodge around him. His fist connected with her temple and her whole body lifted from the ground due to the strength of the connection. For an instant, Kazuki felt his heart stop in his chest, 'Don't pass out.' He wanted to yell, but the words didn't come. Instead he could tell from his vantage point that her eyes had rolled into her head.

There was an instant there, a split second where Kazuki wasn't sure he was going to be able to do something, or just sit idly by and watch. Thankfully his body was already in motion by the time he made his choice. Elli was flying through the air at the pile of rebar. Without being alert, without channeling she wouldn't be able to flex her muscles at the right time to repel any damage. And with the velocity she was flying she was sure to be impaled.

Running so fast, the sand and dirt felt like ice. Kazuki struggled to maintain traction but it was nearly impossible. Every step was a gamble. His heart surged into his throat, Elli only a few steps away. He leapt forward, catching her in the air, feeling her weight and warmth in his hands. Her momentum transferred to him and they took a new course, colliding with the ground, tumbling - end over end. With Kazuki positioning himself every chance he got to take a brunt of the force. Finally, the two of them tumbled onto the ground, Kazuki sprawled out, back and neck hurting, his arm feeling like the bones inside were beginning to splinter.   But when he looked over and saw Elli breathing comfortably he let out his own sigh of relief.

"Nice save!" Casey yelled from the sidelines.

Kazuki smiled to himself despite the pain and raised his hand, giving a thumbs up as he once again pushed himself wincing to his feet.

"It's   on!"   Kazuki   turned   toward   Bailey, momentarily distracted. The radio… Kazuki recognized the song. A moment later it tuned out of the radio frequency, disappearing.

Alden rushed up, "I've got to take care of this guy right now but I'll get around to you later Mr. Japan!"

Kazuki ignored the comment, suddenly feeling more able with the backup. He let Alden rush in, scoring the first few hits, and taking a few in the process. If every hit from this guy felt like getting hit by a car, Kazuki had to wonder what he felt. How much damage could Noise really take?   He had to be approaching his limit. He just had to.

"Bitch!" Alden's expletive brought Kazuki back to the present, "A little help here!"

Kazuki decided against the snide comment about him wanting to do it alone and leapt into things. "My song is almost over!" Kazuki yelled from the other side of Noise. "Unless you want to take him on, on your own we need to do something!"

Alden stepped in for the attack and took a hit to the face, his nose bloodied anew; he kept his stride however and brought his own foot down on the instep of Noise, hobbling him, if only for a second.

Kazuki started attacking from Noise's side, forcing him toward the other side of the construction yard, toward where Bailey and Jayson were with the radio. Meanwhile Alden kept up his frontal assault, taking more hits from Noise than Kazuki had ever landed on him. Alden kept fighting though, if you wanted to call it that.   He looked more like a punching bag, his head rocking back with every blow, but he wouldn't fall.

Finally the three of them had worked their way across the packed depression of dirt. "Now!" Kazuki yelled, "We've got to do it now!" Elli had followed them; at some time she'd gotten up. Kazuki could feel her suddenly start channeling.

"Jayson!" Alden yelled, motioning to the side.

Jayson scurried over and opened one of the doors to the large metal freight container, Kazuki rushed forward and leapt into the air, planting both of his feet in Noise's chest, sending him back several feet, Alden continued the trek, whipping out his foot and pushing him along. Kazuki moved forward as quickly as he could, but Kazuki could tell that Noise had figured enough out to know he didn't want to be forced inside.

Noise didn't have time to react though, Elli sailed in with a kick of her own, causing him to slam into the ground and topple end over end, finally clearing the door and passing into the inside of the container.

"*That's it brother*!" Kazuki yelled, Satoshi running inside the shipping container.

"I'm on it!" Satoshi closed the door to the freight container. And suddenly it was silent. Just the heavy breathing of the former combatants. Kazuki listed intently, he heard a bang on the inside of the container that reverberated through the whole structure, then another, someone was being thrown into the walls.

Elli stumbled over, "You sure this will work?"

Kazuki nodded, "None of us could tune in there. No Channeler can, it's a Faraday cage, no radio in, no radio out." Kazuki let out a deep breath, "Inside there he's normal, and if they're normal, my brother can take on anyone." He said with more than a hint of pride.

"He might be a little stronger, a little faster, but he's nothing like the monster we just fought." Kazuki explained, turning to look at the injured masses behind him. The beating continued for tense seconds leading to minutes, Kazuki's song ended, Elli's song ended. Elli had to lean on Kazuki for support; she might not have taken many hits, but she'd spent herself too much. Moved too fast for too long, she was burning up. "You did good." He reassured her softly and she mewled in response.

There was a clang from inside, the sound of metal on metal, and the door swung open. Kazuki held his breath as he peeked inside. There inside, beyond the door and illuminated by a single overhead incandescent bulb was Noise. His head was slumped, and he was wrapped in the ropes.

"*Is he dead*?" Kazuki asked his brother warily.

"No, I wouldn't kill anyone." Satoshi turned slightly, "Funny he gave you guys so much trouble, you could have taken him easy after he lost the ability to do that channeling thing." Satoshi made a few phantom punches, "Three hits and a slam against the box and he was down for the count."

"Heh, wimp." Alden laughed, drawing a contemptuous look from Elli and Kazuki.

Noe and Irvin hobbled up behind Kazuki, "So, you got 'em." Noe mumbled, feeling the pain of his bruises even worse without Channeling.

"Yes. Can I see your cell phone?" Kazuki asked, turning slightly toward Noe.

"I guess." Noe fished it out of his pocket, giving a sigh of relief when he opened it, probably because it wasn't broke.

"Thank you." Kazuki accepted the phone and pulled a piece of paper out of his pocket with a number for the police department. He dialed the number then held the phone to his ear, "Yes, I found that guy that caused all the damage on the news last night…" Kazuki started, remembering what Noe had told him earlier, "Yes, I'll hold."

Kazuki gave Noe thumbs up, before saying

quietly, "We better start getting people out of here."

Noe nodded and wandered off toward the rest of the Channelers. Alden gave a nod as well, his face a swollen mess of bruises, "Guess I'm out of here too loser." Kazuki scowled at him, "And kick some ass while you're in Japan so that when you come back here you're half a match for me." Alden turned before waving over his shoulder, "Peace out." And with that he half-hobbled half-jogged away.

Kazuki decided that he didn't want to bring up Alden's earlier musings about killing Noise. Kazuki gave him another look over, now that he wasn't actively trying to kill them; he just looked like a normal guy who needed a bath, a haircut, and a new pair of clothes. He wondered if the police would be able to do anything for him.

"I'm going to get Julie to a hospital, you guys okay without us?" Casey asked, still wincing as he moved.

"Yes, we got it taken care of, thank you Casey. Thanks Julie!" Kazuki yelled as he watched her push herself to her feet. She waved back with her good arm.

"Oh…" Kazuki suddenly heard someone on the other end of the line, "Yes, that guy who destroyed those vehicles last night, he's over at the construction site on Jones… Yes, some people incapacitated him; they said he was dangerous and strong." Kazuki didn't want to explain more, and he didn't want to sound crazy.

"Yes, thank you, goodbye." Kazuki closed the phone and handed it back to Noe.

"When are you heading back?" Noe asked.

"The day after tomorrow."

"We'll be sure to stop by, good luck." Noe waved before heading back to the rest of his group.

At some time Satoshi had silently slipped away. Leaving just Kazuki and Elli standing in front of the box. "You… did good." Elli offered, shifting slightly.

"Not really, I hardly got a punch in."

"No, I mean, you were a good leader, you really took charge of things."

"Oh, that." It was embarrassing that she complimented him because he knew he did such a horrible job. Too many people injured.

"Stop being so modest, and accept your reward."

Kazuki swore she must have been tuning because he couldn't have avoided the kiss if he'd tried. It was wonderful, warm. It was his first. She pulled away slightly; her eyes downcast, making him worry for a moment that she regretted it, but the blush on her face saying otherwise. "I'll see you in the morning?"

"Yes, I hope so…" Kazuki trailed off, still a bit shell-shocked.

"I guess we'd better get out of here." Their eyes locked for a moment, those same piercing green eyes before she eventually, achingly turned away and headed toward home.

Epilogue

"You're on your way right... I know, but you said you were on your way ten minutes ago." Noe paused, holding the phone closer to his ear, "Yeah, yeah, just get here, okay? Yeah, bye." Noe pulled the phone away and closed the keypad, "She said she'll be here in a few." He took a sip of his soda before pocketing the phone.

Kazuki nodded, he'd already said goodbye to Casey, Julie, and most of Noe's crew the day before at the barbecue. But Noe had still decided to tag along to the airport. He said he wanted to hang out until Allene made it there.

So it came down to Kazuki, Elli, and Noe sitting in the cafeteria with Satoshi and Miranda at their own table. Kazuki tried to eaves drop passively on their conversation but found himself coming up short.

"Well, I guess I'm going to hit the road." Noe said, drawing it out as he pushed himself from the table. "I'm really glad you decided to come to America man." Noe reached out, offering his hand to Kazuki, "If you ever come back we'd really like to hang out again, all of us."

Kazuki accepted the hand and gave it a shake; rising from his own seat he offered a bow in return, "I am very glad to have met everyone here. I am happy that you enjoyed my stay as well."

"Good luck in Japan man." Noe said with his smile wide, putting down a ten dollar bill to cover his food, "You've got my e-mail, so you've got no excuse not to drop me a line once you get back."

"I will. And thank you again."

Noe waved, "Later." And with that he walked out of the cafeteria.

Kazuki sat back down, swallowing hard, he didn't do well with goodbyes and he'd already had to do quite a few lately. He looked over to Elli trying to keep the sadness from his eyes, today would probably be the last time he would see her.

"I'm not going to see you again, am I?" Elli asked, her mind displaying uncommon synchronicity with his own.

"I… I don't think so." Kazuki replied back after a moment of hesitation.

That proclamation was a lead in to an awkward silence that lasted and lasted. Kazuki would look over to catch a glimpse of Elli's deep eyes only to look away again before anything meaningful could be exchanged. Kazuki looked over again to his brother, laughing, smiling. He wondered why he would be so happy. Why couldn't he be that happy right now?

"Hey."

Kazuki looked up, surprised to see that it was Allene. He didn't expect her to be there so quickly after Noe's call.

"Hey." Elli nodded in her direction.

"How is your knee?" Kazuki asked, looking down at her leg. For once she was in pants instead of a skirt or shorts.

"Nothing broken, just blew it out." She laughed it off, "They put me in this knee immobilizer thing and told me to keep off it but I had to make it here to see you." She laughed, "I can't believe they kept me for so long."

"You missed a heck of a barbecue." Elli said smiling.

"Don't rub it in." Allene sighed, "But at least I made it to see you off."

"Thank you." Kazuki was glad to see she made it despite her injuries.

"Seriously, that guy was tough as stone. Any word on what happened with him?" Allene asked.

"No, nothing on the news or the internet." Elli answered for Kazuki.

"Humm, that's weird." Allene turned slightly and

pulled something out of her purse, handing it to Kazuki, "It's from all of us… except well Elli and Alden." Then she added in a softer voice, "But Elli can always sign it after you open it." She nodded her head in Elli's direction with a grin.

Kazuki smiled and opened the card, "You did get everyone to sign it." Kazuki was happy to not see Alden among the signatures and the well wishes.

"Well, yeah, but it was supposed to be a surprise." Allene elaborated.

"Can I see it?" Elli asked. Kazuki hadn't finished reading it but handed it over anyway as Elli pulled out a pen.

"We're going to miss you." Allene added, "We never really hung out with Casey or Julie or even Elli much, you've kind of helped bring us all together."

"You have Kazuki; you made us realize that this isn't just something random." Elli added.

"Thank you both." Kazuki felt himself blushing from the attention.

"Anyway, I've got to go. My dad's waiting for me in the car." Allene leaned over as best she could with her knee immobilized and gave Kazuki a hug, "See you around."

Kazuki and Elli watched as Allene hobbled away, one leg stiff the other bending ever so slightly as she took one unsteady step as another.

Elli tried to comfort the both of them, "Don't worry, you know how fast us Channelers heal."

"Yes I know."

"You about ready to go?" Satoshi asked, pushing himself up from his seat, Miranda doing likewise.

"I-" Kazuki paused, looking across to Elli, "I guess." There wasn't any reason to delay.

"Just give us a minute." Elli answered for him a moment later.

"Okay, we'll be at security." Satoshi answered

with a wink that made Kazuki uncomfortable.

Kazuki watched the two of them walk away before turning back to Elli, she had one of the biggest smiles on her face he had ever seen. "What is it?" He found himself asking out loud.

Elli bent forward slightly, then a little more, and then closed the gap, planting a kiss on Kazuki's lips. This time it didn't feel as rushed, more sensual, more...

The kiss broke slowly, Elli moving back into her own seat again. "Kazuki, I... I wish you lived around here, this time we've had together... I love spending time with you, and I know that if we could be together for longer-- I don't know, I know what I feel for you would grow." She trailed off blushing, it was one of the first times Kazuki had seen her so flustered. She was gripping the hem of her skirt tightly

"But I've got to go." Kazuki restated, not sure what else to say. His stomach was all over the place. Between Elli's words and his other goodbyes he missed home less and less.

"I know, but... if you ever came back. I talked to Miranda about it; she never thought Satoshi would come back after he went back to Japan... but now. Did you know she's trying to find out what it would take to move there?"

Kazuki was taken aback, "No, I didn't."

Elli nodded her head, "When he left the first time, it wasn't love, but now... it is. And I can't help but see the parallels between them-" Elli paused, "-and us."

For a moment Kazuki held his breath, and then let it out shuddering, it was a lot to take in.

"Just promise me you'll stay in touch. You've got my number, my e-mail, everything you need. I just want to hear from you. I want to see where this goes." Elli said pleadingly.

"But-" Kazuki tried to offer some protest but the thoughts died on his lips.

"There's something special about us, and this area, and Channelers. Let's not close the door just yet." Elli pushed herself to her feet, coming over and giving Kazuki a hug, "You never know what tomorrow might bring." She whispered in his ear before pulling away and putting on her smile again, "Ja Matta."

Kazuki pushed himself up form his seat, reaching out and taking Elli into a hug, "I am going to miss you."

Elli nodded into the hug, "Me too." A moment later she pulled away, "Good bye."

"Good bye Elli."

She gave another smile, this one sadder before turning and walking off into the crowd. Kazuki sighed, bending over he grabbed his bags and headed out of the cafeteria. Following the signs he managed to find his way to the security checkpoint.

"Over here!" Satoshi yelled, waving his hand above the crowd.

Kazuki made his way over to his brother, Miranda standing there as well. "Thank you for letting us stay with you." Kazuki said while bowing deeply. He really was appreciative, considering all the things she went through.

"You're welcome; hopefully I'll be seeing you again."

Kazuki flashed a look to his brother as if he didn't know about Miranda planning to come to Japan, but he didn't acknowledge anything amiss.

Satoshi embraced Miranda with a hug, "I'm going to miss you honey."

"I'll miss you too." Miranda said, going in for a kiss. Kazuki watched the two of them hold each other for a moment before breaking apart. They didn't say anything else; Miranda just gave a little bow of her own and headed into the crowd.

Satoshi turned to his brother, "So, what did you think of America? Would you want to come back?"

Instead of answering on impulse, Kazuki thought about it for a moment. There was a lot of good, but there was plenty of bad too, "Yeah, I would want to come back." The good outweighed the bad. He'd found more friends here than he had in Japan, people like him, and then there was Elli.

As Kazuki's bags passed through the X-ray machine he sighed and pulled out a picture he'd printed from the day before. He gave a short sad laugh. It was the bunch of them at the beach together all wrapped in bandages from their battle, eating and smiling. Miranda, and Satoshi too, the only one that had missed the picture was Allene. He wiped the tear from his eye, everyone looked so happy, especially Elli with her arm draped around his neck. Yes, he really was going to miss the states.

About the Author

I grew up in the Metro Detroit area and from a young age I had a fascination with two things, chemistry and writing. In 2006 I finally graduated with my BS in Chemistry and moved to Wisconsin to pursue my career. Still, my passion for writing has persisted and I vent it the only way I know how.

My idyllic life in chemistry is completed by the presence of my wonderful wife Christina and our two loving dogs Conrad and Silva.

www.ingramcontent.com/pod-product-compliance
Lightning Source LLC
Chambersburg PA
CBHW070559130626
46556CB00001B/217